The Colour of

WATER

Printed in Canada

The Colour of WATER

by

Luanne Armstrong

Caitlin Press Inc.

Caitlin Press Inc.
Box 2387, Stn. B
Prince George, BC
V2N 2S6

Caitlin Press would like to acknowledge the financial support of the Canada Council for the Arts for our publishing program. Similarly we acknowledge the support of the Arts Council of British Columbia.

Layout and Design by Warren Clark
Cover Design by Warren Clark Graphic Design
Cover Photo by Joanna Wilson
Author Photo by Joanna Wilson
Printed in Canada

Canadian Cataloguing in Publication Data
Armstrong, Luanne, 1949-
The colour of water

ISBN 0-920576-70-2
I.Title.
PS8551.R7638C64 1998 C813'.54 C98-91028-4
PR9199.3.A547C64 1998

Acknowledgement

I owe deep thanks to several people for various kinds of assistance while writing this book, in particular, Ian Millican, not only an excellent critical reader but someone who showed up and helped out at a crucially necessary time, Joanna and Alan Wilson, whose hospitality and support are a mainstay of my life and my mother and father, who have assisted me in so many ways. I would also like to thank several people who read the manuscript at various stages and offered advice and encouragement, including Mary Woodbury, K. Linda Kivi, Kaca Hegerova, Juanita Meekis, Dorothy and Avril Armstrong, and Bill Armstrong. I also owe a very special thanks to my editors, Ann Ireland and Melanie Callahan, and to Cynthia Wilson of Caitlin Press.

Dedication

To my family,

especially the young ones...

Section One

The Family

Chapter One

Dana was clerking at the store, and Rob was out in the bush the day they found Mary's canoe in the lake. Rob hadn't even known she was missing. No one had. When she was in a lousy mood everyone had learned to leave her alone. She'd come by when she came out of it. That's what they thought. It became one more thing to blame themselves for.

Jake McFadden phoned Kathryn to say he'd found a green canoe stove in and washed up on a beach on the other side of the lake. Jake knew the canoe. He knew Mary spent time on the lake alone. Kathryn had gone over to Mary's house and found it empty. She'd gotten word to Rob, her grandson who lived with her. He was logging up Sheep Creek. She got the foreman at the mill to call him on the radiophone and he'd grabbed a ride down the mountain with a logging truck. When he got to town, he phoned his girlfriend Dana, to come out to the farm with him.

It was just after spring breakup. Rob was twenty-three. He had just started his first real job, choking logs on a hi-ball crew, making good money for the first time. Spring breakup had been delayed this year. It had been one of those slow, cold wet springs which meant extra snow in the mountains. Then suddenly it warmed up; the snow hanging in the mountains came down with a mad rush. Creeks and rivers swelled and boiled with freezing brown water. Leaves popped out on the trees and almost as fast, blossoms laced the orchards, dandelions, green grass, daffodils, tulips, sprang up as if they were being yanked out of the steaming ground. The roads dried and logging trucks ran again. People put on shorts, marched out to plant gardens, got burnt bright red over their legs and shoulders, burns they displayed virtuously, both rueful and proud of this evidence of their labour. Then they slept, restless, on hot itchy sheets.

The crew Rob was on was working full tilt, making up for the long break, cutting, hauling, decking logs. Kathryn was planting, setting out the last of the pale leggy seedlings nurtured since February in every window in the house.

As well as working, Rob was spending a lot of time with Dana, who was twenty-one and had black hair, long legs, a slim waist and small pert breasts. He was spending more time than he could afford, giving up eating and sleeping, times he should have been home helping his grandmother, to spend his nights with her. He'd drop by Dana's place at night, after going home for a quick shower and to change of his sawdust and mud crusted clothes. They'd go out, usually, for pizza, chicken, hamburgers, then back to her small room over a store on the Colburn street for quick, hot sex. Afterward, they lay, curled together, the smell of exhaust, smoke and burning grease from the Dairy Queen blowing in warm smoky clouds over their bed. Neon colours flashed over their bodies. They'd smoke a joint together, talk, fall asleep, until four, when Rob got up, drove home, dressed for work, and caught the crummy the forty miles up to the logging site on Sheep Creek.

All they had to go on to figure out what happened was the empty canoe, the stuff she'd left in the house, and her journals. Mary was Rob's mother, Kathryn's daughter. None of them knew her very well. She'd just moved back from the city the year before. Rob had grown up with Kathryn. He avoided Mary, his real mother. He wasn't even sure he wanted to know her. She was pretty embarrassing with her crazy clothes and crazier ideas.

Her journals were on a shelf in the closet of the upstairs bedroom in the old house. Dana found them. She had decided to stay at the farm with Rob and make herself useful. She went over by herself, a few days after Mary had disappeared, to see what needed doing, she told Rob later. She looked through all the rooms, her nose wrinkling at the cobwebs, the unswept sawdust and ashes around the stove, the sagging couch and faded rug. She looked through the kitchen, opened the fridge, found a garbage bag and threw out the few vegetables and pathetic plastic-wrapped leftovers.

She went through the drawers in Mary's room, flipped quickly through the few clothes in the closet, and decided she didn't want any of them. When she found the journals she cracked one open, began to read, then closed it up again. She hesitated, thinking of the stove downstairs. Then she put them back in the closet and went back across the field to Kathryn's. She told Rob about them and he went and got them, put them in a box and put them upstairs in Kathryn's attic. One by one, when they thought no one else was looking, everyone in the family crept up the stairs, cracked open one or two of the journals, some in hard bound books, others in scribblers read a bit, and closed them up again.

Kathryn's house rapidly filled up. Her son Colin arrived at the bus station in Appleby. Rob brought him out. Kathryn glared at him like it was his fault, then went and sat at the kitchen table, crying. No one had seen her cry before. Everyone found a reason to leave the house but Colin sat at the table with her, his big hands folded in front of him, saying nothing.

No one really knew Colin. He had left when he was seventeen and he was forty-seven now. He'd rarely been back.

"Guy's a bum," Rob growled to Dana. Colin seemed to have had a career over the years that had included a lot of odd jobs. Now, he said, he was in sales for some printing, graphic design kind of place. At least he had a regular salary. Rob avoided him at first but after Colin took over doing the chores, he decided he'd been too hasty. Maybe Colin was okay. As long as he wasn't afraid of work, Rob could tolerate him. Maybe Colin's years in the city hadn't turned him into some kind of sissy even though he packed around a paunch like a tumour and his hands were soft and white. Rob's were dark, covered with nicks and scratches, smelled of grease and pitch.

Colin got there two days after Mary went missing and stayed on, got on the phone at the end of the week, moved things around, rearranged his schedule. It took him about the length of that week to change back into Kathryn's son. Although he was clumsy and slow at first he took over the milking, feeding the chickens and splitting wood for the cookstove. Every night after finishing supper, he disappeared into his room. He borrowed Kathryn's car every couple of days to go to town. The bottles piled up in garbage bags by the back door.

They all ate together every night. Even Arlene, Colin's daughter, who hadn't spoken to her father for years, and her husband Mike came out every night for dinner. Arlene was only twenty but was already married and settled into town life. Sitting all together, they hardly talked. They could barely stand to be together, but it was still easier than being apart, being alone. They were all thinking about the journals. They talked about the weather, the chores, the farm, what was for dinner. Silence stretched between each remark.

"She was pretty lonely, eh?" Rob said cautiously one night to Kathryn. They were playing canasta together. He felt almost as guilty about how he'd ignored Mary as he did about her disappearance, as they all went on calling it. It took a long, long while before anyone said the words, death and dead, even though they all knew about the lake and its appetite for fools in boats. Kathryn threw down the cards and went upstairs. She wasn't talking about Mary. But Rob went on sitting, remembering what he'd read that afternoon.

The shape the daffodils make, their mouths crying oh, oh, lonely, lonely, small yellow screams. I keep trying to call Rob in my head, hoping he'll hear, pacing the rug, watching the road, unable to work, can't sit down, hungry but there's no food unless I go to Mom's, which I can't do.

Neighbours came by bringing cakes, pies, cookies, jars of canned fruit, meat and fish, stews, and salads. Food piled up in the fridge and freezer, but these same neighbours stayed for coffee and sometimes for dinner so it all got eaten again.

During the search, people drifted in and day. Dana and Arlene kept making coffee and putting out plates of food. One night there were fifteen cars in the yard. People ate, helped with the dishes, organized themselves into search parties, offered boats, dogs, stories of psychics, and miraculous wilderness survivals. In Appleby, someone said they'd heard Mary had been seen in Vancouver, that she'd staged her own disappearance. Someone else said they'd heard she'd taken an overdose of LSD, or was it heroin? Some kind of drug, anyway.

Kathryn wandered in and out of the house, and around and around the farm, down to the beach and then back again to the house, as if grief was an enemy she didn't know how to fight. She and Rob went every day with the search crews, with the RCMP boat on the swollen brown lake. They put ads in newspapers and talked to the local paper or radio station. A reporter from CBC called.

They searched and searched, crawling on their hands and knees through the tangled red willow along the river south of the lake, trudged along the granite shore line on the far side of the lake. They searched and talked to people living along the lake, and finally they photocopied hopeless posters to be sent away and hung in bus and police stations.

The RCMP called their search off after a few days, but Kathryn and Rob went on looking. The cops were sympathetic, but everyone knew the lake never gave back bodies. It rolled them down into the cold thick mud where they disappeared, locked into the black depths there, at the foot of the mountains. They didn't say how foolish it was for anyone to go canoeing when the lake was so high and so cold. They didn't have to.

Even after they ran out of places to look, Kathryn went on wandering over the fields, out to the barn, into the house, then out to the garden, where, for a while, she worked furiously until she started to wander again.

The season was progressing. There was a lot to do. The garden had to be got in regardless of how they felt. They all worked at it. The garden took on some kind of aura, as if by planting, planting, planting, new life coming into being, one seed, one pricked out plant at a time, they were at least doing something.

Neither Kathryn nor Colin nor Rob could sleep. They sat up late, played canasta, drank cup after cup of tea. After two weeks, Rob went back to work. Dana took over all the cooking and cleaning. She went on working at the Safeway in town. She and Rob slept together in his narrow bed in the small room at the top of the stairs. No one said anything about it.

Every night Rob went to bed and woke again in the morning, doubled over with a bellyache. He picked at his food. He mumbled hello to Dana when he came home and then went back out, and worked at something until called for supper. He and Kathryn avoided each other.

Every morning just before he finished waking, he wished and prayed Mary alive again. He wanted her back like he had never wanted anything before in his whole life. Sometimes, he earnestly, secretly, prayed, in a careful whisper, while Dana pretended to sleep beside him. She hadn't known Mary. Privately, she didn't think Mary could have been much of a mother. She was almost relieved she'd never have to meet her. But Rob was growing haggard and thin. There was a gash in the toe of his boot where he'd hit it with the saw. There was a bruise across his shoulder where the cable hook had swung and caught him. He was careless and too slow, out of rhythm with what was happening. Work like his was no place to be careless.

Dana cooked huge meals, cleaned up the house, and tended the garden. Kathryn got grayer and grimmer and more distracted. She went on working as hard as she always had, taking up task after task, only to drop each one after a few minutes. She stood staring at things, then shook herself back to work.

"Why don't you try and rest?" Dana said one day. "I'll make you some tea."

Kathryn glared at her. " What the hell good is a cup of tea?" she said.

Fine, you old cow, Dana thought. I won't ask again.

Even Colin seemed unable to concentrate or fix on anything. He was like a man who'd run full tilt into a wall he hadn't seen and now wandered, dazed and bleeding, wondering what had happened.

Arlene and Dana took charge of packing Mary's things, and cleaning the ratty old house where she'd lived for the last year. The ancient unpainted house was full of paintings, sketches, and half finished letters. There were dishes in the sink, an unmade bed, laundry on the line. They packed everything but the paintings in garbage bags for the secondhand store.

"This is a beautiful place," Arlene said wistfully. They were taking a break on the porch. A hot wind wandered across the field and lifted the hair off their faces. Below the house, an old meadow sprinkled with invading baby firs and patches of buckbrush sloped to the trees beside the lake. “I wish Mike and I could buy it but it’s too far out of town. I couldn’t stand all that driving. And it’s lonely out here. After all, in town, there’s church, and movies and friends.”

“I live in town,” Dana said. “It’s not that great. A place like this you could make into a real showplace. A big house up here on the hill, a garden, fruit trees. A marina and a big boat. You could have parties, show it off.”

“Maybe,” said Arlene. “ I thought someone in Calgary owned it.”

“I don’t know,” said Dana. “Rob will know. He knows everything. I’ll ask him about it.”

One Saturday, the day after they’d given up searching, Dana got up quietly in order to let Rob sleep. She was due at work at the store in town. But when she was sitting on the edge of the bed, putting on her socks, Rob grabbed her wrist.

“Don’t go,” he said.

She pulled at her wrist, annoyed.

“I have to,” she said. “I need the money. “

“I’m working,” he said. “I’ll make the money. Stay here. Grandma needs you. I need you.”

“Piss off,” she said. “I look after myself. I don’t want your damn money.”

He let go, lay back on the bed, watched her without speaking while she continued getting dressed.

“Let’s get married,” he said. She looked at him.

“I mean it,” he said. “ I want us to get married.”

She didn’t say anything. She frowned at the two blouses in her hand, trying to choose between them. Finally, looking at her feet, her eyes drooping like she was about to fall asleep, or start weeping, she nodded.

He didn’t say anything more. His eyes filled with tears and abruptly, he stood up, pulled on his jeans, went downstairs. She heard him out in the yard, chopping kindling.

She went to the window and watched. He looked up, turned

again to the wood, picked up a huge block, split it with one gigantic blow of the maul, grinned at her and went back to the wood. She went on standing. Then she smiled, put her hands up, stroked her breasts, lightly, and wrapped her arms around herself. When she heard him come in, she took off the blouse, put on an old sweatshirt, and went downstairs to plug in the kettle. While she waited for it, she sat at the kitchen table. She took a piece of paper and a pen and began writing, " big log house," she wrote. "Three kids, land for a garden, two new cars." Then she crumpled the list and put it in the wood stove.

She remembered a scrapbook she and some teenage friends had made. They'd spent days cutting pictures of carpet and couches and dishes and curtains from magazines and pasting them in the book. She still had it. Perhaps next time she went to visit her mother, who still lived in town in the same shabby grey stucco house, she would look for it. She hated visiting her mother. The house smelled of cats and loneliness. Her mother always wanted to talk about her latest illness, show off a new rash, or describe a new pain. Dana felt sorry for her mother but the easiest way to deal with her was to stay away. She'd left home at seventeen. She knew already that what she wanted most was a life as unlike her mother's as possible. She wanted a big family, a big beautiful house, with lots and lots of land. She wanted to drive into Appleby in her new car, and buy whatever she wanted. She wanted to invite her friends from high school to her house and discuss drapes and furniture and paint and carpets.

The coffee was ready. As she waited for Rob to come in, she smiled and touched her breasts again, very lightly. Maybe they'd get a few moments of peace together before the rest of the household woke up and cars started arriving in the yard.

After a few days the cars stopped coming. The phone stopped ringing. But that didn't stop people from talking. For a long time after Mary was gone, stories got told and retold at dinner tables, other than Kathryn's, stories of a wild girl with long red hair, and that damned wild horse. Kathryn had got her that horse when Mary was just a kid, just a bit of a thing. The two of them charged around the neighbourhood like they owned the whole damn place, jumping fences they'd no right to jump, ignoring no trespassing signs, closed gates, or growing hay and crops.

Mary grew up all knees and elbows and mad at the whole world. Used to fight with kids on the school bus, get kicked off, walk home, bitter eyed with fury, get home and head to the barn, the horse and being alone. You could see her, almost any day, charging along the road at a dead run, careless of logging trucks and traffic, foam from the mare's open mouth flecking her face. Stupid way to treat a good horse. Kathryn should have known better, should have given the girl hell.

But the girl could always paint. You could give her that. Right from day one, her art teachers raved about her. She won all the art prizes going when she got to high school, even some fancy prize from the Coast, got her picture in the paper for that one. Now that every painting of hers that the craft store had hanging on its walls for months, had disappeared, people began to wonder if they'd missed something. Not that anyone called her pictures pretty; they were all daubs and splashes of colour, nothing that really looked liked anything, but there must have been something to them. Someone must have liked them. Someone had bought them all and not even quibbled about the price. Someone who said she was some friend of Mary's from Vancouver. Word was she'd spent less than a full day in town. Just bought the paintings and left. The woman in the gallery said she was a snobby bitch, just pulled out a charge card, bought all the paintings, loaded them in her car and left town.

But then who knew what friends Mary might have had. Who knew what life she had led in Vancouver, hundreds of miles away. Rumours had flown about drugs, and a man who had kicked her out. But Dana had told Arlene that Mary's boyfriend had phoned, and was going to come up and help with the search but she'd talked him out of it.

Yes, indeed, a very crazy woman The whole family had a streak of wildness. Take Kathryn's husband, old Bill Mangerton—you didn't cross him. Stories were told and retold about Bill, how some guy owed him money for too long a time. Bill stomped into his yard one day and said, "O'Neill, how'd you like to be driving down the road one day with a full load of logs and have your goddamn front tires shot out?"

O'Neill had paid. You didn't mess with Bill. If you were smart, you never laid your tongue on any of his family. Mary had been his right-hand helper until she got big, and then something changed between them, and Colin took her place, hanging out at his father's side as they went around the farm or around the community together. But Colin never gave a damn about the farm. After he left for Vancouver, he never came back, except for the odd birthday or Christmas. There was something about a girl in trouble but she disappeared to the coast as well and came back as skinny as ever.

Dana had heard some of the stories even before she met Rob. She knew who he was. He had been two grades ahead of her in school but he never seemed to have much to do with parties or girls. Then one night, sitting in the bar with her friends, she saw him come in. He looked lonely, she knew about loneliness. She had grown up with a single mother and only a few memories of an alcoholic father. She was drunk enough that night to ask him to dance. After one dance, he left and she thought, well, that was that but the next day he came by the Safeway where she was working, and stood in line at her till, and asked if she was going to the bar again. She said, yes, she thought she'd go after work, was he going to buy her a beer? "Sure thing," he said, and grinned. He had very white teeth in a thin tanned face and dark brown hair.

At coffee break, she asked the other women about him. "Mangerton," one said. "Oh, yeah, the guy with the crazy mother. Ditched her kid and ran off or something. That's what I heard. Lives with his grandmother, on that big place out the lake. Gorgeous place. I know 'cause my mom goes to church with his cousin, Arlene."

Dana asked her mother about the Mangertons. Her mother had known Rob's grandfather. "Mean," said Dana's mother. "That woman, Kathryn, used to peddle eggs and stuff around town. Dragging her little kids with her. Poor little things. They always looked scared to me."

A man without a mother could use some taking care of, Dana thought. And his family had all that land.

Now that Dana was living with Rob in Kathryn's house, she saw even more how much he needed looking after. Rob was working his guts out and worrying about Kathryn and trying to keep up with the work on the farm. He came home with lines of dust caked into his face. His legs were scarred with bruises and cuts, his hands a mess. She asked him what happened at work but he brushed her off.

"Ah, you just got to learn to duck at the right times," he laughed and pulled her onto his lap. He was strong and warm. She rested on his lap, curled against his chest. She slipped her hand under his shirt, feeling the hard strength of his muscles. She wriggled against him in the way he liked.

It wasn't fair to him, that was sure, and if she could so something about it, give him a happy normal life, she would, she would, despite the rest of his crazy family. Any woman, she thought, that would abandon her own son, run off to the city to pursue some foolish career as an artist didn't deserve much sympathy. Now her disappearance, her death, was breaking Rob's heart.

Mary had wasted her life. Rob's Uncle Colin didn't seem much better. A lousy drunk with no real career. Kathryn should have put her foot down, kept her kids under control. The whole family was disorganized, Dana thought disdainfully, the house a mess, the yard full of junk and dead vehicles which had been there since Bill's death. That was the first thing she was going to do, clean up the place and make it something to be proud of.

Chapter Two

The front of the Caterpillar reared up in the air then crashed ponderously onto the newly dug boulders. Within the barred cab, Rob rode the motion with ease. Only his hands moved, dancing from one control stick to the other. Dirt, rocks, young fir trees and stumps rolled in a tangled slow wave over the edge of the logging road Rob was pushing up the steep hill. He was thinking about that spring again, twenty years ago this month.

The Cat banged and shuddered. Sometimes it slid sideways on the rocks or a log that went under the treads but then it went on. Nothing stopped it. The torn gouge it made in the forest grew steadily. Blue smoke jetted from the exhaust pipe. The steel treads left behind the smell of crushed wood, burnt rock and weeping resin.

Mary was never far from Rob's mind. Some memory of her would show up at the oddest times, like this moment, on this intensely blue and green spring day. The willows in the swamp below the slope were bright burgundy, swollen with sap. The fir trees were tipped with vivid shining green candles. On a day like today, he had been known to leave work early, drive somewhere he could walk down a path tunneling under cottonwood trees by the river, or up the mountain to a sun-soaked ledge, and sit there, watching and thinking. At those times, his mother tended to show up. Maybe it was the colours that reminded him. She used to dress in bright burgundies and yellows and greens. Her clothes seemed to float around her, never quite secure.

But today he had no time to stop. The damn road was overdue. He had a crew of men who depended on him. And he didn't want to think about his mother's long ago death because he had other things to worry about. Twenty years ago, she had disappeared but he'd put it behind him. That's what he told himself.

Still today he couldn't stop remembering how strangely quiet it had gotten after the initial excitement died away. Colin went back to Vancouver. Arlene went back to town and her life with Mike. Dana stayed on. She and Rob told Kathryn they were getting married. She looked at them, blank eyed, said, yes, they would stay with her and that was wonderful but then her eyes lost their focus and she looked away again. Their wedding had been a quiet affair at the town hall, just a few friends and Kathryn standing there, shrunk in on herself, not looking at anyone.

People went away regretful at things being left in a muddle, no body, no death, no funeral, not even a memorial service although everyone knew Mary had to be dead and everyone said Kathryn ought to do something because the girl was gone and she'd have to come to terms with it.

Guess she'd been hit rough, people said to Rob. Didn't know as to how she'd ever come out of it, they said. What made it worse was that Mary had only come home from the city a year or so before and had taken over the rambling junk pile of a house next door.

The thing no one talked about was what preoccupied them all the most, the real questions, the real things, like the icy frigidity of the boiling brown spring run off, the idiocy of taking a canoe onto that freezing water. Mary was good in a canoe, had lived on the lake all her life, had been in a canoe since she was a kid, knew what she was doing.

So what was she doing out there? But then she was a crazy, always had been. That's what people said. Rob knew they said it, just not to him.

Rob shook his head. He didn't have time for this. He drove the Cat at a boulder that was too big, looked at it, backed up, came at it sideways until it finally gave way, splintering into crumbled granite slabs.

He loved his work. It made him a lot of money, kept him busy, and still gave him time to think. Up on the Cat or the skidder, ears hidden behind huge protective orange bubbles, the roaring motor still there, but distant, dulled, a steady pressure like running water, his mind could run away along with the noise, wearing familiar grooves like a creek over runnelled granite.

He drove himself too hard, Dana said. He should learn to relax. There were gray lines of dust and dirt in his face which never came out, no matter how long he stood under the shower. But most days, he liked himself when he looked in the mirror. He still looked good for his age. He was balding but his hair was still dark. And despite his lined face, he was still tall, broad shouldered, with arms like braided ropes, no fat anywhere. All this in spite of Dana's huge meals; roast venison, beef, chickens, barbecued steaks, carrot cakes, pies. Almost everything they ate was grown on their place, or hunted, killed by himself and the boys. Their own milk and butter. They ate damn good. Dana saw to that.

He got up at five every morning as he had since he was a kid, and Kathryn had bullied him into helping with the milking. He would light the fire, milk the cow, get out of the yard in the first gray light with time to stop at the Coffee Jug on his way. He'd pull into the parking lot full of 4x4's with fuel tanks in the back, make his way inside, meet with his crew, drink coffee, eat breakfast, bullshit about work, and the latest piece of government bureaucratic stupidity that was coming down the damn pike. Then they'd drive twenty or thirty miles to whatever logging site they were working on, to spend another day of trees thumping to the ground, machines roaring and grinding, trucks loaded at the end of the day. By six-thirty or seven he'd be home, with only time to shower, milk, do chores, eat dinner, and fall into bed with Dana's warm bulk beside him.

Life was pretty good. He figured, when people looked at him, they must think he was doing something right. There was the big log house that he and Dana had built together, had put so much energy into, the landscaped yard crowded with Dana's flowers, the huge garden, orchard, barn, and in back, the shed full of snowmobiles, motorbikes, the new boats, guns, fishing rods, tools, saws, all of which he had bought to share with his sons.

And he had. They'd gone hiking, fishing, and hunting. He'd

taught all of them to hunt, except for Brendan, who flat out refused. Brendan, continuing his lifelong pattern of being a pain in the ass, had decided instead, that he loved hiking all by himself, hated fishing and hunting. He had saved his money from his allowance and bought himself a damn kayak, kept going off alone onto the lake or into the mountains just to drive his mom crazy. Now he wasn't even doing that, just kept hanging around with those goofy friends of his, none of whom gave a shit about working. Brendan, at eighteen, didn't seem to give a shit about much either, certainly not his family, except maybe for Kathryn.

Who, instead of being tough on him like she was on everyone else, spoiled him rotten. Always had. But when Rob yelled at him, or for Christ's sake, tried to talk seriously to him, like Dana said he should, the kid shut up like a steel trap, disappeared somewhere inside himself and walked away.

Just like Mary. After all these years, it had worn a weary groove in his thoughts. Mary, his mother. Mary, and her death, and why. He had missed her every day since she died, and he figured he'd go on missing her. She'd left a hole in him somewhere. Nothing had filled it in and nothing ever would.

When he was growing up, she'd been the most astonishing light in his life. She came home every summer. He remembered her as flashes of colour, bright red, purple and yellow clothes. Even though he spent most of that growing up time with his grandmother, Kathryn, he waited every year for the brief blazing moments when his mother came home.

He and Kathryn got along all right. She was tough on him, no nonsense, work hard, get along in school, no whining. She'd never babied him. And that was good. She'd made him tough and he appreciated that.

Brendan had started going next door to visit Kathryn when he was just a little kid. She'd taken a shine to him, petted him and he in turn had kept her company. They talked a blue streak, the two of them. Brendan went with her to do chores, helped her bake, asked her questions about everything.

"Don't bother your Grandma," Dana told him. "Stay home. You

can help out here." But Brendan always escaped. And Kathryn indulged him, never raised her voice, never sent him home, even when Dana, with frost in her voice, phoned and demanded that Kathryn send Brendan home immediately. For some reason Kathryn never seemed to get mad at Brendan.

But Rob had never forgotten the tone of voice she used on Mary, the sight of Mary's face burning under the lashing of Kathryn's tongue. He had never gotten used to the sound of Mary's voice when she talked to Kathryn. He knew that side of Kathryn far too well. He wondered if Brendan had ever seen it.

Mary had loved him. He knew that for sure. It had taken him a long time to figure that out. When he was old enough to begin figuring things out, he realized that she'd dumped him off like some kind of extra luggage. Summers when she came home, she'd take him on picnics or swimming. After a while, he got too old for such activity and he started avoiding her when she came home. He wondered if he hated her. Her moods scared him. When she was happy, she was very happy, and when she was sad, she was desperate, frantic for light and air. That's the part he'd never understood. He would have done anything to help when she was like that, but he didn't understand. He never knew what to say or do. He'd never been able to move that blackness in which she was trapped like glue.

He remembered once, right after she'd moved home, when he'd been reluctantly helping her move into the old house. When he said he had to leave, she had turned and grabbed on to him, held on and wouldn't let go. He'd pulled away, unwrapped her arms, and gone out the door without a word. Later, she made a joke out of it, how Rob wouldn't even hug his own mother, waved her arms, talked too loud with the bright brassy tone in her voice he hated. But he could see the tight lines around her mouth.

So while he worked and carried on his life, he thought about Mary, but today, he couldn't stop worrying about Brendan. Brendan made him crazy, always had. When Brendan was little, he had always been more Dana's kid than his. Then after a while, he didn't seem to want to be anybody's kid. As a little kid, he had been such a pain in the ass, whiny, temper tantrums, given to running out of rooms, slamming doors. Rob told Dana she spoiled him rotten. He told her what the kid needed was toughening up. But because he was the youngest, because he was always so damn skinny and wouldn't eat anything, no matter what Dana tried to tempt him with, she always interfered, let him get out of doing chores, came between him and Rob.

So now he had taken off altogether, after the fight they'd had last night, when Rob said if he wouldn't go to school, he could work on Rob's crew instead.

"You useless lazy bastard," Rob said. He tried to keep his voice calm but it kept rising. "What the hell makes you think I'm going to support you? You weren't brought up to lie around smoking your fool head off and not contributing a damn thing to this family."

Brendan said nothing. Dana was in the kitchen and Rob knew from the clashing of pots and pans that she was listening.

"Well? You haven't done a damn thing for months. The least you can do is get some job experience."

"I'm still taking math," Brendan muttered.

"One lousy class. I sure never see you work at it."

"I work," Brendan said.

"Work?" Rob echoed. "At what?"

"School...and I help Grandma."

"Jeezus. You call that work?"

Brendan went silent again.

"Tomorrow morning at five. Be ready for work. I don't know what the hell you can do but I'll find something."

"Like hell," said Brendan.

"What? What did you say?"

"Like hell. I'm not going working for you killing trees or whatever the hell you do. And I'm not staying here." He'd slammed out the door.

So now he was staying up at Kathryn's. Shit. Maybe he should go talk to her. She had no sense when it came to Brendan. She even let him smoke and never bitched about it. Rob's face turned red when he thought about it. He didn't mind so much about the drugs and smoking. All kids went through that. But doing nothing, mooching off Kathryn or whoever would put up with him, that was no good.

Yet Kathryn had been so tough on Mary. She'd never forgiven her for wrecking her life, producing a child at seventeen, then running off. Kathryn had never relented, never forgiven.

"Better she had stayed home where she belonged,"she would mutter to Rob whenever one of Mary's letters showed up. Then when Mary had finally moved home, Kathryn had done nothing but bitch at her.

Mary, his mother. Mary, the artist. He still had a whole lot of her paintings, even though people occasionally "discovered" her all over again and tried to buy them. Dana had stored them up in the attic. They'd hung one they both liked over the fireplace. The paintings were tricky. When you first looked at them, they just looked like shapes, dots, blurs of colour, and then, if you looked longer, the colours shifted, fell into place, made a picture bursting with light and movement.

But Brendan didn't paint. Brendan didn't do much of anything. Just sulked, lay around, took off for days with his druggie friends, until he and Dana had to phone around, find him, go fetch him home, feed him, put him to bed where he'd sleep for sixteen hours, get up, eat something, and take off again. Jeezus. Kids.

Brendan, Mary. He loved them, both of them, so damn much it tore his heart. They were tangled up somehow, in his feelings about them. Both of them, in their own ways, lost to him, one to death and memory, and one to someplace he couldn't even reach for, couldn't get a handle on it to understand. Christ, he'd done his share of drugs. Both he and Dana had. But then they'd smartened up, got their shit together, and made a life for themselves. Brendan didn't seem interested in anything they had to offer, just went on living in a fantasy world, not dealing with anything, not listening to a damn thing anyone said.

And yet the kid was so goddamned bright, gifted, his teachers always said, even when they were complaining about work not done, or about rudeness. Brendan. What the hell could Rob do? What could he even begin to offer Brendan that the kid might be interested in. A car, a job? The goddamn kid would laugh in his face.

Chapter Three

Lying still, reluctant to wake, Kathryn tried to will herself back into the relief of darkness, of not being, while part of her listened for the sounds which were the background tapestry of her life, the squirrels in the ancient walnut tree outside her window. the chickens, traffic on the distant road. Brendan was here. He should be up by now, chopping wood in the basement, clanging the door of the furnace. Then she heard the silence. She woke up. The familiar sounds were gone. She was aware the day was upon her. But she was not at home.

Her eyes flicked open, fell on the foolishly bad painting of flowers on the wall at the side of her bed. Who would be bothered painting such a thing, let along hanging it up. Not her painting, not her wall. Striped yellow wallpaper. Good God.

The faintly burned smell of steamed food drifted in the open door. There were curtains, pulled back, on a frame above her bed, tubes in her arm; she looked down at herself. She was wearing a thin blue rag of a gown. So she was in a hospital. But she didn't remember getting here.

Or agreeing to it. I hate hospitals, she thought. She had always hated them. Hated their smell, the smell of cleanliness covering the hidden desperation clinging like soot to the waxed corridors and smooth walls. She took a deep breath. The smell caught her throat, and she choked, gasped for air.

She looked around, still sucking in deep whooping breaths. She had to get out of here, get air. When she could breathe a little easier, she lay back, taking her bearings, eyes closed, trying to remember. What had happened? It must have been Mike and Arlene, interfering again. Maybe they trapped her, caught her off guard or asleep, brought her here.

"You think I'm just a senile old coot," she muttered. "I'll show you. I'm not helpless yet."

She needed to get up and pee. She wanted a pot of tea, wanted more than anything to make her slow way down the stairs of her house, into her familiar kitchen with no stupid wallpaper, only layers and layers of paint and soot and more paint, put on by various hands over the years–mostly hers. She'd put the kettle on the stove, while the cat rubbed its tail on her ankles. Then she'd check to see that Brendan had rinsed the milk bucket, put the milk to chill in the fridge. She'd take her tea to the window, watch the life in the yard, birds, flowers, the sun streaming in the window, and make plans for the day.

She struggled to sit up, panted for breath, hoisted herself with her hands. She was all right. She could tell that. Nothing hurt. Nothing was broken. Why was she here then? She waited for a while, propped up on the pillows and breathing, thinking perhaps someone could come and explain what she was doing here. But no one came. The room was quiet. Far away, down the hall, she could hear a phone ringing, faint voices, and the hum of a floor polisher.

She sat up farther, picked up the water pitcher on the table beside the bed, pulled back her arm, and threw it at the wall. Nothing broke, the pitcher was plastic, unbreakable, only an arc of silvery water rippled over the dull orange plastic chairs.

Her arm still had strength in it. That was good. All those years of pitching hay and picking up hundred-pound feed sacks were still there, usable. She looked around for something else to throw, the pillows, of course, the blankets, an anemic vase of flowers. Dyed carnations. Probably sent by the people who trapped her here. Why then, for God's sake, send flowers? Because they were so glad she was trapped, barricaded at last in a jail she'd have to fight her way out of, despite being old. Well, she wasn't that old. And to hell with the disapproving looks of nurses and doctors and neighbours and God knows who else. She threw the flowers at the picture. Water streaked down the wall, and the flowers scattered on the tiled floor.

Carefully, because it hurt, she unwrapped the tape from her arm, yanked out the IV tubes, and then overturned the contraption that it all hung on. Then she finished sitting up. All the way. Slowly, she had to sit there for a while, breath coming too fast, but breathing was getting easier; she'd been doing it for ninety-one years. The dizziness passed again. She swung her legs over the side of the bed, stood up, then looked around for her clothes. She found them in the cupboard beside the bed, and laboriously got dressed, threw the foolish hospital gown on the floor, went to the bathroom, washed her face with hot water, came back to the bed.

Nobody had come in. She sat on the bed in her red flannel shirt and boots. Her short grey hair was standing up all over her head. She tried to smooth it down with her hands.

"You think I'm losing my marbles," she said out loud. "Who cares what my hair looks like? Who cares?" She grabbed the metal table which stood beside the bed and shoved it hard. It slammed against the wall and made enough noise to finally bring a nurse.

Arlene stood in the door, hair neatly pinned, makeup, pastel pink pantsuit, hands on hips, frowned disapprovingly and said, "I suppose you think you're just going to walk out of here now in a tantrum and I'm going to let you. You just get back in that bed and wait for a doctor. You know you're not well, and you need to just be quiet and conserve your strength. God will help you if you let him but you've got to do your share."

"No," said Kathryn. "I'm going. There's nothing wrong with me. You can't keep me here and you know it."

Her granddaughter stood, bit her lip, frowned, finally said, "Oh, all right. You're not doing yourself or this place much good. But first you have to wait and see a doctor. And then we'll have to figure out how to get you home and keep an eye on you. I'll get my prayer circle working on you as well."

Kathryn shrugged her broad bony shoulders under her red plaid shirt. She was used to Arlene's prattling. She snapped, "Call Rob, he'll come. Or one of the boys."

"They're out working, Grandma. I'll just call a taxi for you."

"And what taxi is going to cart me way to hell and gone out to the farm and not charge me a goddamn fortune in the bargain? "

"No, I mean to my house. I'm off shift in a couple of hours. I'll come and keep an eye on you and drive you home later."

"No," Kathryn said. "I'm going home now. I have to get home. I've got things to look after. I'll bet no one's been out tending the chickens or watering the garden or mowing the lawn. Nobody does a damn thing these days unless they have to."

"Mike and I went out last night," Arlene snapped. "And Brendan's there. Remember? Rob went over there last night to check on him. Okay, I'll go find a doctor to sign you out and see if one of the boys will pick you up, if I can get hold of anyone. It's all going to take a while. So now please just get back into bed and try and stay quiet for a bit, and I'll send someone to clean up this mess."

"I'm going home," Kathryn said suspiciously, but at least consenting to sit back down on the bed. "You know I hate doctors. Why'd you make me come here?"

"Because you were sick, remember. We thought you were having a heart attack. You fainted, when Mike and I were out visiting. You scared us to death. Don't you remember when Mike and I drove you in here? That was three days ago. You've been mostly sleeping ever since. Doctor says you'll probably be okay, just not enough blood getting up to your brain, something like that. But we've got to keep a closer eye on you. What would have happened if we hadn't been around?"

"I been here three days? Goddamnit, Arlene, I got to get home. Things'll be in a mess, weeds all over the garden, chickens not fed."

The younger woman sighed deep and long, blowing the air out through her mouth.

"I'll go phone," she said, turning on her heels, "but don't blame me if no one's around." She left, her rubber shoes squeaking on the polished grey and white tiles of the hospital corridor.

Rob finally came in from work. Arlene had called on his radio phone. He came to the hospital in his muddy sawdust covered work clothes. Together he and Kathryn went out into the bright spring sun. He lifted Kathryn up the high step into his diesel four-by-four.

When they got home, she put the kettle on and then went outside, made sure the chickens were actually fed and the garden watered, then sat at the table and complained about the hospital and Mike and Arlene's treachery in taking her there. Brendan was nowhere around. Of course not, Rob thought, what the hell did he care that his great grandmother had almost died? Useless kid. He said as much to Kathryn.

"You leave him alone," she snapped. "He has his own life. He doesn't have to baby-sit me."

Rob and Kathryn sat at the ancient round oak table that had sat in the kitchen, next to the bay window, for seventy years. Kathryn and Bill had bought it when they were first married. Kathryn thawed some biscuits in the microwave Arlene and Mike had bought her a few Christmases ago, and they ate them with strawberry jam but neither had any appetite.

"I got to get back," Rob said. "I'll call Dana, get her to run over."

"Leave her alone," Kathryn said. "She's got her work. I've got mine. I'll be fine. I just needed to get home, out of that place."

"You sure you'll be all right?"

"Just go," she said. "I hate people making a damn fuss."

Rob drove up the drive to the highway, past the row of ancient cedars, the ancient mailbox which no longer received any mail, leaning slightly towards the road. Once, when he was twelve, he had painted on it, rather badly but with great care, a picture of a cedar tree. He wanted to name the farm then, after the cedars, but Kathryn stopped him with a snort.

"Let them Calgary weekend wannabees name their places," she said. "This is a plain old farm and that's what it's going to stay."

The house, once gleaming white but now dull flecking grey was between the highway and the wide blue lake. The long curving driveway ran between sloping hay fields which were still bordered by silvery cedar split rail fences, now over a hundred years old. Bill's father had cut the cedars, then split them, and then charred them in huge fires built on the beach. Once they were burning, he smothered the fire in sand, leaving the cedar rails almost impervious to rot. He had built the house as well, situating it in a hollow below the brow of a hill, barely visible from the highway, sheltered from the wind off the lake. Beyond the house were the garden, a chicken coop, and an old log barn slowly crumbling to wood dust. Beyond that was the orchard, a brief slope of granite and twisted scrawny firs, and then the blue expanse of lake, stretching to the mountains.

In the summer, people often stopped to take photographs. Kathryn raged when she saw someone with a camera, standing on the highway, looking down. "I should charge them bastards," she'd say. "Maybe I could put up a sign. Cute farm. Ten bucks a photo."

When Rob was a child, the land on either side of the farm had been bush laced with deer and elk trails, occasional clearings where moss was piled thick on rocks and logs, coyote dens, osprey nests, Douglas fir and enormous yellow pine splitting crevices in the granite.

Living on the lake wasn't popular then. Few of the people who had settled the valley wanted to live so far from Appleby over such an uncertain and twisting road. The farms and homesteads along the lake were scattered over two, three, five mile intervals, in pockets of fertile land, the rest of the land too steep and rocky for farming. There were few beaches. The mountains plunged steeply to the black lake water. The main highway to Vancouver ran through Appleby, far from the lake so few tourists visited.

But over the years, the lake community had changed. Rob didn't mind. It was good to have more neighbours. A lot of them disappeared south in the winter. Some of them had no idea how to live in the country, did their best to recreate whatever suburban landscape they had escaped, trailers with coloured plastic lanterns, bad replicas of California or west coast architecture. People built glass and cedar castles on rock bluffs but their sewage drained into the lake; they laced their acres of surrounding lawns with herbicides. Every spring there was an outcry about mosquitoes, and every fall, an outcry about bears in their garbage and deer in their garden.

Kathryn hated every new house, every new driveway, every change. New neighbours had just bought the property on the south side of the farm. They were from Toronto. Rob didn't think he'd ever met someone from Toronto before. The first thing they did was cut down all their trees, then the house had gone up, huge, surrounded with lawn. The people had snowmobiles and motorcycles but no idea of the meaning of fences or gates. When they came asking for permission to dig a new waterline across one of Kathryn's fields, she snarled at them and slammed the door in their surprised faces.

After that, Kathryn had plastered the farm with no trespassing and no hunting signs, which the neighbours generally obeyed, but not their dogs, or their weekend visitors and grandchildren.

With the advent of so many new people, Kathryn's, and now Rob and Dana's land, had risen spectacularly in value. When Dana and Rob were first married, they bought the sixty acres of land adjoining Kathryn's 160 acres. Rob hadn't thought much about rising values at the time. If he and Dana could manage it, they'd help the boys buy land as well, but the way prices were going up it was going to be difficult.

Damned difficult, especially the way taxes were going up to pay for useless stupidity. Like the "improvements" as they were called, to the narrow winding highway which had been blasted and widened at several places. He liked the highway narrow. Kept the bad drivers off it. At one point, it had been announced that the stretch of road in front of the farm would be improved as well, which would have meant cutting a row of sugar maples planted by Bill's father.

Kathryn phoned everyone she knew in the valley, called in old favours and old loyalties, blustered, threatened to face down with a shotgun any highways men that appeared at her gate, laughed at their offers of more and more money. In the end, the highways people went away. They didn't have the heart for this kind of fight; they decided this stretch of road wasn't that important. They had alternatives. Now the road narrowed where it went by the farm and widened again on either side.

Rob drove back to work. He drummed his fingers on the steering wheel. They were going to have to do something about Kathryn. She really ought to have someone staying there, someone other than Brendan who was unreliable, never around, and wouldn't know what to do in a crisis anyway.

She could die like that, he thought. His throat closed, his eyes filled. He fought the tears back, blinking his eyes in order to see, to keep driving. Kathryn was huge, solid, invincible; it was like the world crumbling around him. The very road he drove on seemed fragile, his truck a collection of metal parts, rusting to dust all around him. It was like watching the mountains erode in a few brief instants, like one of those time lapse films, this knowledge of a life without Kathryn in it, and in a few more brief seconds, a life without him in it as well.

Smarten up, idiot, he thought to himself. God, you're being so damn melodramatic. It was only one brief fainting spell, after all. She was probably good for a few years yet. But Arlene had warned him, caught up to him as he was coming into the hospital.

"It's a sign," she had said. "Really, she shouldn't be allowed to go home but she'll just fret and fume if she stays here. It could happen again anytime. She needs to be watched. You'll have to talk to Brendan about it. Or we could get a nurse or a homemaker to come in."

They'd stood there looking at each other. Arlene was his cousin, ten years younger than him. She had grown up during summers spent on the farm with him and Kathryn but he'd never liked her much.

It still amazed Rob that she had become a real nurse. The uniform seemed like a costume, something Arlene put on to play grownup.

"She'd hate that, Arlene. You know she would. Strangers messing with her house, moving her things around. No, I don't think that would work. I don't see why we can't look after her ourselves. I'll stop by every day. Dana is just over the field. Brendan's there. It'll be okay."

Arlene turned away with an exasperated sigh. Rob sighed too. Arlene was always trying to reform them all. She'd gotten involved with some nutty bunch of fundamentalists in Appleby. She had strict ideas about health and nutrition and hygiene. Her other preoccupation was housecleaning and decorating. She and Mike seemed to spend all their spare time fixing up their house, a two bedroom in town. They were also talking about building a cabin on the farm, down by the lake, something "cute" as Arlene put it.

Rob swiped at his eyes, but he couldn't quite make the tears stop. He was amazed. He hadn't cried for years. It was embarrassing. They kept on squeezing out. Thank God he was alone. His throat ached, clenched shut. It was hard to breathe. He had to gasp for air. But somehow he managed to keep driving. By the time he got to work, his face was back under control. He was able to swing down from the truck, yell a rough joke at the guys taking a break, sitting on yellow pine stumps.

Chapter Four

After Rob left, Kathryn went on sitting at the table for a long time. There were things she ought to be doing, the things that had seemed so frantically important when she was trapped in the hospital. Work always piled up if she left even to go to Appleby for a day. Brendan had left dishes in the sink, leftovers on the counter. The compost bucket was full. The garden had a fresh green fuzz of weeds.

But she was so tired. She wouldn't have admitted it to Arlene, or to the brisk young doctor who had checked her over and shrugged at her insistence that she was going home, that she was fine and didn't need any help from him. But now she admitted it to herself. She was more tired than she could ever remember being in her life.

I'm too tired to live anymore, she thought, and then tried to cancel the thought. What a stupid thing to think. She laid her head down on the table.

Mary, she thought. Mary, you went ahead of me. You went down this road. Help me get through this.

Fear, like a great roaring wind, flooded through her.

Goddammit, she thought frantically. I hate this. I hate this. I can't die. The words twisted around themselves, tangled into knots. I can't go. I won't. I won't leave this, this house, my land, my family. She held onto the table. She had always hated leaving the farm to go anywhere. She was damned, she thought, if she'd leave it forever. She held on like a woman in a flood; if she let go for a second, the flood would tear her away, like it had torn Mary, over a precipice somewhere, and she'd be gone.

The light was dimming; it was dark in the room, maybe a storm coming. She wanted to get up from the table, go outside, look at the sky, but she couldn't move.

After a while, she came back to herself. She must have fainted again. Better not tell Arlene or Rob. She'd be all right. She'd get past this, the same way she'd gotten past everything else in her life. She just needed to stop pampering herself, lying around when there was work to do.

She pushed herself up from the table, stood up straight, and went out the back door into the sun.

You're walking like an old woman, she thought. Straighten up, Kathryn. That's what her grandmother had said to her, eighty years ago. Her grandmother, a little tiny spry woman with no softness in her. She had taken over the family when Kathryn's mother died. Kathryn had been only twelve.

Be tough and hard and work and never give in. Never let down. That's what her grandmother had defined as life's purpose.

"The devil finds work for idle hands," she told Kathryn sharply. "If you see what needs doing, turn your hand to it," she had said. "That's a woman's life." And that had been Kathryn's life. There had only ever been time to work, first for her parents, when she was a kid, growing up on a rock and poplar farm in the northern BC bush, and then when she had married Bill, there was the same life she was used to, always too much work and never enough money. There were fruit trees, the garden, cows, chickens, baking, cleaning, the children, always more work to do than she could ever possibly have time for. But it was work she knew how to do. Her hands flew without ceasing.

She had met Bill when he was working on a railroad gang, and she had her first job, cleaning at the only local motel. She married him because she admired his tough exterior, his gruffness, his lack of sentimentality. She felt she could match him. They fought, long and often, but they made a team, worked together, survived. When she was first married and new in the small lakeside community, she had made an effort, made time for choir at church, or the occasional afternoon tea, and a few times a year, trips to town for movies. But most of the other women she met were soft, silly people. They twittered and gossiped. Kathryn had gradually stopped seeing them.

Over the past few years, her life had narrowed, pared down to bare bones; there was the farm, Rob, Dana, their boys, Arlene and Mike. Sometimes, these days, though she hated to admit it, she lost track of people, couldn't remember names, who was who.

Now she stood still in the hot sun, in the middle of the shaggy lawn which she'd need to remind Brendan to mow. The sun penetrated her head, her flesh, her bones, punching her full of holes, until she was transparent, as airy and light-filled as a feather. The yard vibrated silently around her, as if somewhere, a great gong had been struck. She wondered if she was actually awake.

"Mary," she said out loud. "Mary."

The sun shook the enormous walnut tree that stood near the back door. Leaves and twigs sifted down onto the grass. "Mary," she said again. Behind her the back door slammed. The house muttered on its foundations.

I want her back, Kathryn, thought. I want it all back. It's gone too fast. I never had time, I never knew. I will stand here saying her name until the earth cracks open and gives her back to me. She was mine, and I didn't know that.

She pulled herself straighter, considering. Then she went back inside, got a hat, and a blanket. She went down the long path beside the hayfield, over the rocks and under the giant Douglas firs, to the beach. It was a shame and a sin to sit on the beach in the middle of the afternoon, with work waiting for her but so what. She was too mad to care. Besides, she was old and tired. She had earned a damned afternoon in the sun.

Carefully, she lowered herself down to the blanket on the sand. She closed her eyes to the bright sun. Her whole body flattened out under the pressure of the light, softening, dissolving, seeping into the earth beneath her like rainwater after a drought. This is what she wanted, she thought drowsily, to just be absorbed into the ground like leaves after winter, tiny hair roots tangling around each molecule of flesh and absorbing it, pulling it down and down, into the soft dark crumbly soil, just right for planting, smelling of secrets and abundance for another season.

Chapter Five

"My dad's a killer," Brendan told his friend Johnnie. "He thinks nothing is worth anything unless he can kill it, eat it, or fuck it." They were lying side by side in someone's basement, smoking cigarettes.

"He's cool," Johnnie said. "He's tough."

"He's a pig," Brendan said. "I wish he'd drop a damn tree on his head one day." Then he wondered if he meant it. Later, when the acid they'd taken sang bright purple siren songs in his blood, he wished the words back, terrified they might come true.

Now, a week later, Brendan was walking in the middle of the highway. It was night and pitch black. He could stay on the road by following the faint sheen of the lines in the middle of the pavement. When he heard a car coming, he didn't look or turn around. The drivers hit their brakes, and drove around him. Some honked.

He was wearing a black denim jacket and three t-shirts layered over top of one another and cut-off denim shorts. He had long black hair which hung down his back. His face was thin and white with large dark eyes. His hands and feet were huge with long thin fingers and toes. His brothers always teased him about his feet. "Bigfoot," they jeered. "Gonna grow up to be a sasquatch."

He was walking the fifteen miles from his home to town again. He hadn't been able to get a ride. No one had driven by that he knew, and now it was freezing cold and dark. He didn't mind, he told himself. He liked being out at night. He liked the blackness, the sense that everyone else was shut away in lighted rooms, and he was outside on the edge of everything.

He was living with his grandmother because he couldn't stand his father. She wasn't actually his grandmother, but his great grandmother, but he had always called her Grandma. His own grandmother, Mary, had never seemed much like any kind of grandmother. He had never even known her. She had died long before he was born, before his mom and dad got married. She was too impossibly remote and beautiful and fantastic to be a grandmother. She had been an artist. One of her paintings hung over the fireplace in his parents' house. Brendan had grown up with it. He was too used to it to know what he thought of it, except that sometimes, when he was younger, he used to lie on the couch and stare at its misty wandering whirling paint, and wonder where it was, what part of the world it represented, or if it was some magical imaginary place.

He knew, in the bitter centre of his heart, that he was only living at his grandmother's because he was chickenshit, because he didn't have the guts to do what he really wanted to do, which was to go to Vancouver or somewhere even farther, get any kind of job, get a room, start to live.

But when he thought about it, his heart sank. He didn't think he knew how to run away. He had tried and tried to picture himself getting on the bus, or hitchhiking into a strange city where he knew no one, job hunting, looking for somewhere to live. It didn't seem like living, it seemed like desperation. Sometimes he thought about running in the opposite direction, into the mountains, along the trails where his dad had taken him and his brothers hiking and fishing. He liked that fantasy a lot more. He even got to the point, sometimes, of planning what to take, but that was as far as it went.

He still had to finish his damn Grade 12 math, a subject he hated, so he could graduate from high school. It was so damn stupid to have to go back to school when everyone else he knew had graduated, gone off somewhere, was travelling, or going to university. He hated math. That's why he hadn't finished yet. But at least he had an excuse for still being here, hanging around the town like some nerdy loser. Plus his grandmother needed someone to do chores, and keep an eye on things.

And he liked her. He liked her a lot. Ever since he could remember, he had been going over to her house, running across the expanse of hayfield between the two houses, stooping under the pole gate, then slamming the screen door behind him, crawling up on the stool by the kitchen table. She always had great food. He remembered chocolate chip cookies and hot chocolate with marshmallows, or gingersnaps, or pie, or carrot cake. She always had something. And he could ask her questions. She never minded him sitting there asking dumb kid questions. It seemed like they could talk about anything. She always talked to him like he was smart and knew what was going on. After he ate, they'd go outside, and he'd stay beside her as she worked. She told him about plants, chickens, the mysteries of new calves and milking.

Now she was in the hospital, and no one seemed to know what was wrong. He'd tried to stay at the house without her there, but it was too spooky. He did the chores and then headed for Appleby.

Sometimes he forgot she was so old. He had never thought about her getting old and one day dying, because he didn't want to and it was impossible to imagine. It would be like a mountain falling. One night, just before falling asleep he had, just for a moment, let it in, that she was old, that someday, she would die, and found himself, there in the dark with tears in his eyes. He turned on his back until the tears dried by themselves and the raspy ache in his throat subsided. But of course, it was impossible to stop keep thinking about death, about his mother, his father, even himself, growing old and the disappearing into nothing. What a stupid way to have a world, he thought. It made him frantic and slightly breathless, because there was so much to do before such a distant time.

But for now, here he was, stuck in the valley until June, anyway, and now it was still only April, spring at last, but still two long months to get through before summer. At least he'd finally got the jam to get the hell away from his parents and their endless nagging.

"Get a job," his dad had said. "You lazy asshole."

Brendan clenched his fists. He'd been going crazy, living there with his insane family. Or maybe they weren't insane, but if that was normal, they could keep it. Anything was better than living there, fighting with his dad. His mom was always trying to keep both of them away from each other. Her whole trip was to stuff everyone with food as if that was the answer to everything. His two older brothers had left home and were living in Appleby. So he was the target for all the shit.

When they did come around, they sounded like his dad. "Get a job. Do something with your life." They only came around for free food or to bullshit with his dad about cars.

His father spent his life killing trees and fixing machines so he could kill more trees and make more money. His brothers didn't seem to think any further than the next job and the next round of beer drinking. They littered the yards with machines and parts of 4 x 4 trucks and tires and nuts and bolts and buckets of oil. His mother's whole life revolved around her house and around food, growing, picking, canning, freezing, cooking, and then cleaning up. She never stopped, never rested, never relaxed. Even in the summer, when she was outside, lying in a lawn chair, her eyes kept moving restlessly from plant to flower bed to tree, until she couldn't stand it any longer and she got up and began to prune a tree or weed the garden or go in the house and start cooking.

His father went hunting every fall, brought home dripping carcasses of deer and elk, more food for his mother to make something with which to stuff them all, like pigs in a pen. Every Sunday, his father and brothers, and now, somedays, their girlfriends, sat at the table swilling down the huge amounts of food his mother cooked, and the men talked about work, and machines, and chain saws, and the other men with whom they worked. The women said hardly anything until they were out in the kitchen, cleaning up. Then they bitched away to each other about everyone they knew.

What Brendan depended on were his friends. The ones he hung out with. The people he played with, smoked dope with, partied with, stole stuff from 7-11 with, the ones he trusted. The ones he cared about, that cared about him.

But his friends would hardly ever come out to his grandmother's house. They were afraid of her because she was so old, and because she looked at them from under her eyebrows and said unexpected, ungrandmotherly things. Perversely, he liked to bring his friends there when he could talk them into it, watch them shifting, uneasy and grinning, their assumptions about this little old lady rapidly fading as she got on them right away, asking questions, making jokes, cackling away about hideously embarrassing subjects like sex and drugs and fast cars about which she should have been expected to know nothing at all. His friends would stand there, shifting, mumbling answers, hardly able to wait until they could safely get back outside, into their cars, and away.

Yeah, Kathryn was all right. He was proud of her, even when he was fleeing, laughing with his friends to the safety of the car, the road, some beer or dope, a hit of acid, an all night session of some role playing game in someone's basement, dice and game notes littering the floor. When the game finally ended, they would all sprawl exhausted on a couch or mattress, falling asleep at first light, when the dim grey silhouettes of trees would show across somebody's lawn and the rest of the world began to wake up.

Yeah, friends were what mattered. He and his best friend, Johnnie, had been friends all through high school. Johnnie was tall, good looking with brown curly hair, and full of hell. That's what his grandmother said. "What a hell raiser, that boy," she said. She always asked about Johnnie. "How's the hellion?" she'd say. "Still getting you into trouble?"

She told Brendan to be careful, that Johnnie liked having him around as a follower, someone to admire and look up to him, and that if he followed him long enough, it would mean trouble. Brendan didn't know how she could know all this. But he thought she was probably right.

His grandmother didn't drive him crazy like his mother did. His mother gave his advice all the time as well, but then she had to reinforce any thing she told him by touching him, kissing the top of his head, rubbing his back, endlessly anxious to make sure that he was still her last baby, her youngest son. His mother drove him crazy.

Everything did. When he looked around his world, he couldn't see much to be happy about. He'd grown up listening to people agonize over the possibility of nuclear war, and now, as far as he could tell, everything was going to hell anyway. The environment was toast, there weren't any jobs worth doing, especially for someone his age. His mother and father both said, together and separately, over and over, that he had to go to university, but to Brendan, that sounded like another long boring waste of time, just another more complicated version of high school. And then on, and on, into a boring job, a sort of job, and a boring life in an apartment somewhere, with maybe a wife and two whiny kids, and then death.

All of which meant nothing, as he walked down the centre of this black-iced gravel littered pavement, holding his cigarette to his lips with one numb hand. Words ran like skittering bugs in his head, shaping themselves into something he could almost, if he had the nerve, call a poem.

Chapter Six

Brendan was the one who found Kathryn passed out on the beach. He'd come home finally, after sleeping at Johnnie's for a couple of days. He found the house quiet, but he could tell she was back, things had been moved around.

He put the milk in the fridge and then went outside. The sun was shining and he was hungry. He went down the path to the beach, whistling bird calls. The beach was his favourite place. Whenever he was home, he would wander down the path to the edge of the sand, stand looking in the water, glance at the clouds piled up over the mountains, their familiar blue silhouettes carving a space in the sky, listen to gulls, ravens, and the odd trout struggling up out of the water for a brief rainbowed arc of air.

When he saw her, at first he didn't know what to do, or how to react. He tiptoed over, very secretively, and sat down beside her. He took her hand, which was warm, noticed how she was breathing, the laboured wheeze. His eyes filled up. "Grandma," he whispered. "Wake up."

She opened her eyes, but didn't seem to recognize him. She looked at him, said, "Mary," and went back to sleep. He bent down, tried to lift her but couldn't. He covered her reddened skin with his shirt. Very gently, he leaned over, kissed her forehead, and whispered, "I'll be right back."

Then he ran faster than he had ever thought he could, across the field, under the barbed wire, over the old stile, through his own yard, to where his mother was making supper, and waiting for Rob to come home.

"Grandma," he gasped. "The beach. She won't wake up."

Dana was always calm in any emergency. She moved to the phone, called the ambulance, grabbed a blanket and pillow, and ran with Brendan. She couldn't keep up. He tore the blanket and pillow away from her, ran ahead of her, back down the path.

Kathryn looked old and shrunken, lying under his torn plaid shirt, as if she was melting away into the ground, disappearing in front of his eyes. He covered her over with the blanket, put the pillow under her head and called her, but she wasn't there somehow, had been replaced by some stranger, someone helpless. His grandmother would never lie here on the beach in the late afternoon sun, grotesque and graceless. His grandmother was always moving, busy, in charge, fixing things, cleaning, cooking, restless as a mother hen with a brood, scratching, clucking. His grandmother was never overcome by anything. The world had thrown all kinds of shit at her, and she'd looked at it and contemptuously thrown it back.

When the ambulance arrived, Dana went with it to the hospital. Brendan stayed back at the house with instructions to call his brothers, tell his dad when he came home, phone Arlene, and watch the roast that was in the oven.

He did the calls, feeling grave, important, and terrified. When Rob drove in the yard, Brendan met him outside, said breathlessly, "It's grandma, she's sick again, she was on the beach, I mean, she fell asleep or something. I didn't know she was home, I mean what was she doing on the beach? That's so weird, that she'd go to the beach in the afternoon."

Rob gave him that look that Brendan always hated, the look that said he was not making sense. Rob didn't even ask him questions, strode in the house to the phone, called the hospital, listened, hung up and looked at Brendan.

"Goddam," Rob said, and sank into a chair. He covered his face with his hands. After a while, Brendan realized his dad was shaking, maybe even crying. He knew he should go over, should say something, do something. He stood there frozen but the phone rang.

Rob answered, "Jeezus God, Dana, why'd the doctor let her come home earlier? Doesn't that goddam hospital know anything? Didn't they know she wasn't in any shape to come home? And what the hell is Brendan babbling about, her sleeping on the beach or something?"

Rob's face crumpled. His voice choked. He listened again, struggled to get control of himself, said, finally, "I'll be in as soon as I shower and change." He slammed the phone down, breathing hard, turned, didn't seem to see Brendan, then, panting like a man in a race, went upstairs without saying another word. When he came back down, he nodded to Brendan, who went out to the truck with him.

They rode to town together in silence. Brendan stared out the truck window at houses, gardens, fences. The grass was just starting to turn green. I've got to call Johnnie, he thought. He scrunched himself into the corner of the truck, as far away from his father as he could get, wanting a cigarette.

There wasn't much they could do at the hospital. Kathryn lay shrunken and pitiful on the bed. They expected any moment that she would wake up, look around, furious at the fact that everyone was standing around and no one was doing anything useful, that she was trapped in the hospital again and they'd let it happen again.

Brendan went to slip out the door of the room.

"Where the hell do you think you're going?" Rob snarled.

"Johnnie's," he mumbled, staring at his shoes.

"Come home and have dinner," Dana said. "I'll drive you in later if you really want to go."

When they drove home together. Brendan sat between his parents. When he was younger, he would have curled up, his head on his mother's lap and gone to sleep. Dana reached over and took his hand.

"Baby," she murmured. "How are you doing? How's my sweet boy?"

"I'm okay," he said. He let his hand stay in hers.

"You'd better stay with us tonight," she said. "We'll go over to your grandma's in the morning, do the chores together."

He shook his head. "She wouldn't want the house left empty. There's the cat and everything."

She said, "I hope that roast hasn't dried out. And I made a carrot cake, just in case you might come by."

He shook his head again, but he was hungry. He had a hard time remembering when he had last eaten, a sub at 7-11 sometime, maybe yesterday some chips and beer at Johnnie's. He wanted a joint, a beer, maybe lots of beer, and his friends to talk to.

When supper was ready, he sat in his usual chair, next to his father. His mother fussed, she always fussed, but he ate all the food she gave him, had extra dessert.

After supper, he went back across the pasture to Kathryn's dark house. The cat came to him, and he was glad of the company. He stood in the middle of the darkened kitchen, listening. The house was full of small secret noises. Most of them he could identify. He carried the cat upstairs with him to go to bed.

During his sleep, he dreamt that he was trapped in some strange country, run by a dictator, who took pleasure in pain and torture. He lit people on fire, strangled them with piano wire. In the dream, Brendan was working in a store and someone gave him a poster with a picture of himself. He tried to run away, got up on the mountain where there was a kind of old cabin in which he thought he might hide. He felt in his pocket for the poster, and realized he had dropped it in the store. They would be coming after him. They would know he was to be tortured and killed as well. There was no escape.

He woke up, sweating and terrified. The house murmured and shifted around him. The door to his room creaked and his whole body jumped. But it was only the cat, coming to curl up under the covers with him. He lay still, thinking about the dream. He didn't know about dreams. He didn't know about anything. He thought about Kathryn, drifting away from them all, into an unknown country, an unknown darkness, a place to which he could no longer follow, as he had followed for so long behind her on her way between the kitchen, the garden, the chicken house, the beach. Now she was leaving him behind.

There was a picture on the wall of him and his brothers when they were children. It was taken outside under the old walnut tree. There had been a tire swing. A friend was with them, four boys of different ages, caught by the camera in attitudes of detachment and surprise. Someone must have called to them, said, "Look up, smile," and they had looked but not smiled, looked and gone back to playing.

Brendan stared at the picture. He had been around four when it was taken. His two older brothers were hanging on the swing; he was standing off to one side, staring out of the picture, in the scene but not part of it. The picture hurt him. He didn't know why. He remembered being four. He even remembered boy who had come to play that day, a boy who had died later from leukemia.

He had been happy then. He wondered if he would ever be happy again. These days, his life seemed to be one long shifting of moods through every shade of grey, a grey that never lightened and let the sun come through. He and his friends shared this greyness, hung on to each other through its manifestations, played games all night to keep away its darker shades.

His mother kept trying to sign him up for various kinds of lessons, tried to get him to take a lame Creative Writing course in town, piano lessons, karate lessons. She was always full of ideas for what he could do with his life.

He never bothered to tell her he didn't plan to do anything with his life. He couldn't think of a thing worth doing other than hanging out with his friends and surviving with a minimum of effort. He wondered what he would do now if Kathryn didn't come home. He'd have to find somewhere to live. For a while, he could stay with Johnnie. But living there would drive him crazy after a while. Johnnie's parents were cool. They didn't care about smoking dope or cigarettes, or drinking beer. They didn't care about housework or cooking either. Maybe he could go pick apples or something, get enough money for the bus, go to Vancouver like he had always planned, hang out there, learn to skateboard.

He got out of bed, turned the picture to the wall. Then he got his notebook out from under the bed, drew cartoons in the margins, pictures of a mouse with fangs, a snake with rabbit ears, a person with a head that was only a question mark.

Chapter Seven

Brendan wanted to go to town. But his dad was in at the stupid hospital, and his mother was off somewhere, buying groceries and he felt compelled, for some stupid reason, to stay home. A sense of imminent disaster hung over the farm, a distant cloud, a thunderstorm brewing. At the same time everything was depressingly normal, the sun went on shining, the grass stayed green, the lake was, as always, glinting through the fringe of trees along its edge.

There was nothing at all to do but sit and watch the boring sun on the boring lawn in front of this boring stupid house which you couldn't do anything in because you'd get it dirty and then his mom would look at him and frown and run around cleaning it up. He got up and went prowling through the house, stood for a long time in front of the fridge, opened the cupboards, went into his parents' room, looked at the two different piles of books, beside their bed, left that room and finally, did something he had wanted to do for a while, went and pulled down the ladder, climbed up it into the attic. When he and his brothers were growing up, they had occasionally played up here on rainy days but it was too dark, dusty and uncomfortable to be much of a playplace.

He looked around. He didn't quite know he was doing here, but he had an idea; the box with Grandmother Mary's diaries had always sat in a corner. He had looked at them before but without interest. They were scribbled all over on the outside; some were hard cover, some were child's scribblers, some were coil bound notebooks, and some were drawing books, both large and small. Some were dated and some weren't.

Brendan pulled one at random, a drawing book, full of bright scribbles, bits of leaves, a tree trunk, a canoe, something that looked like rocks, a dog's ear, a horse hoof, the edge of a window. The drawings were clear, precise, one or two to each page, done in pen or black ink or pencil.

He pulled another, a journal, dated 1974, the spring that she died.

Crawling towards spring, he read. *No money. No money, no money. Went over to Mom's today. She had a lot of ideas for what I ought to do with my life, as usual. But I've tried everything I know how to do. All I can do is make pictures. and right now, it's all I can stand to do anyway. Why isn't that enough? Why isn't anything I do enough?*

He put it down, picked up another, an older one, and then another and another. Finally, he piled them all back in the box, picked up the box, crawled back down the ladder, and took them to his room. He crawled under the patchwork bedspread, lit a cigarette, then got up and opened the window. Then he crawled back into the bed, which was piled with pillows. His hair fell into his eyes and he kept flipping it away as he read. He curled down farther under the blankets, pulled the sheet over his head, so he could barely see.

It was like reading a mystery, a puzzle, a story he couldn't put down, full of moments like dreams, moments he felt he had also lived through, had seen through this woman's eyes .

The sky catches and eddies around the tip of Steeple Mountain. My life trails after me, catches and eddies in this moment, this room, where the grey light solidifies into late afternoon.

He heard the car in the yard. It was Johnnie; he had managed to borrow his parent's car. Brendan read one more entry.

There's nothing as easy as sitting here, warm, the fire singeing my knees, with coffee, a book, a pencil. The day slides by like oil, gone before I can grasp it. I am frightened of time sliding so fast, and yet so relieved to just sit, here, at last, to only be here, to see no one, go nowhere, to listen to silence crowding the room.

He could come back. He could read more. But now Johnnie had come to take him out of these shadows. With a sense of enormous relief, Brendan scrabbled up, unwrapped himself from the blankets, grabbed his pack with his notebook, his cigarettes, and his game playing cards, took the stairs two at a time and slammed the door hard behind him as he left.

Section Two

Mary

Chapter Eight

The small restaurant hummed and buzzed with voices. A drift of blue smoke hung over the tables. Behind Mary, the radio buzzed static, ignored, but never turned off. Charlie, the ancient owner of the cafe, was at his usual table, a full ashtray, a cold cup of coffee and a stained deck of cards in front of him. Over the years, he had both expanded and shrunk in various places, so now in 1955 his huge belly protruded, strained at the front of his blue buttoned cardigan, but his arms and legs were thin sticks that stuck out at odd angles. Mary thought he looked like a giant bug. She avoided him as much as she could, but his half slitted cold blue eyes watched her as she worked.

She worked, half asleep, in a kind of trance, carrying food, emptying ashtrays, avoiding hands, and checking the room for empty plates, or a raised hand beckoning for a refill. Right now, in the late afternoon, she was the only woman in the room. Occasionally, one of the neighbour women came in with her husband for lunch or dinner, and in the summer tourists came, but usually the coffee shop was full of truckers, loggers and miners.

She hated this place, the rank greasy smell of it got on her clothes and hair and never went away but it was work and she couldn't afford to turn it down. But the work meant she never got to see Rob, which was the whole point of working in the first place, so she could stay here, keep on being his mother, instead of going back to the city, where she belonged and needed to be so she could keep painting and be the artist she had always dreamed of being and needed to be – was always meant to be. Instead, she got home after he was in bed. The next morning, she slept in until nine, took him for a walk or had a snack with him before she went off to work again at noon. In the morning, while she slept, he'd be out with Kathryn in the garden. He was a large, tanned, quiet child, content to spend hours on the bank beside the creek that flowed down hill near the house, under the walnut tree, playing with trucks and bits of wood, making roads and houses. His other favourite things were helping Kathryn cook, or riding with his grandfather on the tractor, steering it while the old man kept one helpful hand on the wheel.

Mary hadn't meant to love him but she did. She loved the smell of his sun-warmed brown hair, the feel of his round tough muscular body. She loved his body snuggled against hers, his lazy assumption of the comfort she offered. His coming into existence had ruined her life, destroyed her hopes. She shouldn't love him but she did.

Plans for paintings formed in her head while she was working in a semi-trance, answering back to the men when it was called for, but on the whole paying no more attention to them than she absolutely had to. The pictures tormented her like burrs caught in her clothes next to her skin; she imagined paint, colours, an expanse of white canvas gradually filling with colour. The pictures came out of somewhere mysterious; each was born with a surge of hope and adrenaline and she tried to think when she could find time to paint, at least sketch out some ideas. Every day she brought a sketchbook to work with her but never opened it.

There was never time to paint and one by one, the pictures died again. Sometimes they died just as she had made five minutes to herself and opened her sketchbook. Or they died in the sad yellow light from the light over the outside door of the restaurant, as it opened one last time each night, letting go of Mary along with a cloud of exhausted blue air. They died in the long slow afternoons, before the after-work rush, when there were only a few old men sitting in the corners and a few hopeless flies buzzed against the frosted glass windows.

But she had Rob. Since she was seventeen, and his coming had destroyed her life. She never told anyone what happened. No one ever asked. She had wanted so desperately for them to ask. She wanted desperately to tell someone, but she never would. Everyday the memory invaded her thoughts, tinged with a stinking green scum of humiliation and fury.

It was her own fault. She had done it to herself. But she hadn't known, had never dreamed that the repercussions could ruin her life so fast, so easily. Curiousity, stupidity, ignorance. That's what she knew later. Later. Her only defense was that she was seventeen and impatient and curious. No one else she knew had as little experience as her. She hadn't had dates in high school. She wasn't part of any group, or clique. She lived too far out of town; didn't belong to any clubs, no one wanted to drive that far to pick her up. She wasn't part of anything, didn't have real friends, only a gaggle of misfits like herself that she hung around with at lunch to stay camouflaged and not be alone. She was only really at peace in the school in the art room. The art teacher was a little bustling man with a thick accent. He never gave up on his job even while the kids made fun of his accent and threw paint at his back and spent their art room time drawing obscene cartoons and giggling. But he had had enough sense to leave Mary alone and not try and teach her anything beyond how to mix paints and wet clay. Sometimes he looked over her shoulder and nodded.

Kathryn and Bill got a new neighbour that year. He had rented a ramshackle summer cabin that sat beside the lake just north of the farm. He had a beard and his clothes were scruffy. People along the lake road who saw him hitchhiking sniffed disdainfully. "That smelly beatnik," they said over coffee to Kathryn. "Probably freeze to death next winter."

Mary heard them talking. She knew what a beatnik was because she had read everything in the school library and had found an article about beatniks in *Life* magazine, complete with pictures of brooding dark men who wrote poetry in restaurants. She had hardly ever been in a restaurant. Bill, her father, hated restaurants, said they were a waste of money.

She saw the stranger one spring day as she was riding by on her red mare. She was nearing the end of school, and spent most her days restless with fury and fear and worry, wondering about her future when she graduated from high school. She wanted to go to art school but she didn't know what she had to do, how to get there, how to afford it. Her parents would laugh at the idea.

He was chopping wood, swinging awkwardly at pieces of driftwood he had hauled up from the beach. Probably would freeze to death, she thought. No heat in driftwood. He'd be better off borrowing a saw from her father and cutting some real wood. Someone had said in her hearing that he was a writer and Mary had woven fantasies around that. She had never met a writer, never met anyone who wrote anything more complicated than letters to relatives. The writers presented to them in high school were old, long dead. Mary had the vague impression that writing was something people had done a long time ago but no one bothered with now.

There were lots of books in Kathryn's house, old books, classics that Mary's grandfather George had collected, huge heavy books, and there was also a collection of dusty-looking books collected behind the glass that had been left to Kathryn by an elderly neighbour. There were *Reader's Digest* and *Maclean's* magazines, the local newspaper, the *Star Weekly*, and her father's *True* magazines. There were books in the library at school, poetry books that no one had ever taken out but Mary, but there were no writers alive in any world she knew about.

So this man was a curiousity. She took to riding often that way during the spring. She took to washing her long red hair and riding with it down, flying behind her. She saw him watching her. One day, the mare stumbled as they were going by his yard. Mary stopped, slid off the mare to check her leg. He came up behind her.

"You okay?" he said. "That's a pretty horse."

"Yeah," said Mary, keeping her head down. Her silky hair swung over her face. She straightened up. He was standing right beside her and she flinched at his closeness. She turned back to the fretting mare, trying to calm her.

"She seems all right," Mary said into the neck of the horse. "I'd better go." She hesitated. She needed a lift to get on the horse but she didn't want to ask this man. He saw her need without her asking.

"Here, I'll give you a lift," he said. He bent to grasp her leg and she scrambled onto the mare. Now she could look safely down on him.

"Do you write books?" she asked.

"Sure," he said. "I've got a whole library here. Do you like to read?"

"I guess so."

"Come back then. I'll loan you some books if you want."

Up close, he had blue eyes, a sun tanned face, a black beard. He was wearing a torn green jacket. He smelled of woodsmoke.

She waited for a few days, then went by the cabin again. He invited her in and she tied the mare in the yard and went. He was polite at first. He was much older than her, but she couldn't tell his age because of the beard. The cabin was not very clean. There was an unmade bed, a table, a typewriter, a few tin dishes in the sink, and cans of food on shelves, and a long row of paperback books. The place smelled of smoke and something mustier, old clothes, dirt, pack rat. He made her tea and she looked through the books, asked if she could borrow two of them.

She knew Kathryn would skin her if she found out what was going on. Mary found herself dreaming about the man, imagining things about him. She knew almost nothing of his life. He had told her very little. After the tea, she avoided him for weeks on end, then she took to riding through his yard again, tossing her mane of red hair, stopping occasionally to talk but not getting down off the dancing impatient mare.

Then one June day when the leaves were a bright fizzing green overhead, he stopped her. "Come inside," he said. "I have something to show you." She got down, tied the mare moving restless, pawing in the yard, wanting to keep going.

"Look at this," he said smiling. "I have to show someone. You were the only person around here that I thought might care."

He showed her the poems he'd been writing, a magazine she had never heard of which had published three of them. They were incomprehensible to her but she smiled, handed the magazine back, impressed.

Oh my God, she thought. There is a big world and someone I know is a part of it. I want it. I want it too. I want to go there. The man, who had told her only that his name was Paul, took her hand, ran his hand through her hair. When he bent to kiss her, she let him, stood still, bewildered, unable to think of what to do, torn between running and staying. When he pushed her down on the bed, she let him, then too late, she began, weakly to struggle and push against him but he laughed. He held her down with one hand and undid her jeans with the other. It didn't take long. She lay panting and exhausted on the bed like an animal in shock, like a deer running hard into a fence. He let her up. She ran from the cabin to the mare, rode home again, sore, bleeding and terrified. She lay in her bed at home and cried but she said nothing. She sat in her room all night without sleeping, terrified.

The next day, Bill said at breakfast, "Funny thing, that writer guy, saw him driving out this morning, car all loaded. Thought he was going to spend the summer, but guess he changed his fool mind."

She spent the summer, dazed, unable to think, barely able to go on breathing. She went to the public library, and terrified that someone would see, looked in a book on pregnancy. She was paralyzed. How could her life, in full flood in one direction, be so suddenly stopped, turned, sent spinning off in another direction entirely. She thought of suicide, of running away into the woods, of running away to the city. She felt most betrayed, not by the man, but by her body. Her body had always been something she could rely on, had ridden horses, climbed trees, swum, canoed, fished, put up hay beside her father and Colin, beat the boys at school in softball and races and green apple wars, kept her safe.

Now this body had betrayed her, turned female, and was about to betray her idiocy and humiliation to the world. She stayed at home. She stayed in the house. She lay on her bed, day after day, enraged and befuddled by her own stupidity. Eventually, she didn't have to tell her mother. By the end of the summer, when Mary had made no move to go anywhere, Kathryn guessed somehow. She'd seen so many pregnant animals, she knew the signs without even thinking.

She came upstairs one night and sat on the bed.

"You'd better tell me," she said. "I don't know when you did it or who you did it with but if there's a baby coming, we've got to do some preparing."

Mary pulled her hair forward over her face.

"When?" said Kathryn.

"I don't know," Mary whispered. "Maybe after Christmas."

Kathryn didn't lecture or reprimand Mary. She treated her like a small child, cooked her food, looked after her, but never looked at her, or talked about the baby, the birth, or Mary's wrecked future.

Colin, her older brother had gone ahead of her, and was already in university. The year before, after he graduated from high school and went off to university, she begged and pleaded and was allowed to go on the bus to the city to visit him. She came into the city in the morning with the sun glowing on the towers; Colin met her, took her to the university cafeteria for breakfast. The university was awash in light. Ancient gnarled oak trees covered in vines grew from emerald velvet lawns. It was a dream. She made Colin take her through the art department. She lusted after it all, the smell of paint, the sight of easels, student work hung on the walls. She belonged there. She knew that. She belonged to the whole university, to the books, the ranks of brightly lit classrooms, to the trees, the ordered gardens. But she didn't belong with the students, with the blond and happy students all walking briskly somewhere.

Now everything was gone. She wandered around the farm like a ghost, haunted, unspeaking, unspoken to. Day after day, she waited for her mother to ask her what had happened but no one asked her anything.

When she went into labour, Kathryn delivered her to the hospital and left her to the ministrations of the nurses and the ancient doctor. They looked past her, barely spoke to her. Mary retreated; she listened to her body, disappeared into the pulse and storm of its rhythms, finally disappeared altogether to a somewhere away from shame and blood and pain and humiliation.

When Rob was born, she looked at him lying beside her in the hospital bed. She unwrapped his tightly swaddled blankets and examined him. She wanted to hate him but she didn't. She felt about him as she felt about her body. It was hers; it had betrayed her but she had nothing else to depend on. Kathryn brought them home, installed them back in Mary's old room, crowded with a secondhand crib and stroller. She didn't seem unhappy and she treated the baby with loving kindness. She seemed to take it for granted that now Mary would stay, continue to help on the farm, bring up Rob, live a hidden, shamed life.

She stayed home for a year. She nursed Rob and looked after him, and wandered around the farm like a ghost. But the following August, she left Rob with Kathryn and left on the Greyhound bus for art school. It had taken her months to do the application and get a student loan. She'd done it all in secret. She told them at the dinner table. The silence that grew after her words was like the heavy black silence before a summer storm.

"I have to try," she said. "It's my life."

Kathryn's face was pinched with fury. "When you have a child," she said, "that is your life. You don't count anymore. Your life is over. It's the child that matters."

"No," said Mary. "No, I have to try." Those were all the words in her head. She wanted to think of more, to say something else, but there were no other words. They continued sitting together in silence, ate their supper. Mary and Kathryn did the dishes and Bill went out after supper as always. Mary put Rob to bed and then sat on the bed in her room. Then Bill came in, turned on the radio to listen to the news, and then he and Kathryn went heavily up the stairs to bed. The next day, they drove her to the bus and watched her get on and stood with Rob as the bus went away. She didn't look out the window at them. She kept her head down, and clutched her stomach. She thought lightning or boulders from up on the mountains might crash down on the bus, but nothing happened. She sat on the bus all night, awake, drawing doodles in a notebook and writing Rob's name over and over.

Art school was a dream of happiness. She had no money and she barely understood most of what her instructors were saying to her. She didn't notice that all of them were men, that most of the other students were male. She avoided most of the other students. She began wearing all black, black leotards, long ragged black men's sweaters she found in the basement of the Sally Ann, huge clunky men's boots. She wore her hair long and straight and combed forward to hide her face. After a while, she found other people who looked like her; she went places with them for coffee, beer, whiskey, listened to jazz music in smoky basements. She smoked cigarettes. When people asked her where she was from, she learned to laugh, wave away the question.

She thought how ugly the city was and she missed Rob with a constant ache. She got brief weekly letters from Kathryn with news of the weather and the farm. The red mare went lame and Bill shot her and buried her in the hay field. New neighbours, another subdivision of summer cabins going in where she had once laid down in a log cabin with a strange man, a calf born dead, the garden doing well, Bill had torn down the old chicken shed and built a new one.

Her instructors smiled tolerantly when they looked at her work, and then moved on and paid more attention to the ambitious young men standing before energetic sketches of nude women. Mary painted and painted. She read books about painters. She walked the streets and thought she was part of a tradition that included Rembrandt, and Titian and Van Gogh and Breughel. She painted in her small housekeeping room on the top floor of a dingy hotel. She told no one about Rob.

At the end of two years she got a diploma saying she had completed art school. When she walked the pavement in the rain, she could smell the cool clear waters of the lake. She saw the shadows of the mountains between the office towers. She gave notice, packed her things, caught the bus and rode sleepless through the whole long night, longing for Rob, the farm, the lake, the ancient cedars beside the road, the pine slopes on the mountain, her mother and her father. She stared out the window as the dawn rose light hit the mountains. She was moving inward through circles of familiarity, moving towards the shape of the mountains against the sky, the salmon, orange, rose, pink light of the sunrise on the snow covered peaks, the black spiky spruce, then the lighter green of cedar and fir along the creek, the layered grey green wedges of ice against the bright green moss on the granite walls of the creek. She pressed her face against the glass. She felt she had been starving and was now looking at food, food that was colour, texture, light, she could feel it all within her body, the glassiness of ice, the rough kiss of moss, the rigidity of tree bark.

She came home again and the two years vanished. The mountains rose up and set their wall against her, against her memories, against the knowledge that for a brief while she had dreamed she was an artist.

Rob didn't remember her, but he came to her, after a while. After a few days, he screamed and fought to run after her whenever she left the room. She let him sleep with her, despite Kathryn's disapproval. She smelled his hair and stroked him and hugged him and hung onto him as he hung onto her. After a while, he got used to her, and went back to spending most of his time with Kathryn.

Mary, with her new grown up, city educated eyes, saw what she had never known before, that Kathryn and Bill were poor, that they were getting by on their summer sales of fruit, on selling milk, and on the bit of logging work that Bill picked up, which was steadily decreasing.

She also saw that while Kathryn still seemed ageless, her father was getting old. She watched him slump in his chair after lunch, fall asleep again after dinner. She and Kathryn talked about it while they were making dinner together. Kathryn was worried as well, but Bill hadn't been to a doctor for thirty years and couldn't see any reason to go now.

She tried to figure what she could do to help. She'd gone to school on a combination of starving, mooching off another students, and working part time in a coffee shop near the university. She'd gotten the job through another classmate; she wouldn't have had the nerve to ask for herself. But now she thought perhaps she could do this again.

She got dressed in a skirt and blouse, tied her long unruly hair back with a scarf, went to town with Kathryn and Bill on their town day, and while they bought groceries, she went to the three coffee shops in the town, first to the bus depot with its grey formica counter and a row of red topped stools where she and Colin used to spin on the rare occasions when Kathryn brought them in for ice cream.

The man there listened to her request for employment. He didn't so much look at her as look past her.

"Got no use for anyone right now," he said. "Maybe try later. Next month maybe." Mary backed away, conscious that there was some kind of threat in the room, conscious of a sense of trespassing.

The other restaurants were the same. They knew who she was before she asked. She could almost read the words in their eyes, "unwed mother," "bastard kid." Their eyes slid over, past, around her. "Nothing now," they said. "Maybe next month."

There was a tiny art and framing store in town. Mary knew the woman there, knew she had been a friend of Kathryn's, once. She knew framing, knew she could do better than the crooked frames around the muddy prints which hung in the windows.

The woman in the store looked flustered. "Yes, I do need help sometimes," she said. "I guess I could call you if I do. Say hello to your mother for me." Mary went out. The woman would never call. She had the same blank wall in her eyes as everyone else. She left town with Kathryn and Bill, said nothing about what she had been doing, hid her humiliation, got home, changed her clothes, went out to the barn, but the red mare was gone. There was only her old torn bridle, stiff with dust and disuse.

But the next day, a miracle happened. The country store owner just a few miles away had a small coffee shop attached to the store. He had been in the valley forever. He and Bill had gone to school together. He had been at Bill and Kathryn's wedding. He needed help, was Mary interested? She went to see him and was told to start the next morning.

She made plans to buy paints and canvas, set them up in the corner of her room. But when she finally got there, finally sat down in the afternoon of her day off, with Rob asleep and her mother outside, her father working on the tractor in the lower field, for the first time in her life so far, she found she couldn't paint, had nothing in her head, no voices calling, no colours, textures, nothing presented itself.

She sat there for a long time. Rob woke up, she called him and he squirmed out of bed and came to see what she was doing. She picked him up, sat on the floor with him, smelled his clean salty hair, held him to her and rocked back and forth, until he got bored and ran away to find his grandmother. Mary remained, rocking on the floor, not looking at the white canvas that loomed overhead.

She had always painted, but she had always painted for someone, something, for a teacher, for applause, for contests, for the diploma which said she had gone to art school. No one was around to talk to about painting, about this new fear, about how it felt. Kathryn always looked at her work, said something vague, hung it on a wall already crowded with her work. Mary thought about school, the people she had met there, the city, the classroom at art school. They were all so far away, unrelated to her life here. She put her head on her knees for a while longer, then pushed herself off the floor, went downstairs. Kathryn had started bread that afternoon, but since she was outside, the dough had over risen. Mary punched it down, formed it into loaves, put it in the warming oven of the wood stove for another rising, then went outside. She found Kathryn in the garden, told her about the bread, worked beside her until it was time for tea and then time for chores, getting supper, and after supper, reading to Rob before putting him to bed.

On her next day off, she avoided the bedroom, went for a walk instead. There was place where she used to go, where she used to ride the red mare. It was across the highway, up on the mountain above the farm, a granite knob stuck on the side of the mountain; there was a nest of red tailed hawks there, just below it.

When she was in high school, she and the mare had gone there almost every day. She'd get down off the bus, nauseous, her head pounding from the trip, the noise, the stink of kids and leftover lunches and exhaust. She'd come in the house where Kathryn would always have tea ready. Mary drank it as hot as she could stand it, feeling it burn all the way down, burn out the sick cold humiliation left over from the day, there were always cookies or cake as well. Then she changed and went out to the barn.

The red mare had saved her life. Kathryn had bought the horse as a sad filly with burrs matted into its mane and tail, an infected eye, mud and manure caked on its coat. Mary didn't care. She wanted the mare and the mare took her on. They shared their craziness. The mare had been mistreated, beaten into submission, hit in the eye. She trusted no one. She had two gaits – dance and run. Mary rode her without a saddle for the first few years, staying on by balance and determination. The mare bucked the first few times she rode her, but then decided she was more interested in running than bucking and Mary decided it was easier to stay on when the mare was running, so that's how they went, on the highway, up and down the mountainside, over rocks and trees, across the creek through gullies, and into the lake. Mary's legs grew into steel hooks which gripped the mare's ribs and drummed on her sides as they flashed through the brush and up the hill.

She made the mare walk home though, dancing and sidling, or Bill would smack her. He had hardly ever hit Mary, in fact, he hardly talked to her, so the first time he saw her bring the mare home dripping wet and turn her loose, he shocked her speechless when he backhanded her across the bum. "You'll ruin that horse," he said. "From now on, you walk her home. Cool her down."

Mary couldn't see how the mare dancing her wild sideways home under a tight rein was cooling her off, but she did what she was told. She never argued with her father. No one did. Not even Kathryn.

But now the red mare was gone and so too had many of the places where she used to ride. Someone new to the valley had built a house just below the granite knob, had bulldozed a trail to the top of it, had planted flowers and made silly rock walls which held nothing. After she looked at it, Mary went away back down the mountain, down the trail to the beach and sat there with her head on her knees.

I could swim out, she thought. It was still spring, the water freezing cold. It wouldn't take long. It would be easy. I could swim and swim. She thought of the black freezing depths of the water. It would be peaceful there. It would be dark and fine and peaceful at last. Her mom would have Rob which would be fine by the two of them. They'd hardly miss her. The embarrassment to the family would be gone. They could all hold up their heads again. If I could die, she thought, just sit here and will myself to die.

But she went on breathing. Far away, Rob hollering about something drifted down on the wind. Bill was plowing. She could hear cars on the road, the creek rushing crazily down the hill, swollen with spring water.

I want to paint, she thought. A picture formed in her mind, a new picture, not even an image, a sense of an image. Very carefully, she stood up, holding it in her mind like a full and fragile glass of water, went back up the beach trail past the hayfield to the house, went in the back door so Rob and Kathryn wouldn't see her, found her sketchbook, blocked out the picture, enough to hold it, keep it from flying away. She worked until she heard Kathryn calling her to supper, until the good warm meaty smells of gravy and roast beef drifted up the stairs and woke her hunger.

She came back from where she'd been. She'd been a long way, but she was excited. This was a new kind of work, a new kind of feeling. Maybe, she thought, I'm growing up. Maybe this is the work I really want to do. Lightheartedly, she went downstairs to find Kathryn cross with putting up with Rob, snapping at Bill, Bill hiding behind his *Farmer's Weekly*. Rob threw himself on her legs, howling. She felt his head. He continued to sob. She looked at her mother helplessly, but Kathryn just shrugged.

"He's mad because I wouldn't let him ride his tricycle to the beach. He wanted to go look for you and I wouldn't let him. Then he ran through a patch of thistles and hurt his feet. Well, what do you expect? You're never around when he needs you to be."

She hugged Rob to her and gradually his howling quieted. She didn't want to think about Rob. She wanted to think about her picture. But she couldn't, not right now. But she'd get back to it, it was some kind of promise, hidden there in the pages of her sketchbook and she didn't have a choice about keeping it.

Chapter Nine

Mary was leaning against the counter in the coffee shop in the late afternoon. No one was around. The sun shone down on the road outside. She had been at the coffee shop for nine months now, knew the routine, knew the customers, swung in the door with breezy nonchalance. She had a good relationship with Rob, she'd even finished two new paintings and stacked them behind the closet doors in her room. They weren't what she wanted to paint. She knew that. She'd spent all last Sunday afternoon at the beach with Rob. Mostly she had sat on the sand, staring at the water, at the shifting patterns of light flickering back from the slickly patterned surface off the water. She'd cupped her hands, studied the ways the shadows fell, the light shifted, the colours, mixing them on a palette, trying to get that exact shade of blue green, with the light on top, the darkness underneath.

Then she'd played with Rob, put him to bed.

She'd had a date this week, a movie with a nice dull man who drove a cement truck. She hadn't found much to talk about with him. But that was all right. She'd tied her wiry bushy hair back with a blue scarf, and put on her black skirt and black sweater, put on red lipstick, looked at herself in the mirror. Then she found a bright scarf, flung it over her shoulders. They went to the movie, had a beer afterwards, came home. It hadn't been so bad.

Bill and Kathryn didn't seem to mind her going out. They knew the guy's parents. They'd been sort of pathetically nice to her ever since she'd come home, she reflected. Colin never came home. He'd stayed in the city, was scratching out some kind of living at something, selling vacuum cleaners probably. Bill wanted him to come home. When they got one of Colin's infrequent letters, Bill would only grunt. "Boy should come home," and then he'd put on his hat and go to the barn.

Kathryn too said, "Your brother should come home. Who's going to do the work when your father is too old? Who are we going to leave this place too? Who's going to take over for us?"

To which Mary never replied. What could she say? When she was little, she had helped her father, had driven the tractor, had worked beside him and Colin. Her father never talked to them. She knew he could talk because he talked to his friends when they came over once a week to play poker and drink whiskey. Mary and Colin could hear them from upstairs, laughing. Their laughter got louder and louder. Mary hated these men because they kept her awake. Any kind of noise kept her awake. Kathryn had told her when she was a baby she had cried for hours if some kind of noise woke her up.

But she wanted her father to talk to her. She wanted him to tell her how he knew so much. He gave her and Colin tidbits, tiny bits of information, enough to keep from killing themselves with the farm equipment; the rest of the time they were expected to watch and do whatever they saw that needed doing. They were expected to drive the tractor, put up hay, milk the cows, prune apple trees, weed the corn, gather the eggs every day, lean in under the air of the buzz saw and grab the wood as he cut it, and stack it in the woodshed. Work was her father's life. Mary tried, because she secretly adored him, to make it her life.

She liked the farmwork and she liked to walk beside her father, matching her stride to his. He never paid much attention. She followed him and sometimes, if he was busy, or doing something too difficult or dangerous, he would grunt at her to get out of the way. He was immensely strong; he worked all the time. Sometimes she wondered if he ever talked. Did he talk to her mother? She knew they talked about the farm, about work, about what they needed to buy in town. Did they ever talk about anything else?

Sometimes other men came over and he talked to them. They talked leaning against the tractor, or sitting in the house over coffee and plates of fruitcake and gingersnaps. She sat near them and listened to them talk about machines and work, and fixing trucks. Everything they said was important.

There was always work to do and it was all important and desperate and needed doing immediately and it was never done fast enough or well enough. Things always went wrong. It rained when it was haying season; the rain split the cherries and rotted the strawberries and left mold all over the beans and peas in the garden. Or when they needed rain, it was too hot and dry; lightning danced over the mountain tops and Bill filled barrels with water and muttered about the goddam useless forestry bastards. Every year mosquitoes came and made working in the garden a hellish misery, and when they were gone wasps and hornets and came and ate the raspberries and grapes and plums.

But they worked anyway. It was what you did in the summer. You picked things and helped Kathryn can and jam and freeze, you did the hay when it was time, you weeded the garden, dragged hoses to put on sprinklers and gathered the eggs from under the sullen fierce chickens every afternoon, and gave them food. Mary knew how to do all these things and she did them faster and better then Colin. She knew she did. He worked too, but he slouched and complained and was slow. Their father sneered at him.

When she was thirteen, her body changed and her breasts began to grow. She hated them. They itched and rubbed against her shirt and got in her way. Colin jeered at her about them which made her furious. Haying was frantic that year. Bill had leased a couple of extra fields at someone else's farm, five miles away and they had to drive there, haul equipment back and forth. It was after he built the new hay shed, but before he bought a baler. Mary's job was to help stack the loose hay in the barn as he and Colin threw it up to her. They walked down to the barn together, the three of them, side by side. Her father went to get the tractor and the mounded wagon load of hay.

Mary stood by the barn, leaning on her pitchfork. She looked across the field, squinting at the purple, sun-hazed dusty day.

Remember this, she thought to herself. Happiness filled her, delicious as peppermint, because the day was so full and round. Remember this day. She tried to notice, memorize details – the minty arid smell of cut hay, the feel of the hot stubbled ground through the thin soles of her running shoes, her jeans and striped t-shirt, the enormous beauty of the still lake, the mountains gazing at themselves in the clear water.

Mary loved haying time, satisfied at the sight of the barn stuffed to the rafters, bulging with winter reassurance. It was hard work that her father had picked for her, dusty under the airless tin roof, but she was thin and hard muscled from riding and swimming. It was her pride to eat as much as her father and Colin, to work as hard as they did, to be so thin and tough and wiry. Kathryn braided her hair every morning, but by afternoon, it had escaped and flew around her face in a red cloud.

Colin and her dad threw the hay up to her with pitchforks; the hay came up in great sliding masses, and if she was quick enough, she could catch it with her own pitchfork, and move it to the back of the shed. She floundered through the thick hay on her knees, grabbing hay, shoving and wrestling with it, exhilarated at her own ability to lift a mass of hay with her whole body.

The creek flowed behind the barn and when they were done with the load, they went together, the three of them, to get a drink. Her father stripped off his sweaty shirt and lowered himself to the creek to drink. Colin imitated him, and they knelt together on the creek bank. Muscles stood out under the white skin of their backs.

Mary stood behind them, hardly able to breathe for embarrassment. She could smell their sweat. Their white flesh shone through the gloom under the cedars their skin goose-pimpling in the sudden chill. She stepped backwards. She didn't want to bend down beside them to drink, didn't want to be there with them at all.

She hugged her arms around herself, around her newly budded breasts under the thin T-shirt, turned away, said over her shoulder, "I'm going up the house for a drink." They didn't look up. She didn't know if they heard her. She trudged up to the house, slopping her feet through the white dust, came into the kitchen where Kathryn was making bread. Mary watched for a while.

"Aren't you supposed to helping with the hay?" Kathryn snapped. "Why are you moping around like some loonie in the middle of the day?"

Mary went to the sink. "I'm just getting a drink," she said. She heard the tractor start up, down by the barn.

"There's the tractor," Kathryn said. "For God's sake. Get a move on. The hay won't wait while you're mooning around my clean kitchen like a big lump, shedding hay dust everywhere."

Mary went out the back down, down the steps. She had been going to remember this day. Why? When she got back to the barn, her father and Colin were raking the field for the last bits of hay. She stood beside the field, but they ignored her. Slowly, she went on down the path to the beach, afraid she would hear her father bellowing at her.

But nothing happened. No voices called after her. When she got to the beach, she went along the shoreline for a while, leaping and jumping from rock to log to rock, until she came to a tiny cove a half mile down the beach. A creek ran down through the cove; there was a kind of cave between the rocks, floored with fine sand. Mary sat there for the rest of afternoon. She watched the water, the shadows moving over the mounded granite boulders, the fine grained striated blue of ancient cottonwood logs lying across the sand, and over the creek. She wished her eyes were mouths, so she could take it all in, like food, take it in and make it part of her, flow outwards and dissolve, wrap her flesh, transparent as air, around all of it. She yearned towards it; finally she lay face downwards on the sand, while little tendrils of pleasure and belonging curled like vines through her flesh.

Chapter Ten

The bell over the door of the coffee shop jangled. Two men came in. One she knew; his name was Jim. He'd ridden the school bus with her, lived on a farm ten miles closer to town. He was a tall, shy dark man that she had never exchanged a single word with, but they knew about each other, in the way that rural people knew about each other. She knew that his mother worked in town and his dad was a farmer. His father came to the farm and visited her father, bought hay sometimes. She nodded to them waited until they sat, then came over with the coffee pot.

He smiled at her, and she thought what a nice smile he had. "You're Mary Mangerton, right ?" he said. "I remember you from the school bus."

"Right," she said, flustered. "Yeah, I remember you too."

"Nice to see you again," he said. "Heard you'd gone off to school or some such."

"No," she said. "I'm living here now."

Then she went away, flustered with embarrassment. Why had she said that? Why had she said anything? She served their food but avoided saying anything more.

Mary wiped the tables and the counter, then stood beside the cash register. Mr. Parker, the owner, was gone for the afternoon; the cook, who was, as usual, drunk, was lying on a chair in the kitchen, with his head thrown back, snoring. The bell jangled. Three elderly men came in. They ignored her when she went to pour them coffee. They came in every afternoon. They always ignored her except to point at their cups when they wanted a refill.

Men were a puzzle. She didn't want Rob to become like all the other men she knew, but she couldn't see any way to prevent it. So far, thank God, Rob didn't much like his grandfather, and Bill paid little attention to him. Rob had two women who doted on him and indulged his every whim. Kathryn seemed more affectionate with him than Mary ever remembered her being with either her or Colin. Mary didn't remember her mother hugging her, or singing to her. When she was a kid, Kathryn was always busy. The secret name of the farm was always work. Money, or the lack of it, ruled their lives. Nothing had changed since then. Bill still sold hay, and fruit, and eggs around the valley. Kathryn grew a huge garden. They kept a small herd of cattle, and raised a couple of pigs every year as they had always done. The only difference was that Bill no longer worked at the sawmill or went logging. He and Kathryn just got by. Mary gave them money now. When she was a kid they never minded her going fishing, were pleased when she came home with a string of trout. Now, she realized it was because she had been bringing food; fishing wasn't play.

Now she saw Rob learning the same chores and following at Kathryn's heels, and she didn't mind. Kathryn and Rob seem to have developed a shared language. Mary saw them one day in the chicken yard, Kathryn squatting on her heels, picking up baby chicks with one hand, showing them to Rob, meanwhile fending off an indignant hen with the other hand. Kathryn was laughing. Mary walked away. Kathryn never laughed with her, mostly ignored her, as Bill ignored her. And yet they wanted her there. They needed the money she gave them. They needed her.

Whenever bitterness seeped in, there was always the woods, the beach, the mountainside. She walked and walked, always with her sketchbook, coming back to the house at dinner time, coming into the dinner table, where Rob was crowing and laughing, sitting between his grandparents. Mary sat down silently, took her place at dinner. They didn't ask her where she had been or what she might have been doing. The talk at dinner was about farming, the neighbours, the weather, the crops, machines, and the possibility of a sale at the local Co-op.

When she wasn't walking, or working, or playing with Rob, Mary farmed as well. She stepped back into familiar roles, helping with the hay, holding calves or pigs while her father castrated them, pruning fruit trees, picking and canning mountains of fruit and vegetables, helping with butchering, cutting and wrapping meat, making bread.

There was something about it all that got to her. She loved farming. She loved the farm, but she couldn't figure out why. She remembered once, as a child, standing in silent worship as the late afternoon sun slanted across the emerald alfalfa of the lower pasture, as it turned the lake to gold, the mountains to misted blue shadows. Maybe it was just the look of the place. Maybe that was all that hooked her.

She decided if she got another offer of a date, to turn it down. The farm was enough of a world. She didn't want to go anywhere else. She couldn't bear to go to town. She didn't want to talk to anyone. She passed the day pleasantly enough with the people who came in the cafe, but their conversation never went beyond comments about the weather, or jokes about the terrible nature of the coffee.

She slipped into the old familiar habit of going to the lake alone, of spending her spare time alone. She took a sketch book with her. Without the red mare, she walked and walked, feeling the pines, the granite, the blue hills, breathe with her. Often she simply went and sat, and watched and watched, while nothing at all happened, and she felt, for a brief while, perfectly at peace, perfectly happy.

Then she came home, ate, put Rob to bed, and painted until late at night, until long after her parents were in bed. Winter came again, her second winter back in the valley. The light waned and dimmed, and her spirits dimmed with it. But she made it to work everyday and home again.

When spring did finally come, she asked for time off from work, then she packed up her paintings, caught the bus to Vancouver, called Elaine, the one friend from art school with whom she had kept in touch. Elaine welcomed her, standing in the doorway of her grubby basement apartment, long black hair, long black sweater, a cigarette dangling from one hand.

Mary stopped. She had forgotten that people dressed that way, that they laughed so carelessly, that they could live in an apartment where the walls were painted a whole variety of colours.

Elaine was living on an allowance from her father, who owned some kind of business in the city. In Mary's hometown, she had never considered being friends with the daughter of the local business owners, they seemed to all wear pale blue angora sweaters, and pleated skirts. Some of them left the high school in grade nine to go to private school.

Elaine looked at the paintings with narrowed eyes.

"They're good, you know," she said, "but you've slipped a bit too. I always thought you were the best of all of us. You were always trying something new, something different. I don't know. Feels like something's missing here, some kind of edge. They're too, I don't know, too pretty."

She walked around them some more. "Anyway, leave them with me. I know some gallery owners. So, how long can you stay? And are you really going back to that ghastly hole of a town, whatever it's called? God, why do you live there? Look, I've got an idea. Let's go to the bar, the one by the school. I'll call some of the gang. They'll be glad to hear you're back in town. Oh, my God. Let me loan you some clothes. What are you wearing? What do you do up there in the country, anyway?"

For the next week, Mary stayed up late, slept late, woke up with a hangover, spent the day over coffee and cigarettes, talked about art, went out again to bars. She went to bookstores, and spent the little money she had saved on books and second hand clothes, and then she got on the bus and went home again.

She sank lower and lower in her seat as the bus struggled through the night, through winding narrow mountain passes, and thought about the impossibility of her life. The mountains towered over the noisy, chuffing, whining bus. Black streams ran beside the road, full of white teeth, the bones of the mountains showed through wherever a slide had come down and swiped off the blanket of black trees. The city receded and left her entirely. She curled up, turned and thrashed like a trapped animal on the seat, tried to find a way to sleep, to leave herself behind, dozed and woke again. She put her head on her knees, put her coat over her head, hid there in the darkness, waiting for morning and her arrival back at the farm.

Rob was at the bus station with Bill. Mary gathered him into her arms, held him against her, held him until he squirmed away. He sat on her lap on the way home, silent as usual, ran to his grandmother with a shining face when they got out of the truck in the chicken-littered, spring-barren yard, crying, "Momma, momma's home." Kathryn had bought him a tricycle while Mary was gone, and desperate to show off, he leapt on it, circled the yard, yelling.

"About time you were home again," Kathryn said briskly. Mary felt as if she had been away for a year. "They've been calling from the restaurant and your dad needs your help with the calves. It's been so damn cold. I don't know when I'm going to be able to get the garden in."

Mary sat at the table while Kathryn poured tea, set out chocolate chip cookies, gingersnaps. Bill sat down beside her.

"Bus was late," he said. "I figured maybe you run into some snow."

"No, it wasn't snowing. But it was slow, coming through the passes. Fog in some places."

"Gotta get them calves done this week," he said. "Leaving it late. Should have got it done before now. They'll be too damn big too handle by now."

Mary ate a plate of cookies, had three cups of tea, put her suitcase away, called Rob. They went to the lake, threw stones and sticks in the water. He insisted on taking his tricycle and she had to carry him and the tricycle over the rocks in the path. She watched him kneeling on the sand, hitting the water with a stick, the back of his neck, his slim fragile body, bent over. She knelt beside him, put her hand on his neck; he looked up at her. She looked away.

"Come on," she said. "I'm supposed to be helping your grandpa. He'll yell at us for being so lazy."

She made him carry the tricycle himself and he started to cry, lagging behind her on the path, calling, "Mommy, mommy, wait," but she went ahead of him, slashing at the grass beside the path with a stick picked up on the beach.

That night, at dinner, she said, "I've got to go away again. I can't stay here."

Kathryn looked at her. "And take Rob?" she asked.

"No," Mary said. "He'd have to stay here, at least until I get settled. I'm going to stay with Elaine for a while. Try and sell my paintings. I can get work in Vancouver. Elaine will help me."

Kathryn and Bill said nothing. The rest of the dinner passed in thick terrible silence. She could hardly breathe. The next day she caught a ride to town with the mail truck driver. Bill was away working somewhere. Kathryn and Rob stood in the doorway as she walked up the hill to the highway. She turned and waved, her heart barely able to move, to swell, to keep on beating from within the center of the pain which filled her being.

Chapter Eleven

Mary came back for Christmas. The minute she stepped off the bus, the city fell away from her in dry flakes. Bill met the bus and drove her home. He told her he had been getting up wood, that it had been cold, that he guessed her mother might be cranky because Rob had a cold. She answered in kind monosyllables, yeah, she said, it had been cold in the city too.

When she came in the house, she swooped upon Rob, unable to resist, unable to keep herself from him for one more second. He shrank back, terrified at this loud stranger, who smelled strange, felt strange, who reeked of distance and cold. She sat at the table while Kathryn made tea and brought out shortbread and Christmas cake, as if Mary were a guest who had dropped in for the afternoon, and after a while, Rob came and crept into her lap, curled up there while she rocked him and ate cookies and he grabbed at her teacup and giggled when she tickled him.

Kathryn and Bill talked to her about the crops, the weather, the fall, the haying, all the things she had missed while she was away, and she nodded in all seriousness and asked about the neighbours and the local gossip. Later, Mary took wrapped presents out of her suitcase, and Kathryn said, "Oh, I don't know whether we'll bother with a tree this year. It seems such a bother."

Rob slept with Mary that night, his head snuggled into her chest, just above her breasts. The next day, she made him breakfast, then got him dressed. She found the old pruning saw and they went to look for a tree, slogging slowly across the sodden mushy pasture grass, up across the highway, and onto the old trail under the power line. It hadn't snowed yet. The trees and brush were bare but under the layer of dead grass, the hay field below them still held a hint of green.

Rob prattled. Mary listened absentmindedly. After a while, he got tired and started to whine about being cold and tired. She picked a tree that looked like it would do. On the way back, she had to carry Rob with one hand and drag the tree with the other. He wrapped his arms around her and whimpered for his grandmother, almost choking her in the process. His weight sagged. She had to keep stopping, shifting his weight back onto her hip.

Kathryn had lunch waiting. They ate macaroni and canned tomatoes, biscuits, homemade sausages and apricot jam and the apple juice Bill made a few times each winter from stored apples. Then Kathryn brought out the cookies she had made that morning, green iced sugar cookies shaped like Christmas trees.

During lunch, Rob fell asleep in Mary's lap and she carried him up to her old room. Then she went and found the old tree stand, brought in the tree, hauled the decorations down from the attic. Kathryn came to look. She had been making mince pie. Her hands were dusty with flour and covered with small burns and cuts in various stages of healing. Burns from the oven, from the wood stove, cuts from chopping wood, from slicing and chopping food.

"Put those blue bulbs up higher, where we can see them," Kathryn said. "I always did like them best."

They stood side by side, watching the tree as though it had come to light on its own in the house, a new peculiar kind of being.

"I wish your brother would phone," Kathryn said. "He said he might make it home for a few days."

"I saw him last week," Mary said. "He came over." She didn't say that he'd been drunk, that he'd showed up with some woman, a harsh-faced blonde she'd never seen before.

"It's been so quiet, just me and your father, rattling away in this house. Maybe it's time we sold out, moved into town."

"Mom, you wouldn't!"

"Well, we might have to. Your dad isn't well."

"Dad? He's strong as an ox."

"He's never told you kids, but he had polio when he was young. He got over it, but it weakened his system. The doctors told him then it might shorten his life. He's got to slow down and take it easy. This farm is too much for one man. If your brother would come home, but he's got his own life now."

The coloured lights shone in the gloom.

"Mother, I have my own life too," Mary said. She tried to sound like she knew what she was saying. "I want to be an artist. I am an artist. I want to keep painting. I am painting." The words sounded ridiculous.

Kathryn said, "Maybe we won't even put in a garden this year. We have to start letting something go. Your dad is talking about taking out some of the fruit trees. They're just too much work, all that pruning and spraying and no one wants the damn fruit anyway. They'd rather buy that junk in the grocery stores."

"What about Colin?" Mary said. "Have you tried to talk to him? Do you know what his plans are?"

"He said something about going back to school," Kathryn said vaguely. "Said he was saving up his money."

"He wasn't saving money when I saw him," Mary snorted. "He was out drinking with some floozie."

"Well, he can't work all the time, can he. Men have to have some relaxation."

"Relaxation," Mary repeated bitterly.

"Oh, my pies are done!" Kathryn said. "I'll put the kettle on. You go check on Rob. He doesn't usually sleep so long. You wore him out this morning, dragging him all over the mountain like that."

Colin phoned Christmas morning. Then they had breakfast and filed into the living room to open presents. Rob went from one person to another, sliding from lap to lap, giggling, drunk on glee and chocolate and toy trucks. After the presents, Mary went for a walk to the lake.

In the winter, the lake turned to flat dull steel, reflecting back the white sky. The blue shadowed mountains and the white and blue shadowed pockets among the granite boulders along the lake reached towards each other in the shadowed water. The sand lay, beaten flat gold, lined with silver ice slivers at its edge. Mary shivered. The breeze off the water bit at her face, needle teeth, like a puppy, vicious and gentle at the same time.

She sat on the rocks, her head in her hands, crouched at the edge of the water, dipped her hands in the lake. The water clutched her fingers, bitter, bitter as rancid milk, bitter as the wormwood that grew on the edges of the pasture. The water tinkled and clashed, ice crystals rubbing their serrated edges against each other. Mary sat there until her bones ached with cold. Finally, she forced herself the long slippery walk up through the pasture, back to the house, bursting with heat and the smell of food.

When Mary left for the city again, Rob cried and Kathryn set her lips and Bill jammed the gears on the truck when he took her into town to the bus station. Mary went back to the tiny basement apartment she shared with Elaine, back to her job waiting on tired grey men in a waterfront cafe, and she tried to keep painting. Rob's face peered at her from the centre of the canvas. The smell of fir trees, icy water, cows, drying hay, warm dirt, sifted towards her from the dust laden corners of the room. In March, Kathryn phoned early one morning to tell her Bill had fallen from the hay loft the day before. He'd been restacking bales of hay. He was all right but he wasn't supposed to do any more heavy lifting

"I guess he fainted, the old fool," she said. "I told him to take it easy, the doctor told him, everyone, but when the hell has he ever listened to me?"

That same afternoon, Mary quit her job, packed her paints and black clothing, hugged Elaine, and caught the bus, yet again, to go home.

When she got there, she took over doing as much of the chores as Bill would let her. He grumbled, came out to the barn with her the first early morning, tried to grab a hay bale and sling it down from the loft, stumbled and had to sit down to catch his breath.

"I know what to do," she said. "I been helping you with this since I could walk"

He left, swearing under his breath, and she finished feeding, cleaned out the milk cow's stall, fed the chickens, and went back up to the house where Kathryn had the breakfast porridge, ham, eggs, toast, juice, left over pie, waiting. Rob came and flung himself happily into her lap, still wearing his night-damp pajamas.

Bill recovered. Within two weeks, he began setting his alarm to be sure he got up before Mary, made it to the barn, had the chores done before she was even awake. She went back to the house, feeling useless, leaned against the door.

"Guess I'm out of a job again," she said.

"That silly old coot," Kathryn snapped. "I know, he was laughing to himself just before he got up about playing a trick on you, having everything done before you got up. Well, nothing you can do. If you get up earlier, so will he. He's that kind of man, your father, and that's all there is to it."

Mary borrowed the truck that afternoon and went to town to look for work but storekeepers, restaurant managers, all looked at her, shrugged, said, "No, nothing right now. Call back next week maybe. Might be something later. Never know."

There was lots to do on the farm. She took over the garden, pruned the fruit trees, tried to stay ahead of Bill. More and more, when she came in the house, she would find him sitting at the table, drinking coffee. Once she came inside in the middle of the day, and found him slowly turning over the pages of a book on flowers she had left lying in the living room. She left again, embarrassed, almost ashamed.

She stayed all summer, helped Kathryn harvest the garden, helped with the weeding, watering, picking, canning, jamming, drying, and storing away.

Then in early September, one late afternoon, the phone rang. It was Jim, the man she had met a while ago at the diner.

"Heard a while ago you were back," he said. "Shoulda called earlier. But I was wondering, there's a decent movie on in town for a change. You wanna go?"

It would at least be an evening away from her parents. She hadn't seen a movie for months.

"Yeah," she said. "I would. I don't care if it's any good as long as it's got some laughs in it."

After the movie, they went to the bar and drank beer, smoked his cigarettes and talked. He was easy to talk to. He asked her how her parents were. They talked about weather, farming, and how few jobs there were. He drove her home and didn't try to kiss her goodnight. Instead, he opened the door of his pickup for her. When she got out, she leaned against him. He was warm and strong. She closed her eyes, and held on. Strength eddied from him. Leaning against him was like floating on water, dark and serene.

Later that week, he asked her out again and she went. After several dates, he asked her to marry him. She asked for time, went home, studied Rob's sleeping face on the pillow, phoned him in the morning and agreed.

Section Three

Brendan and his Family

Chapter Twelve

A lot of people came by the hospital to look in on Kathryn, to say hello, and pay their respects. Brendan didn't know who most of them were but they knew him, said, "Hello there, young feller, is your dad around?" Either that, or they looked past him like a piece of furniture, talked about Kathryn in front on him like he wasn't there. He sat there hating adults, their torturous dithering over flowers and the right thing to say. Most of them seemed to be impressed by Kathryn just because she was old.

You're so fucking stupid, Brendan thought at them. He wished he had the guts to say it out loud, yell at them, instead of just sitting in the stupid hospital room full of orange plastic chairs, a television tuned to some mindless soap opera and issues of magazines about mindless junk. But Brendan went on sitting there anyway, out of love and fear for his grandmother.

He listened to the people talking as the waiting room filled up. Mostly they seemed to talk about sickness, the more grotesque and revolting the better. God, he thought, is that what getting old is about, getting sick and then getting to gloat over the details like it was some kind of accomplishment?

I hate people, he thought. His friends were coming by later to get him. Maybe the best thing would be to just go get drunk and stoned and forget all this. It wouldn't make any difference to Kathryn. He had gone and sat by her bed a few times and held her hand but she wasn't there. He knew she wasn't. Just her body lay there, shrunken and flaccid and fragile as a dead leaf. He missed her already. He just wanted her to come back from wherever she was, so they could go home and she could yell at him about the goddam chickens and then make him cookies and laugh with him about how stupid everything was.

Now he'd have to go back and live with his mom and dad. He'd gone back to sleeping and eating there, sitting between the two of them while they shoveled in food and talked about nothing, gone back to his old room. It was too spooky at Kathryn's. For some reason, he kept thinking about his real grandmother, the one named Mary. He didn't know much about her except she'd been a painter and she'd died and his dad never talked about her, and her pictures were hanging in the living room and up in the attic. He'd gone to look at them a few times when he was a kid. Apparently they were worth a lot of money. His mother had told him that. He knew she wanted to sell them, but his dad wouldn't talk about it. He wished he knew more about her. He'd seen her pictures, but that was about it.

God, he wished his friends would hurry up. Maybe he'd go downtown and look for them. He wondered what held him here, uncomfortably pressed into this stupid chair, waiting for something to happen. Kathryn would die. He knew that. He'd overheard the doctor talking.

"Well, she's had a good long life," someone sitting several chairs down said comfortably to someone else. Brendan thought if he heard one more person say that he'd smack them over the head with this damn chair.

"You know, she never got over her daughter's death," someone else near him said.

"Yeah. Twenty years ago. Drowned or something, didn't she?"

"In the lake one spring. A terrible thing."

"I heard she had some terrible disease so she killed herself. Didn't she leave a note?"

"Wasn't no disease. She had some kind of rotten love affair. She was real wild anyway, always running off with some guy or another. I don't know how Kathryn stood it, or why she never laid down the law to the girl. She was married a couple of times, never could stick with anything. A real little tramp, that one."

"Well, Kathryn was no angel."

"No, she led her poor husband around by the nose. Old Bill, just worked and worked until he died. Laid down and died in harness, I guess Kathryn never did let up."

"Whereabouts is their place anyway?"

"Oh, you've never been out there? That big place on the lake, in below the road, old house, huge cedars, hay fields, cows. One of the real old places. Amazing, one family with all that land. They've hung on to it somehow. I heard Kathryn used to run real estate agents off with a shotgun."

"Hmmp. She would. She got stranger and stranger as she got older. Not really senile, just a bit gaga, if you know what I mean."

"Hardening of the arteries, probably. You know my Aunt Jessie, she went that way. Happens to old people."

"Probably."

Brendan got up and walked down the hall, feeling sick. When he saw Mike coming towards him, he just said, "C'mon man, I gotta get out of this place. You got any smokes?"

He waited until he was out in the car before lighting up a cigarette and then a joint. He took a long drag, inhaled, passed it back to Mike, then stared out the window.

"Let's go man," he said. "Let's get the fuck out of shitty place." Abruptly, to his embarrassment, his eyes filled with tears. He looked away out the window. He'd never felt lonelier in his life.

Chapter Thirteen

"I'm so furious," Arlene said on the phone to Dana. "I don't even know who I'm maddest at. Myself, I guess. I let her walk out. I should have known better. I should have talked her into staying."

"You know you can't talk Kathryn into anything," Dana said patiently. "She would have left anyway. And maybe it was the right thing for her to do."

But Arlene wasn't listening. She rarely did.

"And what was she doing down at the beach? That's not like her, to go to the beach in the daytime. Why wasn't someone there to keep an eye on her? She must have gotten confused. God, she is so stubborn, and you know, Rob is just like her. I tried to tell him she wasn't well, but he's like all the Mangertons, thinks he's invincible so everyone else must be too."

"He said she seemed fine . . ."

"Oh, she'd say that, wouldn't she. And he'd believe it, just because he wanted to. Well, I'll get everyone at church to pray for her ."

Dana sighed. Arlene had just joined a new church. She and Mike had changed churches several times. Each new church was a little stranger than the last. Mike went along with whatever Arlene wanted. He never said much of anything.

"You should come with me sometime, Dana. You'd just love everyone there. I know you would. And we have such a beautiful choir."

Arlene never seemed to remember that she had said all the same things the last time she changed churches. She changed her style, her clothing, her reading, sometimes even her speech patterns, according to who was in the church.

Dana put it down to insecurity. Arlene had had a lousy life. She'd spent her childhood shuffling back and forth between Colin, his ex-wife, and the farm. She had hero-worshipped Rob until Dana had entered the picture. She and Mike had no children, despite years of trying and a battery of medical tests. Her talk rattled in Dana's ear like beans in an empty shell.

"Sure, come to dinner," Dana heard herself saying. Rob was used to Arlene and liked Mike. He just sat and listened to her. Dana sighed and braced herself for a long evening. Arlene would complain to everyone about how they had all ill-treated and ignored Kathryn, then try and lead them all in a prayer. Dana began planning the food. She'd have to make sure Brendan was there. The boy was so skinny.

Arlene was beginning to show signs of slowing down. Dana sighed again. "Sure Arlene, I'll tell Rob you're praying for her. He'll be glad to see you. All right. See you tomorrow."

Gratefully, Dana hung up the phone. Rob was upstairs asleep. She was restless, went to the kitchen, made tea, sat in the living room with it, looking at the painting that hung over the fireplace. It blazed with colour. Dana loved the painting. It warmed the room, bringing it to life. She wondered again about the woman who had painted it, and her mysterious death. Rob hadn't told her much, just that Mary had come and gone all of his life. He was so loyal. He'd never say anything against someone he loved. Kathryn had driven him crazy the last few years, demanding more and more help, always complaining about what he did, never grateful for anything, complaining more and more about the neighbours, noise from the traffic on the road, stray dogs. He was always there, helping her with something, adding her workload to the heavy load he already carried.

The phone rang again. It was Luke, Rob and Dana's oldest boy.

"Mom," he said. "Hi, how're ya doing?"

"I'm fine, honey. What's up?"

There was a long silence.

"How's Kathryn?" he said. Dana had already phoned everyone once to tell them the news.

"She's fine," she said. "No change. What's going on honey, it's kind of late."

"Mom," he said again, and stopped.

"All right, whatever it is, you'd better tell me," she laughed. "You know if you don't, your brothers will. No secrets in this family. You're all such terrible gossips."

"Well," he said, "It's Andrea."

"She's pregnant!" Dana exclaimed.

"How did you know?"

"Why else would you phone and say 'Andrea' in that tone of voice ? And why didn't you say something earlier?"

"She made me call. She said you'd want to know. I couldn't tell you earlier. You were so upset about Kathryn and everything."

"Oh, my God," Dana said. There were a whole lot of things she wanted to say. She waited while they rolled through her head in a dark wave and she bit her lips to keep them inside. "Well, that's great, honey. I mean, if you're ready, if you think you can cope, I mean."

Oh what could she say? "It's great news, honey. But what about getting married? Surely Andrea wants a little more security."

"Oh, God, Ma. We'll think about it. Actually, we've even talked about it. Maybe, after the baby's born. You know how it is."

Yeah, she did. "But are you sure you're ready for this? I mean really ready?"

"Well, who knows. Guess I'll have to be," he said ruefully. "Guess it's just one of those things you deal with."

They said good-bye, and Dana sank back into her chair. Luke was like that, impatient with thinking about things. He simply dealt with what came. She wished he was a little more thoughtful but he was a good boy, she thought, steady, hardworking, a good man. Plus, she liked Andrea. She was level headed enough as well. The two of them had started going together in high school. But she and Luke were too damn young to have kids. And not married. And Luke's only job was working for his dad. Andrea worked as a waitress. A baby.

She still had some baby clothes, left over from the boys, stored in the attic. She could organize a baby shower. They'd need so much help. They were so young.

She wanted to tell Rob but she didn't want to wake him. She went upstairs, crawled into bed beside him, curled against his brick solid back, which radiated heat at her. A baby. She smiled. She'd plant a little extra in the garden this year. They'd need so much help, she thought again. They were so young, just babies themselves.

Chapter Fourteen

Once Dana had asked Rob about Mary. She wanted to know, couldn't imagine, being driven to suicide, to drowning.

"She didn't commit suicide," he said patiently. "She drowned. It was an accident."

"But Rob, out in the lake, in a canoe, in the spring, that freezing cold water, that's pretty crazy."

"She wasn't crazy," he snapped. "And she didn't commit suicide." The door slammed as he left.

But Dana wondered. There were the journals, which she'd looked through once, briefly, long ago, just after that horrible time when they found the canoe, just before Rob decided they should get married. The journals were in the attic, with the rest of the stuff they had packed up out of that dreadful old house. Really, how could anyone have lived like that. It was more like a nest than a house, dreadful bundles of dusty cobwebs in each corner, holes in the walls where the wind whistled through, cracked windows, no food anywhere.

But the journals didn't really say anything either. They were like reading shadows, a pastiche of dreams, notes about how Mary had been feeling at any given moment, random words about colour, a description of leaf shadows against a wall, murmuring lines about water, the colour of water, the shadows and reflections on water, bits of drawings, sometimes words, one page which she remembered for some reason, which had read *sad, scared, scarred, sacred,* and bright leaves around the edges, curled into each other. There was a stack of them. The journals covered all the years after Mary had left home, moved to the city, come back, gone back and forth, never really stayed anywhere, never really belonged anywhere.

Dana shuddered. She couldn't live like that, wouldn't have survived a life like that. She looked around her house, the living room bound by bright polished logs, huge windows looking out over the fields and down to the lake. The fireplace. She and Rob had gathered those stones together, had picked out the patterned rug laid over the polished wood floor. They'd bought that rug together on a vacation trip to Mexico. Her kitchen—the dark green counter tops, the cherry wood cabinets, her matching pots and pans, her perfect cotton curtains, the maple table Rob made himself. Upstairs—the boys' rooms, her and Rob's bedroom, the queen size bed with the expensive duvet, the expensive carpet, all paid for by dead trees, acres and acres of dead trees, long gone, sawed into lumber and plywood for other homes like hers.

And nothing wrong with that, she thought. Someone has to do it and Rob is good, he's good, fast, people like to work for him.

But it bothered her. She sent money to environmental groups without telling Rob. She read books and magazines. She had stopped using pesticides on her garden. She bought more and more of their food at the new health food store. She read health books, took vitamins, went on specialized diets. She worried about the amount of meat they ate, but she figured Rob needed it, a man who worked as hard as he did couldn't survive on vegetables.

But she still worried. Nothing could stop the worrying. She had talked to Rob about getting out of logging. If they had the use of Kathryn's land, she thought, they could do something, plant an orchard, or grow garlic, or maybe raspberries, or strawberries. But Rob wouldn't quit logging. Sometimes, waiting for him to come home, pictures twisted through her mind, pictures of the skidder turning end over end and Rob's body flung out like a doll's to crash against the ground.

Sometimes Dana thought that Mary's shadow, Mary's death, Mary's sad and despairing life, stalked them all, reproachful, lurked just outside the windows, under the ancient cedars along the border of the hayfield between their house and Kathryn's, staring in with hungry eyes at all they had and all they had created together.

Section Four

Mary

Chapter Fifteen

Jim came into the cafe the next day while she was working. They had done some serious necking on their last date and she let him. She let his lips ride over hers and she waited to feel something. He sat up after a while and drove her home. All night, she watched the dark wash in and in the windows until it was finally replaced by dawn's filtered grey.

She tried to plan what to say to him about Rob. She knew he knew. There were no secrets in this community. Kathryn always said that. But she would have to tell him something. She had never talked to anyone about it. She knew enough now, from reading to give it a name. An ugly name. Rape. But she didn't think of it that way, couldn't. Not Rob. Rob was no part of that. He was her child, only hers and he had come to her, miraculously, and his life was bright and unstained and miraculous as well. Jim would see it that way as well. And Rob could be their child. Their miraculous shared child. She lay awake watching dreams flow in and out the window with the light.

But when Jim came in the cafe she went out to the kitchen, stared at the greasy blackened pots and pans, and went out again, forced herself to smile. She didn't know this man, couldn't even begin to think how she might share anything with him.

They were married in the town registry office April 15, 1957, by the Justice of the Peace. "Good man," said Bill, slapping Jim on the shoulder. Mary wore a white suit she had bought on sale at the store down the street. Kathryn had bought her flowers. They went to the Lotus Grill for Chinese food. After supper, they got in Jim's truck and drove to his house. He kissed her hard when they came in the house.

She kissed him back, pushing her stomach against him. She could feel the bulge in his pants. "Come upstairs," he whispered.

They fumbled around with clothes and got into bed. Mary was freezing cold and she was glad for the warmth of Jim's body. She began to like kissing. She liked lying in the dark warmth, next to him, feeling his body. She let her arms and legs go soft.

When he pushed himself into her, she turned her head and bit at the pillow. He pushed and grunted and finally collapsed. She said nothing while his breathing quieted.

"Okay?" he asked.

"Sure," she said. She laid her head on his chest. It was still there, the warmth, the reassurance. She drifted, rocking in his embrace, into sleep.

She tried so hard. She smiled and she did housework and she went to the doctor and got fitted with a messy smelly rubber diaphragm, and laid down with Jim in their wide and sagging bed, in their rented house, and slept beside him all night smiling the smile of the just and peaceful, a married woman at last, a righteous woman, part of her community, her mother and father's good girl at last, a family, just the three of them.

Fortunately, Jim wasn't home much. Truck driving for the local gravel plant kept him on the road early and late and he had to stop at the pub for a beer or two. When he was home, he wanted food, and then sleep. Sex was for weekends. But he was endlessly kind, surprising her with presents when he did come home, playing with Rob, building him a sandbox and a go-cart, taking him fishing.

When he was gone, Mary spent most of her time at Kathryn's, helping out. She pruned the trees, planted and weeded the garden, picked and picked and then canned and pickled the results.

She didn't paint anymore. She stacked her easel, paints, brushes in one of the upstairs closets. Jim asked her, slightly worried, why she didn't paint anymore. She shook her head and laughed, and shrugged. He was relieved, said, "That's all right, but you know, there's a painting club in town. A lot of the girls go, if you want to try it out."

For a moment, she had to struggle to bite back a retort. She wouldn't be caught dead in the same company as the women in town who "painted." Then she turned away.

"It doesn't matter," she said. "Come on, it's time for lunch. I made broccoli soup."

Somedays Mary's kitchen shone, Rob ran into her arms shouting, she gardened and cooked and played with her son. No pictures shone in her head. Life had shape. Driving down the road on a spring morning, sitting beside Jim, with Rob in her arms, on their way to Kathryn's for Sunday lunch, Mary felt the shape of things gather around her. The trees sparked bright acid green in their new leaves, the road, the farm, the house, were as familiar as her hands, as her body, as the face she looked at each morning in the mirror.

Vancouver was far away, a distant dream. She had stopped writing to Elaine. What could she say? How could she explain this solidity, the necessity of this life to Elaine?

That summer when they went to the beach, Jim brought his canoe. At first, Mary took Rob for rides in the unfamiliar tippy boat. Bill had always had a rowboat, rarely used except for odd fishing trips. Jim wanted a new boat, with an outboard. He and Bill talked about it a lot. No one else seemed interested in the canoe. Kathryn dismissed it as a menace. Rob was nervous. He sat in the middle and hung on tight to both sides.

After the canoe ride, Mary would leave him playing on the beach and swim out, a slow steady crawl towards the receding black-green reflection of the mountains, wavering just in front of her, pushing her hands through the clear water, just under the surface, the water spilling off her fingers like radiant jelly. Then she would finally tire, turn on her back to rest, lie on the water, alone, luxuriating in being alone. She lay and rolled and spouted water like some awkward kind of sea lion, and closed her eyes and breathed and breathed while the water rocked her.

When Rob went to school that fall, after the garden was laid to bed and October was plastering the mountains with slabs of bright yellow, Mary began taking the canoe out in the afternoons. The canoe's nose split the flat water into fragments, into a multifaceted reflections, patterns of glinting colours. Mary paddled slowly up and down the shoreline, looking at the new houses, the cabins, docks, wharves, which filled up the wild places she had once played. Sometimes people waved to her. She never waved back.

October shone yellow and blue, the days almost too beautiful to stand, the sun hot but with a chill behind it. Mary winced at the nostalgic dying brightness of the sun. The hills were washed blue with gold overlay, the sky turquoise with black behind it, the lake mirror reflecting it all, a flat black, azure, golden eye.

Sometimes she let the canoe lie still, drifting, and dreamed and dreamed, the sun beating hot on her head, and behind it, the chill breath of winter coming. She lifted the paddle, dripping from the water, and saw, in each drop, a picture.

November came with grey, dark, wet days. Days spent carrying wood to the stove, cleaning house, sitting looking at the merciless rain pounding the grass, the empty trees, days spent trying to read. She had emptied the local library of its small stock of books which were neither romances nor westerns. Often she drove to Kathryn's, sat at her table drinking tea, leafing through recipe books, or she and Kathryn went for long walks despite the rain. They walked the graveled edge of the highway while the logging trucks sprayed muddy mist at them and left behind the scent of dying spruce and pine in the wet air.

They talked about the garden, about the endless amusements which men got up to, about what to cook for supper, about Rob and how smart he was, about Colin and his string of women and his erratic life.

Mary didn't tell Kathryn about the black fog that was rolling towards her. She could see it coming. Somedays it hovered at the edge of her life, making her slow, dull, sending her to bed at nine, exhausted, and waking her, restless and anxious, at four in the morning, listening to the rain on the roof, and Jim breathing easily beside her.

She didn't tell her either, about the despair that lived inside the fog, that crept into the house in the afternoons and crouched in the all the corners, and spread over the freshly vacuumed carpet like a stain. She didn't tell anyone. She cooked and cleaned and read to

Rob at night and lay down beside Jim and carried the weight of her despair, a weight so heavy it bowed her shoulders and kinked her back until she bent and sank down to rest on the nearest available surface and then got herself labouriously to her feet again and went on.

She'd thrown away the damn diaphragm but she wasn't pregnant again, yet. Jim wanted kids, kids of his own. Another baby, she thought. Her body was hollow and echoing. She had been so cheated of Rob's birth. She barely remembered it. She hadn't really understood much of what was happening. When Rob was put into her arms at last, she was dizzy with drugs, turned her head away, ashamed of what her body had produced.

Now, everyday, she waited for him, waited for the bus, for his small body hurtling off it and towards her. She'd have more children, she thought fiercely, dozens of children, she didn't care if they were Jim's or anyone's, as long as they were hers.

November drifted on and December came, the first snow. She got through Christmas. They had dinner with Kathryn and Bill and Colin came home, and Kathryn got Rob a new bike.

Jim got laid off after Christmas. That meant he was home except when he went to the bar.

In January, they fought. They had never fought before. Mary had always told herself she didn't care enough about anything to fight. Now something awoke in her and fought like a cornered hurt kind of thing, like the cat, she remembered once, that had caught its foot in a rat trap and when she went to free it, sank its teeth deep into her hand.

Then she stopped fighting. She stopped having sex with Jim. She barely talked to Jim. When she did, she talked in a carefully normal voice about the weather, the prospects for work, what she'd made for dinner. In the afternoons, she went for long walks by herself. She stopped going to Kathryn's.

Sometimes, she went canoeing on the icy flat shimmering surface of the lake. The water dripping from the canoe paddle burned her hands. Pictures bloomed and grew inside her head and died between one stroke of the paddle and the next. She cracked open the freezing water with her paddle and then went home in the dim blue dusk and made supper and ate in silence, and then sang to Rob and told him stories when she put him to bed.

They got through the winter, and when spring came, Jim went back to work and Mary started gardening. The black fog receded and Mary came outside into the sunlight and felt contentment seep towards from the bright laughing mouths of the flowers. She went to Kathryn's for coffee.

"Where the hell you been?" Kathryn grunted as she came in the door. "Jim said you been feeling poorly. He's come by a few times without you. Made some fresh bread. You'd better take some home with you for that boy."

Summer came, and the land blossomed; food grew and swelled and dripped from every branch and bush cultivated piece of ground. Coming into Kathryn's back porch one late summer day, carrying buckets of peaches, heaping the table with corn for freezing, green beans for canning, with Rob running ahead of her, grinning and laughing, a large healthy red faced boy, she thought, it's okay now, I've put it all behind me. I was such a child. She could only feel amused and parental at the thought of that child who had gone off to art school with such naive hopes. Fall came, and she was still contented, so contented she wondered at times if she might be pregnant again and she had missed the signs. November came, and the sky darkened, rain poured down for days on end. The mountains disappeared behind thick walls of cloud.

The walls closed in around her again. In the mornings, after Rob had left on the bus, and Jim had left for work, she sat at the table in their small house, which she had cleaned and decorated until she was sick of the smell of paint, and drank too much coffee and watched the rain.

She stopped talking again, stopped looking at Jim, cooked and cleaned and read to Rob at night and read to herself at night, lying beside Jim as he tossed and turned, trying to sleep in spite of the light.

One night, when she came downstairs after putting Rob to bed, Jim was standing in the kitchen, a blind and helpless look on his face.

"What do you want, Mary?" he said, almost whispering, "goddamnit, what do you want? I do the best I can."

She waited for a while, took the dishtowel from his hand, began to dry the rest of the dishes.

"I don't want to have to hate you," she said. She reached to put the dish on a high shelf and he took it from her hand and did it for her.

She shrugged. "I'm a dead person," she said. "I have nothing left in me to give you. I've tried, I've done my best. What do you care anyway? I cook, I clean, don't I ? I'm a fine little wife."

"That's not fair," he said evenly. "I've tried too. I work hard. I don't have a lot of fun. I took on you and Rob and I've tried to be fair."

"Took us on," she said bitterly. "We're not some lousy charity."

They were both silent for a bit. Mary finished the dishes, and wiped the counter. Then she stopped and leaned against it.

"I'll die if I stay," she said. "I won't be able to stand it if I leave. What can I do? What should I do?" She kept her eyes closed and hung onto the counter.

He was silent. Then he went over and put his arms around her. She clung to him then pushed him away. She went to the stove, put the kettle on, stood there until it boiled and made them both cups of Postum.

They sat there together under the yellow light from the plastic chandelier Jim had found at a garage sale and carried home like a prize.

"I'll take Rob over to Mom's for a while," she said. "Maybe if I went to see Elaine? Maybe if I got a break, just for a while, I'd feel better."

He nodded. "I'll drive you to the bus," he said miserably, hung his head, sulking, like a boy. "Let me know when you're coming back."

She shrugged. She hated his sulking.

"I don't know," she said. "I don't know what I need to do."

"You just need some time," he said. "It's okay. I understand."

"It doesn't matter," she said. "Whether you understand or not doesn't make any difference. I don't know what will. Maybe nothing will."

They drank the hot muddy drink, went up to bed, not looking at each other. Miserably, he held onto her in the darkness, and she let him but she wasn't even paying attention to him. She was thinking ahead, to what she might do, to what the possibilities could be, in the city, in Vancouver.

Chapter Sixteen

After Mary's first year away, after Kathryn and Bill and Jim, who had fallen into the habit of coming for dinner on Sunday, had given up talking about when she might come back, or what she might be doing, life fell into a pattern. Mary came and went for Christmases and birthdays and Easter. She sent Rob pictures, letters, photographs of her paintings. In every letter, she said how she loved and missed him. She spent what time she could every summer at the farm, helping with the gardening and fruit. Sometimes Jim came to see her and they went out for dinner and he asked her helpless stilted questions about life in the city until they got onto safer, more familiar subjects. Then at the end of a month or six weeks she left again.

"It's not right," Bill exploded at Kathryn one late August night after Mary had driven out of the yard, her ancient car coughing blue exhaust behind it. Rob had gone tight faced up to bed. "It's not right that a woman should leave her child and her marriage to run off for some fancy dancy foolishness in the city."

"She's chosen her life, such as it is," Kathryn snapped back. "And a fat lot we have to say about it."

"Maybe we should tell her to get lost. The boy doesn't need her. Just upsets him. She's don't give a goddam for him or us neither."

"She's your family," said Kathryn dryly. "You can't get rid of family no matter what you think of them. You got to hang on to them. You got to try."

They never criticized her in front of Rob but he heard anyway. Kathryn cleaned and baked herself silly for the week before Mary arrived, but they all fell silent in the face of her exuberance, her strange clothes, her cigarettes, her newly cropped mannish haircut. She would swoop upon Rob, too loud, too fierce and he drew back until he remembered and crept slowly back onto her lap.

The spring that Rob was nine, she came home looking more than usually thin and tired. She held onto Rob for a long time.

This time, after he went to bed, she mentioned that she was thinking of taking him with her.

"What are you living on?" Kathryn said.

"Not much," Mary laughed. She tossed her head. Her short hair and made up eyes gave her an odd kind of goblin look. "Waitressing. . . welfare when I need it . . . plus I sold a picture." She tossed this out as if was of no more account than the other information.

"Welfare!" Kathryn said, spitting the word.

"Sometimes."

"Your dad and I have decided to list the farm," Kathryn said dryly. "The real estate agent said he'd be right out. He seemed real excited."

"You can't," Mary said. "Where would you live? Dad would be lost without the farm. What would you do with yourselves?"

"We'd enjoy life," Kathryn snapped. "No more worries about money. Maybe we could travel, get a little place in town. Your dad was talking to someone about making a trailer park here."

"That's horrible," Mary said. She turned her head away. Her mother would not succeed in making her cry. "That's so stupid, I can't believe it. I can't believe you'd even think about it."

She stomped out of the kitchen before her voice broke and betrayed her, slammed the door behind her. Her mother would be furious but so what. She almost ran to the beach, sat on the sand. The green canoe lay upside down on the rocks where Jim had left it. He had never taken it back.

She turned it over, half dragged, half carried it to the water. The brown spring lake water burned her legs. When she was far out on the lake, she leaned over, looked into the blue-brown water, while icy trickles ran down the paddle, froze her hands.

"I'm sorry," she said to the water. "I've been away. I forgot you. I forgot how you looked." She had the sense that she had been far away and sleeping and that she was just now waking up. "I'm sorry," she said looking back at the farm which sloped like a green and rumpled blanket between the trees. "I won't let them sell you. I won't."

That night, at supper, as a peace offering, she said, "Well, I sold one picture and the guy said he might want to buy another one."

"One picture," said Kathryn. "That'll buy a lot of groceries."

"Might get a start plowing up some garden tomorrow," Bill said. "What do you figure, Kath? Same amount as last year?"

"We don't need that much garden this year, just so you can go ahead and work yourself to death keeping it watered and weeded. Who's here to eat it? That doctor told you to slow down and what do you do, just keep on working the same as ever."

"Yeah, and I guess he's just going to come out here and do the plowing for me," said Bill. "I guess he'll get up in the morning and milk the damn cow."

"Oh, stop feeling sorry for yourself," Kathryn snapped. "All I said was we don't need such a huge garden."

"Yeah, and we got money to buy all that fancy junk in the stores? Stuff tastes like shit. Might as well eat fertilizer and water mixed together. What's wrong with the stuff we grow here, good home-grown food?"

"Fine. Well, if you drop down dead one morning, I'll just have to look after everything myself. Thanks a lot."

As an answer, Bill pushed back his chair, slammed his plate of food into the sink, and went outside.

"Seems like one hell of a lot of door slamming going on these days," said Kathryn.

She and Mary stared at their own plates for a while.

"Go on. Eat, you're so damn skinny," Kathryn said. "Won't do you any good to starve just because he's having a tantrum. I suppose you live on tea and toast in Vancouver. Nothing fit to eat in that damn city anyway."

"I think he's scared," Mary said. "I never thought he could be scared of anything."

"Sure he's scared. I'm scared. It's no picnic getting old. You and Colin don't give a damn what happens to us."

"Selling the farm won't fix anything."

"At least he won't have to work himself to death making money from fruit and milk and beef. Maybe we finally could enjoy life. Maybe we'd have a chance to just relax for a change. All we've done all our lives is work."

"Then maybe it's better if I take Rob back with me."

"Rob is no problem. He's happy here. Why would you take him away from the only home he knows. This farm is his home."

"It's my home too."

"You've made your own life. It's got nothing to do with us. No, your father and I deserve to have a decent life for a change. We deserve to relax."

"Mom, I don't think you know how."

Kathryn was silent for a while, then she shook her head. "Your dad's not himself," she said. "I don't know what it is. He worries and frets over every little thing, blows up and slams out of the house just like tonight. Goes to talk to his damn cows, or something. Never has talked to me about anything. Something is bothering him."

"He's never talked much," Mary said.

"Talk don't solve nothing. Neither does worry. Come on, no use sitting around letting these dishes get sticky. Pull up the anchor there, girl, get moving."

Chapter Seventeen

Kathryn and Bill put up a homemade 'For Sale' sign on the cedar tree at the top of the driveway. Rob walked by it every day on his way to school. He didn't like to look at it; it didn't make any sense and so he stopped thinking about it. After a few months, the paint faded, the cedar boughs and wild roses obscured the sign, and no one paid much attention to it anymore. At least once or twice a summer, someone drove in the yard and asked about the farm and Bill took them around, showed them the place, then they came in the kitchen had coffee or tea and plates of cookies or slices of homemade pie and drove away again, while Kathryn and Bill sat in the kitchen and commented about their car, their foolish leather shoes, their silly city fuss about mosquitoes and cowshit. Land along the lake had stopped selling again, as it did periodically. Land sales fluctuated with the local economy, which generally seemed to be somewhere between bad and awful. Lately, some of the people who had built houses had moved away. There wasn't much reason to live on the lake except for the scenery and over and over people opened little hopeful businesses, TenT Here, or Mom and Pop's Burgers, or Upholstery, only to see them fail and then the people put their land up for sale and moved away.

Only in summer did the lakeside fill up, the cabins which had sat dark and damp all winter, suddenly full of children and dogs, smoke from barbecues, the reek of mosquito spray.

In summer, the lake surface was daily disturbed by lines stitched across it by boat motors, some trailing hapless skiers tied to them by ropes, or children bouncing on top of inner tubes, their expressions somewhere between glee and terror. Children sat all day on the gravelly beaches, running in and out of the water, endlessly admonished by their mothers not to go too far. A few more daring built rafts, or drifted under the sun on rubber air mattresses, stuffed full with burnt wieners and hamburgers and green and pink breakfast cereals.

Bill plowed up a half acre of ground and planted it to corn and potatoes, tomatoes, peas, squash, pumpkins, and enough carrots and onions to last the winter. He went out after dinner to hoe in the garden, only slightly bothered by the clouds of mosquitoes that whined around his leathery ears. Kathryn sat on the screened front porch and shelled peas or clipped beans or sliced strawberries or peeled peaches before going in just as it got dark.

When Mary came home, she worked as hard as Kathryn and Bill; sometimes she went to see Jim, sometimes she made an effort to get involved with whatever Rob was doing, take him swimming or canoeing or fishing, but as he got older, he avoided her more and more. She would watch his retreating back, sigh, pick up her hoe or her hay rake or bucket of peaches.

She and Kathryn talked about it in the long evenings.

"Well, what do you expect," Kathryn snapped. "The boy never sees you. He hardly knows you're his mother. If you'd settle down and live some kind of normal life, give him a home, a father, maybe he'd take to you a little more."

Mary didn't argue. She continued opening pea pods, frown at them a little, as if there was some secret hidden in the narrow green bodies of the peas, then continue,

"Do you think he'd like to go to the movies? I could take him tomorrow. I think there's some Walt Disney animal picture on."

"Oh, for God's sake, leave him alone," Katheryn snapped. "He's got friends. He's got his own life to live. You live your own life. You always have, no matter what anyone tells you. Why shouldn't he?"

Sometimes Mary talked a little about her life in the city, but usually the talk turned back to gardening, work to do tomorrow, the possibility of rain, Bill's worsening health, his refusal to see a doctor.

When Mary went to bed, she lay for a long while in the dark, listening to the crickets and the cicadas in the dusty pasture, watching the stars move over the window, thinking about the dark lake water. She could remember without trying the last dingy room she had lived in, the torn carpets, the chipped doorframes, the raised voices in the next room, the screams of slapped children, the furtive squeaking of bedsprings at night.

She couldn't remember the face of the last man she'd slept with. She'd have to move again when she got back to the city. Elaine was her mainstay, Elaine who now was married, had children, lived in a yellow and white house in the suburbs. But even the suburbs couldn't suppress Elaine, with her wild curly hair, her cigarettes, her easy laugh, her house full of food and friends and beer. She had married one of the teachers from art school, an easy going man whose abstract pastels were now being collected and rising in value. Their house was Mary's oasis. Sometimes Glen got Mary jobs at the art school, jobs modeling, sometimes a job as a teaching assistant, sometimes as a receptionist. She watched the crop of new students, the eager girls, the boys, nonchalant or sullen, the changing styles of clothes. She let her hair grow or cropped it and went home to her shitty room and painted and then went out to the bar for a drink.

Sometimes she brought a man home; sometimes she let one of them buy her drinks for a while until she was disgusted with him and herself and then she left the bar alone. On weekends she went to Elaine's or she walked along the dikes on the south part of town, or the seawall in the park, sketching, or looking at the water. After she left Jim, she had lived like this for seven years and for each of those seven years, she believed that if she worked hard enough, painted hard enough, got to know people, kept going, that something would happen.

At the end of seven years, she woke up one morning, staring at the cracked and waterstained ceiling. Wherever she was living, she left her stuff in boxes, knowing she would soon leave again. When she was at the farm, she stored her stuff in Elaine's garage.

She looked at the room full of boxes, the sink full of dirty dishes, the torn curtains. Then she looked at her latest painting on its easel in the corner. It was a yellow painting, full of light, the sun bursting over the water, light barely sifting through the surface of the water, lighting the dark corners, the rocks and logs and holes of the lake bottom. It was April, sooner than she usually went home. At home, her father would be getting the garden ready and her mother would be sorting last year's seeds and frowning over them. The windowsills would be full of seedlings. And Rob? Her heart turned over as it always did when she thought of him. He would be riding his bike, probably going to see friends, splashing through the mud. She had a picture of him taken when he was a six, when she was still living with Jim, when they were a happy family, when Rob was jumping up and down on a couch on someone's living room. She remembered that day. She remembered going over there with Jim and some woman, a neighbour, whose name she had forgotten, exclaiming over Rob and taking a picture of him with her new camera, which she wanted to show off. The woman had been kind or vain enough or both to get the picture developed and had given a copy of it to Mary. Rob was wearing a sweater Kathryn had made.

She turned over and over in the bed, trying to wrap anything around her, blankets, sleep, her own arms, but nothing kept out the pictures of home, her father's face. The last letter from home, from her mother whom had been uncharacteristically worried. Bill was short of breath, his arms and legs ached so much he couldn't sleep. He kept forgetting things. She had even made him see a doctor, but he came home with a bottle full of pills, took a few, then cursed the doctor for a fool and threw them away. Anxiety grew in her. Her parents had finally gotten a phone, but they hated the damn thing and it cost a lot to call. She laid back and worried some more.

Finally, Mary swung herself out of her weary and restless bed and called Colin. He agreed, somewhat reluctantly, to have lunch with her. Colin and Mary saw each other only a few times a year. Colin was usually very busy when she called. Now he said he was too busy to go home; she would have to do it. But he'd help her with the bus fare, he told her. He had a little extra money.

She went home without phoning, and wandered around the town until she found someone she knew going up the lake road. It had no other name. It was the lake road, just as there was the river road, the black bridge road, or the Sheep Creek road.

Kathryn was sitting at the kitchen table when Mary walked in the door. Her face was grey and bloodless. She said, looking straight ahead, not focusing on Mary, "It's a damn good thing you're here. Your dad had a stroke this morning, just after chores. He got the chores done, came and sat down and fell over. I took him in this morning; they don't say much. They say maybe he'll pull through. They say he might not be able to get around, he can't talk very good. I tried to see him but they sent me home to wait, said they'd call. I came home to do some work. I tried to call but your phone was cut off."

Mary stopped in the doorway.

"I'll have to sell the farm," Kathryn said in the same bloodless voice. "I can't hang on here without your father. It'll have to go. All of it."

Mary stepped across the room, filled the kettle, put it on the stove, got the teabags from the metal canister.

"Where's Rob?" she said.

Kathryn leaned against the table panting like a woman who's been running a hard race. She didn't seem to hear the question. Mary didn't ask again.

She made the tea, brought it to the table, made Kathryn sit by forcing her into a chair, poured the tea for both of them. The long afternoon sun slanted in through the windows, slanted like arrows through the swollen buds on the walnut tree in the back yard, onto the broad black backs of the cows, lazing in the new warmth of the April sun, onto the lilac leaves, uncurling like fists, the opening red laughing mouths of tulips, the wet turned earth of the garden, waiting for seeds.

"C'mon," Mary said. "I'll take you into the hospital and come back and look after everything. You should be there with dad."

Kathryn poured a last bit of tea, frowned, said dully, "But what about Rob. Someone should be here. I'd better say. You go in, stay with your father. Phone me and tell me."

"Mom, for God's sake," Mary said. "He's your husband. I'll take you, come back and pick up Rob, get him some food and then we'll do the chores and come back in and sit with you. He's gonna be okay. He's strong as an ox. He'll come out of this. He's just got to learn to take it easy. He never has."

But Kathryn repeated. "You go. I'll stay here."

Mary stared at her, puzzled.

"Mom!" she said. "What's the matter with going to the hospital?"

"I can't stand that place. People only go there to die. My mother went there. I was twelve. She went in and she never came back. I had to look after my whole family. There was no one but me. That place kills people. You go. Leave me here. I've got to look after things. Your father would never forgive me if I let things go."

"I thought you wanted to sell," Mary said cruelly. "I thought you hated it here."

"Sell? I love this place. I've lived here most of my life. But I can't look after it by myself. I can't just let it go. You've got to keep up with things."

"Mom, what does it matter? Let the grass go. Let the deer have it. C'mon, let's get going. Get your coat. I want to get in there and back before Rob gets home."

Kathryn pushed herself up and away from the table with her hands. She stood there, head down.

"All right," she said. "You're right."

Mary went across the room and put her arms around her mother. She was surprised at how small and bony and thin Kathryn felt. Kathryn held onto her like a drowning person and Mary kissed the top of her mother's head.

"C'mon," she said. "I'll go get the truck and bring it around for you." This was what her father always said, and then she felt a great storm of fear swing her around and shove her out the back door before she could let go and start crying. She made it to the truck, sat there, surrounded by her father's smell, grease, sweat, leather, hay, cattle, held onto the steering wheel, still shaking, but managed to get the truck started and bring it around, still without crying, managed to smile for her mother and keep the truck moving down the familiar road back towards town, the hospital, towards the still white unsmiling body of her father.

Section Five

Rob

Chapter Eighteen

The next day Rob took off work and spent it sitting beside Kathryn. The doctors were sympathetic but not encouraging. Mostly, the room was empty except for himself and Kathryn's still, white form on the bed, her breathing, the fan turning over the bed, the green lines on the cardiac monitor.

He was bored. He realized he hadn't sat still anywhere for a long time. He looked at magazines, walked to the window and back, irritated. He would rather have been working; he was more irritated at his own foolishness in planting himself here. Kathryn would have laughed at him, sitting here like a big lump, out of place, his hands dangling over his knees, helpless to do anything for either Kathryn or himself.

But he went on sitting. No wonder Kathryn hated hospitals. The afternoon wore on and on. He kept checking the clock—noon, August 16, 1995. Arlene had said she would come in at four for a couple of hours before she had to start an evening shift.

He refused to believe that Kathryn was ready to die yet. She'd been as fierce as ever the day before, sitting there drinking tea and eating biscuits at the table like she'd always done. Alive, full of hell.

Reminded him of Mary coming in, when he was a boy, always unannounced and unexpected, pouring tea, looking in the fridge, poking and peering into things, ruffling his hair, grabbing him when he didn't want to be grabbed, asking him a million questions and then outside to look at the garden and the barn before he had time to think of answers.

He had been, what, seven or eight or so, when she left Jim and went off to the city and left him with Kathryn. He didn't remember living with Jim, all he remembered was being with Kathryn and Bill.

He couldn't really sort out the times she'd been there and the times she'd been gone. As he got older, it mattered less and less. When he was nine, Bill had started taking him to hockey, and that was more important than anything. Sometimes Jim came with them and they sat in the stands together, or with the other men, talking. Kathryn laughed at them both, coming home shivering and half asleep late at night from practice or on weekends from games.

"My God," she'd say, hands on hips as they straggled in, struggling with the equipment bag, skates, sticks. She had a rough tongue, even then. "My God, you never drove your own children to town for anything. They had to have a broken leg or some goddam thing before you'd think it was enough of an emergency to take them to the hospital ."

"Boy's a good player," was all Bill would say, in answer to her complaints.

But sometimes she came to the game, smiled at him when he came out of the dressing room, persuaded Bill to stop at the Dairy Queen for the treat of store-bought ice cream.

Rob hadn't figured out, didn't notice until he was older, a teenager, almost grown, how poor they were by everyone else's standards. He began to notice the green Dodge pickup they drove was ancient, the wheel fenders hanging by stringers of rust, began to notice that they got him what he asked for, new jeans and checked shirts, and good boots, but the food they ate was all homegrown, that the rare trips to town for a shared movie were occasions for coin counting. Kathryn waited for the meagre Family Allowance checque to help pay for things like the seed order in spring, or the hockey fees in the fall. When other kids at school began to talk about and acquire televisions, stereos, new records, none of these appeared in his house. Hell, they hadn't even had a phone until he was twelve.

And sometimes, though he hated to think about it now, it bothered him a lot that they were so old. When her hair had turned grey, Kathryn had given up any attempt to keep it in some kind of shape, to keep it tidy or curled. She simply kept it short, trimmed it with nail scissors so it had an uneven tufted look. When Bill's health started to worsen, she began going out with him to do chores, stumping beside him in the mornings and evenings to milk and feed.

Rob would hear them get up, look out his window just to see them, two figures carrying pails into the darkness. From behind it was getting harder to tell them apart except that Bill was taller. Time had rounded, lowered, softened them into a similar shape as they trudged towards the distant lighted barn, huddled against the cold.

He was struck then by a curious tearing feeling around his heart. It was the first time, he thought now, that he had ever realized they were old. Rob always woke when they did, just before they went out to the barn. He had loved those early morning sounds, but he didn't know that, either, until he was much older and heard echoes of them in his own house. The hollow clang of the furnace door as Bill laid kindling and logs on the coals leftover from the night's stoking, the water running in the sink as Kathryn rinsed the milkpails and filled them with hot water, then the clang of the stovelids on the kitchen stove as she lit it, filled the kettle, and set it to heat, then finally the creak from the rusty springs of the screen door at the back porch as they left for the barn.

After that, he'd fall back asleep for the half hour or so it took them to milk, waking to Bill's step on the stairs and his gruff voice which every morning repeated the same words.

"Hey there, young feller, you gonna sleep all day?"

Rob would slip on his clothes, and come stumbling down the stairs to the now warm kitchen where Kathryn would be ladling out three bowls of oatmeal, buttering the thick slices of bread toasting on the polished surface of the stove, and tending a frying pan of homemade sausage and eggs. Usually there was also homemade grape or apple juice; sometimes Kathryn bought oranges or bananas but Bill always grumbled about it. Rob would gulp his breakfast, flap a comb at his hair, a toothbrush at his teeth, and then slip on his denim jacket and head for the bus, trying to do the whole long uphill driveway at a run so he could get in shape for hockey.

It wasn't until he was working and supporting a family of his own that Rob figured how poor his grandparents really had been, how much they needed the odd bits of money that Mary sent home.

For years Bill delivered milk to various neighbours, cut firewood, sold fruit in the summer, worked out sometimes with the tractor, plowing or hauling something. They got by, but it was a chancy thing. But Rob never knew. He marveled now, that he hadn't known, that they gave him what they could of a normal life and never complained. There were things that had bothered him sometimes, but on whole, as he told Dana later, and often, they had given him a lot, a great life, a place to live, the freedom to run around on it, and the skills he needed now to survive and make a life for his own family.

When he was fifteen, Bill gave him a hunting rifle that had been Bill's father's and taught him to shoot. Rob also took over the green canoe, spent hours on the lake fishing, bringing home strings of trout, dolly varden, whitefish, lingcod, food for the table. Kathryn always praised his fishing to the skies, claiming fresh trout was her favourite food. He went snowmobiling and hunting and skating with friends from town, from the hockey team. He was a tall brown haired, brown eyed cheerful boy, the image of Bill's younger pictures.

"You're a damn Mangerton, all right," Kathryn always told him, "tall, stubborn, good looking and full of bullshit." He was the kind of boy who sat in the back of the classroom, who handed in his homework on time, but spent his classes dreaming of what he was going to do that day after school, after getting down off the school bus, gulping several cold glasses of milk and handfuls of gingersnaps in Kathryn's kitchen. He was the kind of boy who fixed things, who went outside to join his grandfather on his back on the icy ground under the ancient wheezing pickup, or found him in the basement workshop bent over a chainsaw blade, who watched until his grandfather handed him the saw file and said, when he was done, "Well, now we'll have to see if she'll cut anything harder than butter." He was the kind of boy who split wood and threw hay to the cows and came in the kitchen, whistling, and poking his nose into the pots on the stove until his grandmother smacked his hand with the wooden spoon and said, "Get on and wash those hands, or you're not eating at my table, big lout that you're getting to be."

Their evenings were long, and silent. Rob did his homework; sometimes he listened to the transistor radio he'd bought, up in his room, music from far away and disk jockeys who said clever things in fat jolly voices. He liked that, the sense of the world coming into the room with him through the little box on his desk. Then he came downstairs and Kathryn made hot chocolate and they sat in the living room together, while the wood cookstove clicked, cooling down, and the wood furnace below in the basement kept up its steady distant muted roaring.

Mary was an interruption in their days, an unexpected and unheralded disruption. She came and went with such speed. There was something so frantic about both her coming and then her departures that they all dreaded it. She had a whole series of small cheap cars which always arrived coughing and shuddering with something wrong with them which Bill would have to fix.

When she saw Rob, she always had a whole series of questions for him, his health, what he was eating, his clothes, his friends, sports, his latest triumphs at the hockey rink. She took her right to ask, to know, for granted. But as he got older, he resented it. Who the hell was she, marching in from some life he knew nothing about, cared nothing about, interfering with everything for a few days and disappearing again? He stopped answering, turned his face away, went outside with relief to find his grandfather while Mary dashed off to the garden, or the orchard or started yet another of the myriad of projects which she always started and never finished and worked at intermittently on her trips home—a rock wall in the garden, a new trellis or some plants, bought, left in pots, never planted, left alone by everyone.

He wondered a lot, now that he knew about life, and kids and what it took to survive in this world, how the hell she had survived. He hadn't wondered then. Rules about minor things like eating and sleeping never seemed to apply to Mary. Mary, his mother, his supposed mother.

He moved restlessly on the tacky little chair, bent under his weight. Where the hell was Arlene? He had work to do. If she got here soon enough, he could get home and get something done, get over to Kathryn's and get the weeds cleaned out of the garden, still maybe have time for a little fishing before supper.

He stood up and went to the door. The hall was empty and silent. Behind him, Kathryn suddenly gasped, moved on the bed. He turned and hurried to her, took her hand.

"Mary," Kathryn said. She was still asleep.

"I'm here," he said. "I'm here, dammit." He sat back down on the bed. She kept moving, spasmodic jerky movements. He wondered if he should call the nurse. She mumbled something he couldn't catch.

He stood up and went to the window, then came back to the bed. He picked up Kathryn's hand again. It was warm and strong. The knuckles were purplish and stuck up above the tendons and the blue veins. He rubbed his thumb over the skin which wrinkled under his touch like thin paper. Her hands were covered with scars.

He couldn't stand the sound of Kathryn's troubled difficult breathing. The green lines on the monitor never changed their pattern. He went back to the window, began pacing the floor.

After all those years that Mary had run back and forth from the city to the valley, and never settled in either place, she'd moved home again, rented the ancient crumbling farmhouse next door. After Mary's death, he'd driven a Cat through the damned thing and lit it on fire. Then later, he'd built a house for himself and Dana on the same site.

When Mary lived in it, the house was a wreck, siding aged to light silver and streaks of rust brown around the nails, surrounded by lilac bushes gone wild. The kids had broken off the back door and tramped around in the empty rooms full of torn wallpaper, broken glass, layers of ratshit and dead flies.

No one could believe it when Mary announced she'd rented it and was going to move in. He'd gone over and she was shoveling out the rooms. She'd tracked down an old woodstove and called Jim to help her set it up. Rob remembered Jim coming by to take a look, coming back to Kathryn's shaking his head, disgusted. "Damn place ain't fit for pigs," he said.

Rob had strained his back dragging an ancient iron bathtub up those narrow bent stairs, while Mary ran around, talking and laughing and being excited and happy and full of plans for the house, most of which he could have told her were too expensive, or not feasible.

He stopped going to see her. She phoned Kathryn's looking for him but he was busy, working, chasing girls, living his life occasionally playing hockey, but men's hockey now, just for fun, given up all dreams of the NHL.

After she died he thought about how he hadn't gone by, hadn't gone over, hadn't considered what she was going through, or had gone through. He guess he'd never understand it. There was just the diaries which Dana had hidden away somewhere and the paintings and his memory of how she had looked, the helplessness in her shoulders, in her rounded back. He'd been so young. She'd never been his mother, more like a big sister or a distant aunt. And so he'd lost, he thought, his only chance to get to know her, maybe he might have saved her. Maybe not. Who could tell?

Chapter Nineteen

Kathryn lay dreaming. She knew she was both dreaming and awake. The problem was telling the difference. She drifted. Sometimes she knew clearly what was to be done, that it was time to stop this nonsense, get up, get her clothes on, and go home, but her body was far away and ignoring her. Or rather, she was too far inside her body now to make it do anything. She always commanded her body, made it work, made it get up when it didn't want to, when it wanted to be lazy, wanted to lie in bed, wanted to be warm just a little longer, wanted to be sick, or wanted to be tired. But now, in a strange way, she was her body, right down to the cellular level, she was living in every drop of blood and pore and hair and gurgle and drip of fluid and the part of her that had commanded was submerged into dreaming, and she had no power, any longer, to command the dreaming to stop.

Shadows moved and blended in the room, came and went, looked at her, went away. She could see them clearly though her eyes were closed, could see everything clearly, could hear, far away and close at hand, the inner workings of everything, could hear the strain in the walls that held up this building, the creaking, the rubbing upon rubbing of splinters of wood.

Could hear, farther beyond, the cars moving smoothly and silently on the roads, the people walking and talking, their faces luminous moons under the neon lights of the town, and now she was young and swinging her hands, a whole nickel in her pocket, a treat that came maybe once a year, walking down the wooden sidewalks, past the movie theatre with its new plush red velvet seats, the meat lockers, reeking of ammonia, and the pharmacy, with its ice cream counter, the tall frosted glasses, and the ancient wizened pharmacist peering over the counter from within his jungle of bottles. Farther down was the store that sold wool and knitting needles and fabric and beyond that the garage, the grocery store with the green sign and its endlessly tipping teapot, and the end of the street, the vacant lot with the wagons hitched to patient drooping horses where sad looking Indians stayed on their weekly trips to town, where they lit small fires and left behind a litter of bottle and bones and horse shit.

She could hear and see beyond the town, the mountains, lumped blue, their coating of trees, the hidden shadowed secret places the trees made, the granite shell covering the thick layered ground wrapping the earth around like a warm wrapping, and layered in the hollow between the mountains, the blue shining lake, the lake which would someday take Mary and hide her forever, but no, she would not let that happen, would hide her instead, keep her safe, and how could she be so young and still remembering Mary.

"Mary," she said in confusion and moved restlessly on the white stiff sheets. A shadow between her face and the light.

"Kathryn," said a voice. "Kathryn, are you awake?"

But she didn't want to listen to this voice, this shadow, she was far away and pursuing something important. Mary was somewhere, smiling. She was somewhere near and there was nothing, nothing more important that Kathryn could think had ever existed in her life than that she find her and tell her something, something she had been meaning to tell her, something important, and when she found her she would tell her and peace would be there at last between them, oh God, the peace she had longed for. And all the times she had tried to talk to Mary, tried so hard to tell her what she knew was important, what she needed to know to survive. Mary was so foolish, Kathryn was always afraid for her, afraid of what she knew was coming, some kind of disaster. She had tried to save her in every way she knew, and nothing had worked.

She left the town, walking steadily down the road; the sun was shining and the wild roses were blooming all along the road, mounded tangled thickets of glossy green leaves and pink perfumed blossoms. She walked and walked. It was very far, and night was coming and along with the night was a storm. The road was rough and full of holes. She had to get home. Mary would be there waiting and she would be there all alone. Mary had always been afraid of thunder. She shouldn't be left alone in the dark.

Chapter Twenty

The next morning, there was still no change in Kathryn's condition. Rob phoned the hospital as soon as he got up, around five o'clock.

"I'd better go to work," he told Dana. She turned over in bed, sleepily, mumbled something at him. "I'll go over to the hospital as soon as I get home."

Rob headed, as usual, for the coffee shop before work, meet the boys, finish waking up. Hell, the truck could damn near make it there by itself. Some mornings, he'd wake up as he drove in the parking lot, couldn't remember a thing about the trip in.

He headed for the small noisy dingy room full of men, drinking coffee, the standard ritualized greetings, "Hey, how's it goin', eh?" took his seat at a table where Mike and Russ were sitting. The waitress, a solitary woman in a male domain, poured his coffee, took his order, and went back behind the counter, leaning against the ice cream machine, chewing gum, watching them all.

"Jeez, tough news about Kathryn, eh?" said Russ. "How's she doing?"

Rob shrugged. "You know fucking doctors," he said. "Never tell you anything straight. She's old. What the hell. None of us can live forever, eh?" They were all silent for a moment. He drank his coffee in one gulp, held out his cup for the automatic instant refill from the waitress.

"She's a great old lady," said Mike finally. "Tough, though, Christ almighty, I remember one time I was over there, she got mad at some damn thing or another, gave the whole bunch of us such a chewing out. Jesus Christ, I ain't heard nothing like it before or since."

"That sure as hell is one Christly beautiful place," Russ said. "All that lake front. Make a fortune if you subdivided. You gonna be able to hang on to it, you think."

Rob shrugged. "Dunno," he said. "There's gonna be hell to pay on the taxes, I guess. Then there's my Uncle Colin. He'll probably end up with it. None of us has seen Kathryn's will. She never would talk about it. He hasn't lived here for donkey's years, doesn't give a shit about the place or the family, but he's next in line. Dunno what the hell is going to happen."

Someone else flopped into a chair next to them, the kid they had choking for them, who said cheerfully to Russ, "Hey, shit head, gonna drop another tree on my head today?"

"Ah, piss off, punk," said Russ, the faller. "If you'd move your goddam lazy ass once in a while, maybe I wouldn't have to try so hard to wake you up."

"Better head out," said Rob, "getting late. Nobody's paying you assholes to sit around here all day and drink coffee." They headed outside in the grey light for their respective trucks, sitting like obedient warhorses, side by side on the gravel. It was cold and it had started to rain. Up where they were working, it would probably be snowing, which meant they'd work all day in rain, sleet, wind, and cold. But what the hell. It was always some damn thing and the weather was the least part of it. Weather, you could dress for, get in the truck cab on break, drink a thermos of coffee, keep moving.

It was the unexpected things, the broken cable, the skidder coughing into silence, broken chains, wheel drums, transmissions, hydraulics, all the mechanical things that could go wrong and did, and worse things, trees not falling where they should, branches crashing, logs rolling where they shouldn't, and the absurd softness of the hard male bodies that should never get in the way. Rob had hurt himself a few times, nothing serious, all his fault, should have been faster, more alert, ended in the hospital a couple of times, Dana coming in, furious at him in order to keep from crying. There was that one time Rob had landed in the hospital with a leg slashed to the bone, and the guy next to him had a slashed arm. They'd stolen wheel chairs and happily made their way to the bar, which bought them drinks all evening. It was getting back to the damn hospital after closing . . . that was a chore, and the nurses falling all over themselves to see them back. He chuckled to himself just thinking about it.

His grandfather had died like that, suddenly, had a stroke and fell out of the hayloft onto the concrete floor of the barn. Rob had been at school that day. Somehow or other, Mary had showed up that morning like a miracle, taken over, organized things, drove Kathryn back and forth to the hospital, sat by her dad's bedside, white faced and still as a statue.

Suddenly Bill wasn't there anymore, just a body in the hospital morgue. His presence lingered around the farm, his footsteps in the barn, doors creaking, and the odd smell of grease and leather and cow. His old clothes and his tools stayed.

Sometimes Rob would come down in the morning, and Kathryn would have a wild haunted look. She told him she kept seeing Bill, just around the corner, kept hearing his footsteps, waiting for him to walk in the house.

"He doesn't want to go," she said. "He died too soon. I can smell him. He comes in the room at night. I can't get any sleep, goddam it."

Kathryn wouldn't hear of him dropping school to get a job. "You're fifteen," she said, "and you got no sense and you don't know nothing."

She drove him harder by trying to take on more of the workload herself. There was a bit of life insurance, and some of the money problems eased for a while. But there was still the garden, the fruit trees, hay, the cattle, fire wood, the old truck to keep running. He gave up hockey, stopped going to his friends. When he was seventeen, he got a summer job slashing brush along the power line. He gave his first paycheque to Kathryn and she handed it back.

"You can pay me some rent when you get ahead," she told him. "Put it in the bank. You're going to need a car, or a new truck pretty quick." That fall, he bought an old Chevy truck, in good shape. He took the motor apart himself and redid the rings and valves, took him all winter, practically, and in the spring, he took it to town and had it painted. It looked pretty good.

Mary phoned almost every week. She was feeling more hopeful. She'd managed to talk a gallery owner into carrying her work. She was taking it around herself to small tourist shops and she'd even had a show that Elaine had arranged through her friends. She sounded happier, more hopeful, than Rob had heard her in a long time. She even had a relationship, someone with money, a new car, loads of fun, she said. She didn't sound anything like herself. She'd bring him up, she said, next time she came to the farm.

Rob figured he didn't much care for meeting some asshole big shot from the city with a big car and the usual stupidity about how country people were somehow downright cute, with their little animals and their funky old trucks. Maybe he'd take asshole fishing in the old canoe, or better yet, take him hiking and get him lost for a while. The guy had actually shown up once, and he was as dumb as Rob figured he'd be. Mary had stopped calling so much, after a while. They hadn't seen her for almost two years, then she started coming home again and then, unexpectedly, she had moved home.

And that was when the real trouble started.

Chapter Twenty-One

Sunita's silver earrings kept flashing in the light from the fireplace. She and Rob were standing in the corner. He had poured her a glass of wine and brought it to her. She had long black hair streaked with silver. She was wearing a sleeveless embroidered black top which showed off her tanned arms. Silver and turquoise glinted at her neck. Her long brown legs stretched from under her skirt. She leaned back and shook her hair, laughing at him.

"You should travel," she said, tossing her head. "Get some perspective on things. If you could see what's being done to the forests in Asia, you'd understand a little more why we have to be careful here. This the last wilderness on the planet."

"So why don't you get out once in a while and enjoy it?" he said.

"I work. I have kids," she said calmly. "But I bet I could race you up to the top of Steeple Mountain."

"Anytime, lady," he said, "Anytime."

He was trying to control his temper. Sunita always made him feel guilty. It's not like he had never thought about the environment. Years ago, he and Dana had talked about taking over Kathryn's place, getting it back in shape, putting in a new orchard, maybe a new dairy herd. They'd gone as far as drawing up estimates, figuring out the money they'd need, and in the meantime, he'd just kept on logging and the money had kept rolling in and there was never a good time to go farming. There was never the possibility that he'd be able to make the kind of money that he'd made all these years—the money that built the house and outfitted the boys and bought all the toys and the new truck and kept them going through layoffs and injuries and hard times. So what the hell.

"I want a cigarette," she said. "Come outside with me."

He followed her out onto the deck. She lit a cigarette and stood away from him, staring down at the lake. Rob turned away. He had never felt like this in years. He wanted to grab her right now. What if he suggested they go for a walk to the lake? What would she say?

"You've got a beautiful place," she said. "I hope you remember to enjoy it."

She went back inside. Rob stood on the porch a while longer.

Jeezus. He was too old for this. But forty wasn't that old. And he hasn't felt anything like the way this woman heated his blood, set his blood and muscles into a very fine trembling, set a tone to the evening where he felt both young and foolish and old and mature and witty at the same time.

And under it all, feeling like a fool, because, if he really looks at it, he knows she probably thinks about him hardly at all, except as a neighbour, a logger, a dumb logger, someone who cuts down trees, wrecks the bloody environment without thinking, is responsible for global warming, the vanishing ozone layer, and the eventual extinction of life on earth. When she's around the conversation always creeps around to the same damn subjects, pollution, shit in the food, garbage in the water, the lousiness of factory chemical farming, the disappearing sky, then of course, cancer, death.

The real problem with the woman was she was too damn smart, and too damn good looking. Next to her Dana looked slow, sleepy, domesticated, with her endless talk of food, gardening, her kids, her kids, as if he had done little more than add the sperm to the rich mixture in her womb which spewed forth such strong and healthy sons.

Chapter Twenty-Two

The road Kathryn is walking on grows longer, rockier, narrow, twisty. There is mist on either side, she can barely see the path. She wishes she were home, by her own fire, her bones contented, sitting at peace, while the world swirls away from her into its own myriad of peculiar patterns of joy and misery.

She wants to call out, but her voice isn't working, tries and tries to call, because it's all confusion here. Even as she's walking she's aware of other voices speaking through her bones, and some are hers, and some are too distant to tell. The one speaking most clearly is someone she knows well but she can't remember quite how she knows, or why she should worry about it. She is here looking for someone, and so she goes on down the path though it's started to rain and the fog on either side dances with rainbows and the voices calling, she's here looking for someone, she has to keep going, though her body is distant, and she is shaking with cold, wishing someone would bring a blanket, help her get warm. She's thirsty, she opens her mouth to drink the rain but the rain is as dry as a desert, and she is as light as dust, dust inside and out, only the voice calling, calling, and she answers "here" and runs, her footsteps light on the path, her skirt bundled around her, through the soft grass, shining with winking bits of light from the new sun, from the new day, from the new hope springing in her at the sound of that voice.

This is the voice she has been waiting for all this long while, her grandmother's voice, calling her home, to sit by the fire with her and drink tea and tell stories and wait for the men to come riding home, all the men, dark and bundled heavy for days of riding, her uncles and her grandfather somewhere in the pack, come home safe at last, again, and all the stories she's heard, that her grandmother told her as a girl, stories of raiding and the peat fires and the stone houses and the final great separation have come true and are living in her like a great broad movie that she has walked into and sat down inside.

Chapter Twenty-Three

Brendan lay on the foam mattress on the floor in Johnnie's basement, watching the window turn grey in the dawn light, watching the room dance and fizz. They'd taken something last night, some stupid drug or other, plus beer and a bag of bud that appeared with another their of friends. Johnnie's parents had gone out somewhere, a dance or something, left them with admonitions to look after the house, turn out the lights, left them with bowls of chips and a bottles of Coke. Nice folks. He never worried about what they might think if they knew what really went on in their quiet basement. That was Johnnie's problem.

His head hurt and the light jumped around behind his eyes. He felt his spirits shifting, sliding down, flattening out, flatter than his body under the torn brown sleeping bag. He didn't want to be awake anymore, there must have been speed in some of that shit they had taken, he could feel his nerves jumping, he wished to God he could sleep, but instead he tossed and turned on the hard concrete floor which the mattress barely softened. Finally he got up, went to the bathroom, stood in the harsh yellow light, peeing, and spent some time looking in the mirror, twisting and turning his head. A grotesque scowling stranger stared back, black hair, brown eyes, thin white face, high cheekbones on which the freckles stood out like mud splatters, like flecks of blood on a sheet, like holes in his skin to let the light in. He wondered if he looked like his grandmother Mary, the one whose memories were stuck in his head like some kind of repeating record.

Since his afternoon reading Mary's sketchbooks and diaries, they had filled his head. They coloured what he saw around him. It was like living in two worlds instead of one. He wondered why no one else had read them, or at least, if they had, they never talked about it. Maybe there was something in there that he hadn't found yet, some black secret no one wanted to talk about.

He remembered a phrase from the last page he read, *the duality of my life* she had written, *torments me endlessly, being two people, living in two places, never settled, never home.*

Finally he realized he'd been standing there too long; he was shaking with cold, his feet icy on the floor. He got back under the sleeping bag, shivering, closed his eyes, watching paisley purple cartoons, felt himself sliding down towards sleep, a soft abyss where demons waited. He jerked awake, sweating and shivering, feeling sick. What was in that shit?

Despite the curled sleeping bodies of his friends, he felt an immense loneliness, a loneliness so all encompassing he knew he had always felt it, was always dwelling in it, and always would. He could spend a lifetime running away from it, distracting himself from it, playing foolish games and it would be there anyway, waiting for him whenever the distractions were gone.

He began trying to describe it to himself in words, the purple demons lurking, waiting, no that wasn't right, and they weren't really purple, weren't even describable. Maybe forces, or devils. Despair swept over him at his own feeble ability to ever say what he wanted, to even figure out what it was he was trying to say. He didn't even know how to begin.

For a vivid moment, he saw her floating, her face clear under the rushing green water, her long red hair tangled around her. He had seen pictures of Mary before, but she hadn't really looked like this, her eyes were open, looking at him, her mouth seemed to be moving. She was trying to talk to him but all he could hear was the sound of water rushing in his ears.

The image faded, and he lay curled in a tight circle, put the blanket over his head to shut out the light; the little bright devils gibbered and danced, laughing at him, but they were only cartoons with no power to hurt him. No power, he said to them, you have no power, go away, I am strong he said, I am invincible, I am Brendan the magnificent, a litany he had used when he was little, but which now seemed puny and out of place. He waited, began falling again, as if from a great height, but backwards, falling upwards into the sky, speeding faster and faster away from earth, away from the blue light and into soft darkness.

He woke at noon, groggy with irritation. Johnnie's mother was calling from the stairs. "Brendan," she said urgently, "Brendan, it's your mom. She wants to talk to you about your grandma." She handed him the phone and he sat up, hunched over, the phone clapped to his ear like a poultice.

"Yeah?" he said.

"Brendan, can you sit with your grandmother this afternoon? She shouldn't be alone, even though she's sleeping. I've got to go over to your brother's and your dad's working "

"I dunno," his automatic response to his mother's questions for years, then waking a little more, yawning, he said, "I guess so, when do you want me be to be there? How long do you want me to sit with her?"

"For God's sake. This is your grandmother. Your great grandmother. She's ninety-one. And she's been awfully good to you."

"You'll have to come and get me," he said.

"I'll be there in an hour."

"Jeezus, I just woke up. I haven't even eaten."

"I'll take you for lunch. One hour." She hung up.

"Christ, fucking parents," he muttered. "Fucking guilt trips."

Johnnie groaned and rolled over. Brendan lit a cigarette, handed it to him, lit another one for himself.

"I need some smokes, man," Johnnie yawned. "Let's go to town, get some food, hang around."

"I can't," Brendan said. "I said I'd go sit with my grandmother."

After a while, Brendan said, "The last time she was in the hospital, she tore up the place. Said she hated it there. Said they'd hauled her in there to die."

Johnnie's long brown hair hung down in his eyes in matted curls. He had bright blue eyes. He wasn't wearing a shirt and his ribs hung over his caved in stomach. His skin was a greyish green under the dull light and he kept blinking away the sleep the clouded them.

"Wow," Johnnie muttered. "Dying. Fuck. That's cool."

Brendan squirmed a bit inside. He hated it when Johnnie got going on suicide.

"I gotta get dressed," he said. "Man, I had a lousy night. Must have been speed in that shit we took. Fucking nightmares."

"No way," said Johnnie. "I slept like a fucking baby."

Brendan shrugged, bent to put on his clothes. He remembered again the odd feeling of falling through the sky. The next time he was at his mother's, he would spend some more time reading the diaries, maybe slip a few in his pack and read them later. No sense asking his parents about it. The less they knew about what went on in his life, the better for everyone.

Chapter Twenty-Four

Dana stopped at Arlene's on her way to get Brendan. She asked Arlene how Kathryn was doing.

"She's holding on," Arlene said. "Sometimes I think she's too mean to die."

"It's hard on Rob," Dana said. "He's very tense."

"When Rob and I were kids, we were scared of her. That woman had a temper on her like a mad dog."

"I've done my best to be good to her. Not that she notices anything I do. If she can find something to criticize, she does."

"Rob never seems to mind. He used to protect me from her. She always liked him a lot better than me."

"Must have been hell for her kids. I can't imagine having her for a mother."

"Sometimes I think about Aunt Mary getting pregnant like that. She must have been sneaking around somehow. No one ever figured who the daddy could have been. But he must have been someone from around here. People talked about some tramp that had been staying in old cabin by the farm there, but it must have been some boy in town, don't you think."

"Someone around here could be Rob's dad? I've often wondered," Dana said.

"I bet Kathryn knows," Arlene said as she stuffed a cinnamon bun in her mouth. "She knows a lot but she keeps a closed mouth. What are you and Rob going to do with the land when she goes?"

Dana paused, considering. "You know," she said, leaning forward, "we've actually never seen the will. I've gotten after Rob about it, but he won't say anything to Kathryn. He's just as stubborn as she is. She might leave it all to Colin."

"What would my dad do with it?" Arlene said, stuffing more bun in her mouth.

"Sell it, I guess. He hasn't even come home to see her."

"It must be worth an awful pile of money by now . . . at least a few hundred thousand. All that lakefront . . . it would make nice places for cabins. I wonder what you could get if you subdivided?" Arlene's round face went a sudden pink.

"A lot," said Dana. "But it costs money to do a subdivision. Rob wouldn't want to live next door to a whole bunch of people."

"I'd better go," she added. "I'm going to take Brendan for lunch. He never gets enough to eat."

It was true, Dana thought, driving towards Johnnie's house, Brendan never eats a decent meal any more, sleeps in a decent bed. She knew he took drugs, although drugs were an open secret in this community. Not that she cared. Some people smoked pot and some didn't. A lot of the big shots in town now were people she had grown up with and had smoked pot and got drunk with. Most of them hadn't changed their habits much over the years. She and Rob didn't do drugs anymore. Somehow it had drifted out of their lives without any big decision to quit and that was fine although they joked together about the lousy memories of their friends who were still stoned and the people who grew drugs and paid cash for everything and spent winters away in exotic places like Thailand or Costa Rica. It was one question it took outsiders a while not to learn to ask, what someone who had money but no job did for a living, though most people had a story of some kind going.

But Brendan was her bright boy, her laughing boy, the one who looked like her, everyone said when he was born, the one who had followed her around the kitchen with big eyes asking endless questions, instead of following his father outside into the world of men, or at least he had until something changed. Then somehow, she never had quite known how it happened, he was a sulky teenager, answering questions with monosyllables, or "dunno." Then he was living over at Kathryn's and she hardly ever saw him unless he made it home for some special occasion or other; he never missed anyone's birthday, she had to give him that. He was good to Kathryn, doing her chores when he was there, but still, what was he doing at that old biddy's when his own room was waiting for him, clean, made up, all his wild rock band posters still on the walls. When she would have done anything, done his chores, cooked and cleaned, if only he would come home, eat three square meals a day and tell her something, anything, that was going on in his life.

If Kathryn dies, maybe he'll come home. The thought was unbidden and unwelcome but present nevertheless. She tried to push it away but it buzzed around her head like a damn horsefly in the sun. Seemed like most of her life she had been running into that woman. Rob running over there at any excuse, the boys, her boys, trotting over there to hang out despite their yard full of toys at home, and now Brendan moved there.

When she first moved in with Rob, she had tried, very hard indeed, she thought, to like Kathryn and she had no doubt at all, that Kathryn had tried, outwardly, anyway, to like her. Granted it had been a terrible time, what with Mary disappearing into the damn lake and making Rob so crazy with guilt, but they'd been polite to each other, eventually got around to exchanging recipes and talking about babies. Still, the relationship had never taken, and after a while, they gave up making up reasons to spend time with each other and were merely polite.

Although, after she and Rob had built their own house, she'd tried to interest Kathryn in fixing up her own house, painting the place, putting a new roof on it, anything, but the old biddy would rather be out in the garden, or cleaning the chicken shed, knee deep in manure. Anything outside. She'd never cared much for houses, Kathryn had said one day, and the place showed it.

But as she got older, and her body settled into itself, she looked more and more like a man, stumping around in rubber boots and an ancient torn man's jacket, her grey hair sticking out in tufts all over her head. She even went to town like that, although Dana had tried, tactfully enough, to get her to fix herself up, offered her the names of hairdressers, tried to take her shopping. Not interested enough to even look at something new. Stuck in her same old ways and stubborn as a hen on a nest.

And now she was dying at last, but leaving a whole host of new problems. What if there was no will at all? She and Rob were left looking after everything. Their sons were facing having to assume huge bloody mortgages just to have a house and a bit of land for themselves and their families, and all that land over there across the fence sitting empty, growing weeds. There was Luke and Andrea, pregnant, living in a rented shack, a dump really. Probably Kathryn's house would sit empty, full of ghosts and bats and cobwebs until Colin saw fit to do something with it. It wasn't fair but she knew if she tried to talk to Rob about it, he'd just say it was Kathryn's business and that would be that.

Goddam. Her whole day was screwed up. This was supposed to be her day for the Young Women's League, and she'd had to break at least five promises to people about one thing and another in order to take the time to run into town. She'd promised a cake for the church rummage sale, God knows when she'd get it all done and her own garden going to rack and ruin because she and Rob had to spend their time at that old lady's cleaning up the mess in her garden, full of chickweed and pigweed and every other damn thing it had been. Kathryn must have been feeling really feeble to let things get in such a mess. And the house wasn't much better. Dirt and dust had accumulated in the corners and the dishes in the rack by the sink weren't even clean. God, just what she needed, another burden in her already busy life, and having to arrange for people to sit at Kathryn's bedside and wait for her to die was almost the last straw. But at least now she had an excuse to see Brendan, take him to lunch and make sure he was eating properly.

And then there had been the dinner last night. Why were men such complete fools they couldn't tell how obvious they were being? In twenty-five years of marriage, Rob had never made quite such an ass of himself. She knew he was still damn good-looking and well-built, a hunk, actually, and she generally knew when some woman was making a play for him. In fact, he usually told her about it and they had a good laugh and that was that. But he hadn't told her about this one, which meant that he was taking it at least somewhat seriously and that was not good news at all.

And the woman, Sunita, what kind of dumb name was that, sitting with her long legs stretched under Dana's table, dominating the conversations and proclaiming her oh so well informed opinion on absolutely every topic. When she and Rob had first met her, they both thought she was so wonderful, admirable, had both been bowled over by her, a single mother, bringing up two boys by herself, running a farm, well educated, a Master's degree in something or other, had decided to be a farmer, was writing a book in her spare time. They were rubes, naive to be so easily impressed by someone so superficially impressive just because she was from somewhere else. Somewhere in the States. But then half their friends here had once been American.

But after she'd been here a while, Dana thought, she didn't look so damn impressive. She'd run out of money, couldn't get a job despite her fancy credentials, no one in the town was going to hire her, she'd make them all look stupid, and she ended up being some kind of gardener or glorified lawn mower at the new golf course at the far end of the valley although she didn't seem to mind that either. And her boys were little hellions, now getting to be big hellions. The stories told about them in the valley were legion; they did the same drinking-drug-taking-shit that everyone else did but somehow with more flair; they had a rock band and an old bus that they'd converted, one of them juggled, they stripped half naked and sang together on stage, they drew obscene cartoons and published them around town. They had a father somewhere exotic, Mexico, or South America, that they occasionally went to visit, and came back with weird clothes and weirder haircuts.

And now she was making calf eyes at Rob. Her, supposed to be the big feminist, going after someone else's husband. Although, to be fair, most of the calf eye making seemed to be on Rob's side, which was even more infuriating, that he couldn't see through her, see what a hypocrite she had turned out to be, pretending to be so liberated and unconventional and knowledgeable about every damn thing and what was the difference between her and any cheap floozie waitress down at the jug, pouring coffee and hoping wistfully that some man would come along and rescue her from her fate just as soon as possible?

Well, she'd wait for a cold day in hell before Dana invited her back to dinner. And she didn't suppose Rob would find any good reason to see her, unless he happened to run into her in town. And he didn't have time for sitting around making polite conversation with so much to do and his grandmother lying up there in that hideous yellow stuccoed up box on the hill with her mind gone blank and only the shell of her body lying there still breathing in and out like a motor that didn't know enough to quit even when the key was turned off.

There had to be some way to get Rob to find out about the will. That land should be his, should be hers and the boys. Her boys needed it. It was only fair.

Chapter Twenty-Five

Kathryn sat long and silent by the fire in the small dark house. The fire warmed her hands and her heart. She realized she had been desperately lonesome and tired for a long while, and sick at heart from being so alone, and she wondered why no one had come to her aid but let her struggle on and on, so alone and so exhausted. She tried to tell her grandmother about it all and how hard things had been.

She opened her mouth to speak but the old woman merely smiled and laid another chunk of good pine on the fire, which crackled and spit pitch and sparks through the black smoke roiling in the chimney. Kathryn sat there a long time, listening to the rain on the roof and against the stone walls and the thick wood door, while the fire made shadows in every corner of the room. She must have dozed or slept because when she looked around, the room was empty and the sun was breaking in through the tiny leaded windows and under the door.

She rose and went outside, flinging a rough black cloak around herself and humming under her breath. She knew where she was to go next, had been there so many times before, fled gaily, singing, her hair flying long and foolish behind her, down the path under the pines, along by the broody rocks which made faces at her and dripped noisily from the rain and then farther up the trail, still dark here under the pines, and up onto the grass when the wind broke loose from its fetters and played around like a dog set loose from a rope, and the tall grass bent and swayed in purple satin waves like an elegant lady's cloak such as she had never seen but had only imagined.

She went singing to herself, an old song she only half recognized, and she wondered, far away in her mind, where the song had come from and how she knew it, and part of her remembered being a child and sitting on her grandmother's small bony lap, listening to the song, and the stories of people who survived as best they could in these dark hills. She wondered what she was going to, for she was sure it was a meeting she had been waiting for, for a very long time, and she remembered then, that she was looking for someone, that this search was very urgent, and she tried to hurry along the path, which was growing dark again, and was twisty and slippery; moss over queer round granite stones, like cobbles, like skulls. The path began to descend a steep bank. Far below she could hear the water running, the smooth brown water over the granite shelves and jade green algae streaming in the water, and she went down and down towards it, holding on in some places, stepping carefully on the path, placing her small strong bare feet among the stones. The air was cool, mist was in it, thin fingers brushing her face.

She followed the river upwards to where the water drooled in a thin silver line from the cliff above into a pool, wide, black, surrounded by birch and willow dipping branches in the water. She sat on a green velvet mossed boulder. It was like something she'd seen somewhere else, somewhere far away, and she tried to puzzle this out, but then forgot, for she could hear something far away, something coming over the hills. She knew this was what she had come to hear, the sound of the piper coming home from a weary hard day, the sound of the harsh brash music bringing the men home, the sound of the drums bringing relief and peace to the ears that could hear. She watched the black water, watched the colours flash and dance, watched the colour of the water, the deceiving mask it wore, the surface shining silver and black, the depths underneath, hidden full of green shadows, and lighted by shafts of brilliance reflected from the bubbles which burst out of the waterfall, and drifted serenely past her, sitting on the bank, waiting for the piper to come sliding down the rolling hill, through the pebbles tall and smiling with the sun at his back.

Then it got dark again and she could no longer find the path. She was cold and freezing, full of fear, in the dark, with only the sound of water, wind flowing over the surface, and all about her, blackness. She had to go on, go on. Even the path had disappeared, and she was weary, weary, wanted only to rest, to sink down and down, lie here in the blackness, her head pillowed on the cold ancient ground which hurt her bones.

And angry that no one had come and she was lying here, alone and helpless in the dark, and freezing, they could have given her a blanket, goddam it. Mary, she said, Mary, and a voice said, Kathryn, and another voice said, let her rest, and that made her angry enough to push her creaking bones up from the ground and go on, though where she was going at this point, she had no idea.

Section Six

Mary

Chapter Twenty-Six

Mary is swinging along the street, being happy. Happy, hell, she's ecstatic. And terrified. Never been this ecstatic. Never had this moment, this kind of moment, before. This is it, this is the moment that transcends all others, that unravels all the hurts, that glues epoxy over the cracks in her heart and lets it beat again.

This is it, she thinks to Rob, about Rob, this will make up for all the reasons she left him and couldn't be a normal mother and broke her father's heart, for she has taken that on as well, her father's recent death, her mother's despair over the untended garden and the weedy hayfields, Rob and her mother left to cope, alone, together, with the monumental business of surviving on the farm. All she gave up and the mistakes she made are justified now, merely because. Because someone has looked at her work and pronounced it good, hell, pronounced it brilliant, told her to bring the rest of her work, told her she would consider buying some of it if it was all of that same quality.

Tomorrow, she thinks. Tomorrow, she will take the her paintings to the gallery owner. Now, she and her new man are going to dinner, and then they will go back to his luxurious apartment and make love in his bed with the satin sheets and the miraculous view. Gordon, Gordon, Gordon, Gordon. She wonders if she loves him, if this is what she has been waiting for through all these years , through all the men, to find it now in 1972. She wonders and wonders. He wants to take her to Italy, he says. He wants to show her Florence. He teaches history at the university. He seems to have a lot of money. He has an ex-wife, but by now, that no longer matters.

She is modern, grown up, liberated, taking birth control pills, and having a decent relationship, for a change, with a man she doesn't even need to use to survive. She no longer has to worry. She won't get pregnant, but even if she did, it would be all right, would be part of this new inevitable onrushing flow of things, where her life is taking shape and making sense at last. She is an artist, a painter, and someone, someone who should know, who has money and likes her work, someone else has said so.

And this one didn't even need Elaine's help to set it up. This she had earned, sent her work into a contest, done it right, with slides and a portfolio, and a well typed letter, and she had won, not only a prize and the right to show her work, but the attention of this woman, an art buyer, a woman who was more important than any show because she actually paid money for art, bought for collectors.

Even if it is so late in her life that all this has come, even if she is thirty-seven and her red hair, which she has grown out long and straight again, is thinner, and showing streaks of blonde which might be almost grey and even if she is still living in a shitty apartment with cardboard walls, and a view of the concrete wall of the building next door with a tiny sliver of harbour beyond. Even if she has finally, she thinks, gotten used to the city, which she thought would never happen, gotten used to the stench, the noise, the greyness, the intrusion of signs and stores and people's avid faces and empty eyes, wandering the promising vacant corridors of department stores forever, hands forever reaching, eyes forever roving, seeking, restless. She's gotten used to the late night horrors and the fact that she never, never, never has enough money to cope with this shitty life she has chosen, gotten used to Rob's absence, reconciled herself to it, even got used to the moments when all the acid bitterness of her life overwhelms her, when she is paralyzed by it, as if bitten by a snake and all she can think of at such moments is that dying would be far easier than living with her skin burnt, corroded, curdled by the acid bath of choices which is her life.

Even so, in such a life, there have been more than a few moments like this one, when every male eye on the street swerves to notice and she knows they swerve, when her feet come down toe to heel, sauntering, on the pavement and her back is straight and sweet with power. Times when she can win, she can win, she can turn loose the power within her and keep it going and go where she's aiming, collected, coiled like a spring, and measuring herself against the helplessness she senses all around her, because there is something she wants to do. By God, she's doing it, in the teeth of fear and discouragement and misunderstanding, and her family never understanding or giving a shit about what she's doing, and even Elaine wondering, not so covertly, when or if she's ever going to settle down. All this despite all the doltish men she's slept with, just to get meals, money for bus fare, and the pride in her walk and the swing in her red hair, she who once could have ridden her red mare straight into the jaws of hell itself and laughed in the devil's face.

And thank God for such moments, or she'd never get through the dark times, never have survived so long, with only herself to believe in, herself as her own cheering section, coach, general manager, janitor and broomboy.

She's gotten this far and now she's going to dinner, wearing new clothes, actually new, flashing purples and oranges and browns, bought for this occasion, her hair long and floating free over her shoulders, and her brown eyes mysterious and distant, as befits an artist who has taken this long to arrive. Oh God.

The fear eating her underneath that no one is allowed, no one can do this, stride along the street with head up, and red hair like plumes and her feet in red high heeled shoes and toss her hair and say, here I am and think it justifies anything at all. The dread eating her underneath, that it will vanish, not be there waiting at the restaurant, the gallery owner, her face, like stone, sorry we made a mistake, the owners with money, laughing, buy this, not a chance.

But she keeps walking because it's what she's learned to do, makes it to the restaurant, smiles when she sees Gordon, keeps smiling all through the meal, smiles because she's happy, because he stands up and kisses her hand, because he's handsome, the restaurant is expensive but what the hell, smiles loftily at the snooty headwaiter, and makes it to the washroom in time to throw up, wash her face, sweating, lean against the wall, dizzy, until someone asks her if she's all right, and then she pastes the smile back on, goes out through the heavy door, because they're going to a movie and then back to his place to make love, where she will smile and smile, and tell him, yes it was great, it was wonderful, the best, she's never felt like this before.

Chapter Twenty-Seven

What the hell was wrong with her? Things were too good, that was it.

She wanted to take Gordon home and introduce him to the land and the lake and the farm and her mother and Rob. She wanted a house with both of them, Rob and Gordon, a house with a studio lit by morning light, with flower gardens outside in a yard of her own, a house with light and space and white walls lit by her paintings, a house beside the lake so she could see the water gleaming between the trees. She wanted so much and had wanted it forever. She had privately made lists of her wants, writing them down in the back page of one of her notebooks. She allowed them to come into her in all their varied shining pictures. She saw curtains and rugs and an expensive car. She tried to imagine driving somewhere in a car off which nothing at all was going to fall clattering to the road. She tried to imagine stopping somewhere, going in a restaurant without worrying about the cost, walking in a store and buying something new. It was unimaginable and yet, she thought, Gordon did it, every moment of the day. He had no idea how obsessed and worried she always was by money, by the constant lack of money, by the things she craved and couldn't buy, the things she was embarrassed by craving, the clear cold iron curve of a designer lamp stand, the rounded sensuality of green velvet on a couch, the languid sheen of old oak, the muted colours of expensive carpet, the stateliness of good china, oh, there was so much.

And Gordon took it for granted, doing all those things, everyday, living in a world where such was possible. She wanted to live there as well, occupy that world, not as a sojourner, but command it, demand from it favours and adulation, all the rewards the world could finally give her, that had been withheld so long. Publicity. Little articles in magazines. Leisure. Someone else to move aside the floating crud and crap so she could swim freely in her life, someone else to wash the windows of this fantastic big dream house, someone else to answer the phone, tell people to go away on her behalf. Above all, she thought, above all, she would stop smiling and being nice to people she didn't care about, or want to care about.

What she would do instead was shut herself up in her huge light filled studio and paint and paint, the kind of pictures she always knew she could paint if only she had time and space and didn't have to worry about buying paint and buying time away from work. Work. She would work. She would paint.

Lying one night with her head against Gordon's blond chest, in his huge wide bed, she had told him about Rob. She'd told him the truth but in such a way that it was true even while she knew it was all a lie and a cheat. She told him that she and her mother had an agreement to share the raising of the boy, that she went home every summer, that she and Rob were pals in those summers, went canoeing and fishing and worked on the farm together, that now because her father was dead, she was concerned about him, thought he should have some positive male influence in his life, perhaps he could come and stay some time, perhaps he and Gordon would get to know one another, could become friends, to all of which Gordon amazingly, generously, smilingly agreed. Of course. In any normal world, that is just what should happen. And might. And still might. And hadn't, wouldn't, couldn't tell, how, and in what fashion Rob was conceived, would never tell, even though, lying with her head against Gordon's blond chest, she longed, was frantic, to tell him the whole story. Knowing she could never take the chance.

When she went home the next morning, she curled up on her own bed. The lumpy pale green flowered cover which she had bought secondhand was unraveling and losing clumps of white batting all over the place. Oh God, she thought, triumphant and terrified at the same time.

God, she thought again. God, God, God, God, have mercy, mercy and the dreary uselessness of that litany echoed off the walls in her mind. She drifted uneasily into sleep, and woke again and got herself up, groggy because Gordon was going to phone and before that, she had to get dressed, get made-up, get going, get energetic, and lively. Get back to creating this new life which continued to fall into her lap despite her fear and which, God help her, she might even start to believe in one of these days and far too soon.

Chapter Twenty-Eight

Gordon was going away. Gordon was going away, "for a while," he said. "A few weeks." Mary felt the cold winds of despair wrap around her and in answer, she smiled and laughed and announced that she would be fine, she needed time to herself, she'd use it creatively she said, and get lots of sleep.

Gordon was going away to Toronto to see his family, and Mary thought to herself, but didn't ask, why he hadn't invited her to go, why she wasn't good enough to meet his family. He'd said, looking worried, that someday he would like to go to Toronto with her, but this was a difficult trip, something to do with managing the family money. He seemed to think she'd understand without him having to spell it out. He seemed to think she'd understand why it was important. When she made some crack about wanting to have some money to manage he looked even more worried and said, oh, no, money doesn't solve anything, it's just a terrible headache. When she persisted, sullen, even remarking, somewhat under her breath, that there weren't many problems that she or her whole family had that money wouldn't solve, he changed the subject, and tried to talk to her about her painting, which she hated to talk about and would never say anything but flippant monosyllables. Then she stopped talking altogether and began caressing him, so that nothing much more was said about the trip or anything else.

Later, when he was sleeping, Mary studied his face, the fine, curly, sandy blond hair and wispy beard. He has a weak chin, she decided. She liked that. She didn't want him to be too strong. She wanted him controllable. She liked it when he lost control of himself during sex, when he panted and gasped and said how he loved her. She said much the same things with much the same noises but with the satisfaction of knowing that she was still in control of herself; it gave her an edge, a crucial piece of knowledge he couldn't possibly share.

They went to the train station together, walked hand in hand down the long long platform, through the crowds of people hurrying incomprehensibly in all directions, milling and striding and pushing past one another, but politely, saying sorry and excuse me if they bumped or pushed against each other. Finally Gordon got on the train, but the train didn't start for a while.

She stood on the platform, feeling awkward, trying to smile, wanting to run, feeling sick, feeling the panic start, the trembling deep in her bones, the sick loneliness, the sense of the city lying all around her, huge and uncaring and with no one in it who cared how she felt, no one to whom she could go and sit and say, God, I feel so bad, I feel so shitty, I feel alone, alone, alone. Elaine would listen sympathetically enough but she didn't want to go whining to Elaine again. She was ashamed of whining to Elaine, of always appearing to Elaine as this weak whimpery person, when Elaine's life went on being so normal, the nice house, the kids in school, coffee and bridge in the afternoons. Elaine was putting on weight, she was getting boring, she had grey streaks in her hair and she never even talked about painting anymore.

In fact, Mary thought savagely to herself. Elaine is boring, that's what, she's become stupid, boring and normal and stupid, and that's why she couldn't go out there, because, no matter how sympathetic Elaine might be, she would never understand the sharp vicious sawing of the knife blade within Mary, the razor edges she walked, the hideous choices she made every day, just in getting up, in staying alive, in walking to the latest boring job in the latest ghastly restaurant. They all looked the same despite the potted plants and changes in upholstery and curtains.

The train pulled out and Gordon was gone and there was nothing to do. She had the afternoon to fill somehow. She walked down the street towards the downtown, under the tired ancient chestnut trees, past the people who littered the sidewalk begging, or playing the guitar, or hanging around, smoking, or dressed in awkward grotesqueries of beads and feathers and burgundy velvet and leather vests and hats and shawls.

"Spare change," someone said, planting himself in front of her. Because she was lost in the city on a Saturday afternoon, with no one to talk to and nowhere she had to be, she stopped and looked at him.

He was tall, younger than her, thin serious face, long hair, not too clean, a grey flannel blanket with a hole cut through it to serve as a poncho. She shook her head at his request for money.

"Got cigarettes then, dope, food?" His grin was disarming. She shook her head.

"Hey, lady," he said. "You looking pretty downcast, for such a nice lady, on a nice day. Hey, come on, life is groovy, got to live in the moment. Hey, wait a minute."

He left her, went over to the nearest group of people, some lying on the sidewalk, propped against a store window, some standing. He came back with two cigarettes, handed her one. Resigned, she took it. He motioned to a stone wall, under the shade of the trees, and she followed, sat, let him light the cigarette.

"Watch now," he said, "watch the numbers of the buses. When your number comes, you got to get on, ride it, ride the number in the I Ching. You know the I Ching?"

She shook her head. He took a book, and three pennies from under his poncho, squatted on the ground, three the pennies and studied them.

"See, that's the Creative, very auspicious, means this is very important, very important time for you, got to use it wisely, got to use the energy. You know the Tarot?"

She shook her head again, bemused by his nonsense, his youth, his pinched white serious face.

"Oh man, that's too bad, 'cause in the Tarot, you know, you'd be like the Empress, or maybe the Queen of Cups." He studied her, cocking his head. "Maybe the Queen of Wands."

She finished her cigarette, sitting in the sun, feeling so much older and more weary than the other people in this small park. When she got up to leave, he followed, walking beside her with such calm that she was somewhat reassured, and uncertain as to whether she wanted him there or not. But he was a distraction, as least, from the black pit inside left by Gordon's departure.

When they got to her basement suite, she unlocked the door, and he followed her in, sat at her table while she made tea. He looked at her bookcase, examined the pictures hanging on the wall, turned the canvases around that she had stacked in the corner with their faces to the wall.

"Man, that is so cool. Those are far out paintings, far out," he kept exclaiming, and she was somewhat reconciled to his intrusive presence by his wildly expressed enthusiasm for her work.

They had the tea. He took the I Ching coins from his pocket and tossed them over and over again on the table, studied the results. They exchanged bits of information. He told her that he lived on the streets, slept in shelters, panhandled for food and money, had no cares, didn't want to work, wasn't interested, threw the I Ching to decide where to go and what to do each day.

She took him out for Chinese food and afterwards, he followed her back to the apartment as though he belonged there, as though he had always lived there. She began to get a bit alarmed; she didn't want him staying, for God's sake, silently cursing herself for being soft-headed. He took something from his pocket, unwrapped the tin foil and Saran wrap. She looked at the tiny piece of clear plastic on his finger he held it out.

"What's that?" she said.

"Clear light," he said eagerly. "It's the best. Man, it's so fine. Come on and trip with me. Come on. It'll be so clear."

"No," she said, alarmed. "I haven't. I can't."

"Wow, far out. It'll be great. Come on, come on, come on." He was dancing around the room like some demented fairy prince, the fringes on his cape flying.

She took the tiny flake onto her own finger.

"What's it like?"

"Ooh, it's well, it's like being high, you know, colours, lights, you just know stuff, you understand things, you get, well like insights, cosmic insights. Everybody oughta do it."

She put it in her mouth, where it dissolved almost instantly, like a flake of snow melting on her tongue. She tried to spit it out again but it was already gone.

"What's going to happen?"

"We have to wait. It takes a while, you know."

She was already regretting it, terrified, wishing it back out of her system, wishing he would go, leave her space, her privacy, so that she could crawl into her rumpled bed with a book, a magazine, anything to distract her before sleep coming.

She turned away from him, made herself tea, and sat at the table to drink it. He kept wandering the apartment, exclaiming over things. She should throw him out, she decided. She would, in a few minutes.

She went into the bathroom to get away from him and when she looked in the mirror, her face swam away from her and back again; the eyes became huge, became mirrors, black pools in which she swam, pools with no bottom. She surfaced to a knocking on the bathroom door.

"Hey, you all right?"

"Fine," she said shakily. She went out and sat down beside him, terror rushing through her. What a fool she'd been. What a fool. What a fool. The words reverberated, became lost.

"What's . . . what's the antidote?" she said, wondering if that was the right word, if she had said what she meant, if it had come out as language or merely gibberish or if she had said it at all.

But he understood perfectly. "Vitamin C," he said, "but hey, don't waste a good trip by freaking out. C'm here. It'll be all right."

She sat by him and held on to his hand while the colours danced and fizzed around her. She held on and held on while things began to rush at her. Time gathered speed, roared past her, stretched, and contracted like an insane rubber band. She tried to gather her thoughts, she needed to talk, she wanted to talk, to touch down in the familiarity of talking about what was going on, the familiarity of shared, compared experience, and she tried to gather her thoughts and pull them into words and the words into sentences, a laborious task, and when she thought she was ready, she turned to him, and then turned away again quickly and shut her eyes. The sight of his face, his strange gaunt face and staring eyes, was too much; the words fled somewhere, squawking to themselves, but his face, the glimpse of it, went on reverberating behind her shut eyes and she forced them open again, and tried to smile, and pretend that she was doing fine, just fine, so that when he took her and led her to the bed and pushed her down on it, she went on smiling, still wishing she could find a way to talk, something to say, and then they took off their clothes, and he put his penis inside her and left it there for a long time, and from far away, far away, she could feel her body and his body meshing together, connections knitting and meshing together, tiny electrical vibrations, as they fell backwards and backwards through time which melted and looped like a great purple soaring glowing galaxy.

Then she began to be afraid, the fear grew and grew, it was orange, it had teeth, it was hideous, it was coming towards and she lay there, not moving or breathing, only feeling the fear coming to eat her, her belly sliding and popping, the skin melting off her in the heat. She was burning, she could smell the burning, and she screamed and twisted. He fell onto the floor, and she sat there, her head on her knees, shaking, hoping it would all stop.

He said her name and she looked at him. His face had changed again, matted hair, and thick brow, he was old, old, older than time, and so was she with her matted hair and her strong body. They sat deep in their underground lair, their den, this warm protected place, and she looked around the room with her many-thousand-year-old eyes, at the strange artifacts, the many useless bits of colour and soft coverings and the useless row of books ranged along the wall.

It was the paintings that drew her back, the stack of paintings with their faces turned to the wall, like so many abandoned neglected children. She crawled over to them, turned their faces to the light, their dull, dull sad faces, stared and stared, trying to find what was magic in them, what was their intention, what they were supposed to illuminate, but they were without light, without form, only flat bits of colour with no meaning.

She turned away from them and laid down again, and watched the colours dance and play in her head, pictures which moved and shook like wind over water, which danced and escaped her, which could never be captured or even remembered, pictures of unsurpassed and heartbreaking beauty. All she could do was follow them as they moved and broke and shifted into new forms and new colours, and disappeared again.

After a while, the colours dimmed and left her alone and finally, she slept.

When she woke in the morning, he was gone. She rolled over, relieved, glad to have her house back, her space back to herself. Her vagina was sore. She lay still for a long long time, thinking about the night, trying to remember what only came in bits and flashes. She remembered that she had sex with him, she remembered being terrified, watching pictures in her head, but she couldn't remember what they looked like, only the sense of something terrible coming towards her.

So, that's acid, she thought with disgust. She'd never do that again. Terrifying, to be so out of control, to not know what was going on, to be out on that kind of edge. She got up, had a shower, coffee, looked at the food in her fridge and turned away. Her stomach hurt.

The day stretched away ahead of her. There was nothing to do. She sat by the window, staring out at the lawn, while loneliness rolled over her, filled her nose and throat and eyes and dripped down her nose onto her shirt, unnoticed.

Chapter Twenty-Nine

The ragged hippie was named David. He refused to disappear so easily from her life. He came back the next day, marched into her apartment, apparently prepared to stay the night.

"I think you'd better go," she said coldly. "This is not some fucking crash pad."

"I got nowhere to go. No money today. Bummer, the whole day. All the wrong numbers."

"Go wherever you went before you met me," she said.

His face crumpled and he sat down on one of her chairs.

"It was so cool," he smiled, hopefully. "You had a great time."

"I'm sorry," she said. "I need to work. I need time alone. You'll have to go."

"I'll sleep on the floor. I'll get up and leave first thing in the morning."

"Please go," she said. "I don't want to argue with you."

He fumbled around with the strap on his pack and rearranged his ragged poncho. Outside, he looked like a beaten hound pup, trailing dejectedly down the sidewalk, looking back over his shoulder as if in the absurd hope that she would change her mind and call him back. She watched him go, went to strip her bed, change the sheets, and have a shower.

Two hours later, as she was working on a sketch, he phoned. His voice sounded odd. Something was wrong with the phone. The wires sang and screeched and crackled behind his voice. She could hardly hear him.

"Please, Mary, please," he shouted. "You have to let me come over. I'm freezing out here. I'm freezing to death. I can't find the right bus. I can't find the right number. Please, let me come home."

"It's not your home," she said coldly. "Leave me alone. Don't phone me, I don't want any more to do with you."

She hung up the phone on his anguished howl, but the echo of the phone lines rang in her ears.

For the next two weeks, while she waited for Gordon to return, she wondered, bitterly, at how big a fool she'd been and why she'd done it. When she discovered she had crabs, she was only glad it wasn't something worse. She made sure, by going for a VD test, and she vowed that she would never do anything so stupid again.

She met Gordon at the railway station, terrified that she would see David on the street among the litter of colourful, lounging figures. Mary looked at them as she walked by. Whatever else they were, they looked so carefree, free, lounging in the sun, nowhere to go, nothing they had to, no rules to follow, only the dancing colours of the strange and wonderful substances they were taking.

Mary had put on a dress, high heeled shoes which made her feet ache and burn, combed her hair back into a roll, clipped the side-hairs down with barrettes, so that she looked trim and businesslike, professional, brisk. She had on nylons and makeup. She felt plastered inside a shell of some kind, like a sea creature. She felt embarrassed and self-conscious in front of all these self consciously conspicuously free people. She wanted to apologize, point out that of course, she wasn't anything like the rest of the city, she was as free as wild, as colourful, as interesting, as anyone could be. But she averted her face, kept it still, walked by. One of them said something and someone else laughed, and it might have been at her. But of course she was so much older than them, had once been free and blown it. They were right to laugh.

Gordon swung down off the train, wrapped his arms around her. She leaned into him, closed her eyes, and felt calmness and security wrap around her like a flag, like the warmth of his huge grey expensive coat.

"I missed you," she said. "I missed you so much."

He grinned, squeezed her harder, went to collect the luggage off the cart, and then they went together to the parking lot where his car waited, to carry them back to his soft spacious apartment. They went out to dinner and held hands, Mary hungrily, hanging on, being flirtatious and coy for his benefit. Then they went back to his apartment and went to sleep, curled up together, and she kept something, her hand, her knees, something, touching his warmth all night.

In the morning, they both got up. They both had to work and they made plans to meet for supper. That night, Gordon asked her to move in with him and she agreed, thinking only momentarily of the peace and quiet and loneliness of her small basement. She went home that weekend, packed, cleaned, gave notice, and moved in with Gordon, and there, for the next five years, she stayed.

Section Seven

Brendan

Chapter Thirty

Brendan was trying to decide whether to get up and walk out of the hospital. After the chewing out his mother had given him at lunch, he sure as hell didn't feel like sitting here, thumbing through stupid magazines, *National Geographic,* for God's sake. How insanely boring could you get? He had a feeling Kathryn would have been laughing at him, if she were awake, for going on sitting here.

The machine over her head kept on beeping like it was measuring something important, and Kathryn's chest kept rising and falling. No way, he thought, would Kathryn go on sitting here like some dummy, she would have walked out. Moreover, she would have told his mother to go to hell at lunch.

God, he hated fighting with his mother, especially when she picked a public place like a restaurant to do it in. Normally, he could fend her off with monosyllabic comments, a stony face, and an excuse that he had to go somewhere as soon as possible. But she'd trapped him perfectly this time and then pulled out all the stops: guilt, blaa, blaa, family, blaa, blaa, stress on her, blaa blaa, school, blaa, blaa, drugs, she knew he was smoking drugs, she said, (fantastic, it didn't take a brain surgeon to figure that one out) and while she didn't have anything against drugs, (oh great, the liberal stuff again) she knew from experience (yeah, Mom the wild hippie druggie, yeah, right, she knew all about it, for sure).

But she got to him. Every time, she got to him. She drove him crazy. She leaned over the table with tears in her eyes.

"Please," she said. "Please, just stick around home for a while, until we get through all this. It's so hard on your dad, you know how he feels about Kathryn, and listen, I understand that your friends are important to you but we're your family, we ought to come first. We ought to have some kind of priority claim on your attention."

Oh God, because of course, she was probably right and he was a lousy shit. He couldn't stand his family, he couldn't make up his mind about anything and he couldn't decide whether what he felt about Johnnie and their friendship was really all right or whether there was something secretly wrong with him. Should he just get out of this dead ass town and get to the coast and find somewhere with some life, some action, some real people? Here was always the same, playing with his friends, walking up in the middle of the night to 7-11 for Cokes and chips and smoking too many drugs and trying to decide if there was anything at all worth doing in the far off distant and dim future.

He kept staring at Kathryn. He couldn't help himself. It didn't even look like her. Her cheeks were sunk in, her hair sticking out and her body invisible under the blankets. There was nothing of her in this room but her breathing and her eyes flickering under the closed lids. Brendan wondered if she was dreaming and if so, if she was only asleep, why she couldn't wake up and talk to him. Then, he thought bitterly, she'd always said the hospital was only good for dying. She had reminded him over and over that they hadn't done a thing for old Bill, his great grandfather, but let him die.

Shit, he thought again, paralyzed in his chair by a terrible sense that nothing he did in the next little while would mean anything anyway. His grandmother had somehow suspended time and whether he got up and went outside and went down the hill to 7-11 or whether he sat here in this disgusting place stinking of sick and dying, it didn't matter. Nothing would happen while Kathryn was lying in this high narrow white bed with bars around the side like some asinine baby crib, only her eyes flickering under the closed wrinkled blue lids, and time trapped and stinking of dust and decay in the corners of the room.

He stood up and walked to the window, looked out at the sun shining off the roofs and walls of houses, off the long white wall of the supermarket down the hill. Then he crossed the room, looked out the door, down the empty hall, turned, looked back at his grandmother, shrugged, and left, walking hunched over, hands in his pockets, stabbing savagely at the floor with each step.

Chapter Thirty-One

Kathryn was struggling up from the depths, a great weight on her chest, the pressure of black water, she struggled and kicked and fought for breath, fought her way up towards the bright light she knew was above her but something was hanging onto her, dragging her back down again. She couldn't see anything, wanting to open her eyes, oh God, open her eyes. She kept trying but they were filled with sand, grit, something, they wouldn't work, wouldn't open, she struggled and struggled for breath, and for sight, opened her mouth to yell, but the water rushed in, the water was winning. She was being inexorably dragged back towards the deep black mouth at the bottom of the water, the mouth that swallowed everything, that had swallowed Mary, and she knew it was Mary hanging on to her, because she hadn't saved her.

And then she woke up.

Disappointment hit her like a fist in her chest, because she had left Mary behind in that black freezing water, and she gasped and struggled for breath. Her heart, there was something wrong with her goddam heart, and nobody around to even notice.

She lay back on the pillows, gasping. It didn't matter because she had found Mary and then lost her again, and the pain clutched her heart and to her horror she began to cry. She never cried. Life was too hard for that. Tears were for weaklings, losers, people who couldn't survive. Like Mary.

Tears rolled down her face while her heart clutched unsteadily at each beat and Kathryn went on crying and crying and no one came, for which she was both furious and grateful and too Godawful Christly broken-hearted to care.

Chapter Thirty-Two

Brendan left, made it as far as 7-11, went in, browsed through the comics which were there, but there wasn't much new, looked at the magazines and checked the articles—nothing looked interesting, browsed through the drink coolers—nothing he wanted, shrugged hello at the geeks rapt and tense over the video machines, finally bought a Coke and some cigarettes. He went outside, checked the parking lot Nobody he knew. Shit.

And his mother's voice in his head, needling, "You shouldn't have left Kathryn like that." His mother was coming to pick him up. She'd know that he'd pissed off somewhere and the next time he saw her there'd be another lecture.

Finally, he walked, again, the long distance up the hill to the hospital, went in and sat down by the bed. Kathryn turned her head, stared at him, they stared at each other. Brendan stared, amazed. Kathryn had been crying, there was still tears on her cheeks.

She kept staring. He noticed how green and bright her eyes were, startling, like green ice in the white and wrinkled parchment of her skin, her iron grey hair sticking out all over the place. She looked like hell.

"Grandma," he said uneasily. "Grandma, it's Brendan. Hey, you okay?"

"What kind of Jeezus Christly bloody stupid question is that?" she whispered. "Of course I'm not okay. I'm dying."

He couldn't help it. He laughed, then caught himself.

"Mom will be along, later," he said, awkwardly. "She's off at some meeting."

"I don't care," Kathryn whispered. Her breathing was funny. "It's you I want to see." Then unexpectedly, terrifying to Brendan, she began to cry again.

"You didn't know her," she said. "You didn't know my Mary"

"No," he said. Oh God, now what was she on about? Fervently, he wished for his mother's arrival, her brisk taking over of this situation.

"She was scared. I knew she was scared and I wanted her to be tough. I wanted her to be able to survive, and I thought the world would be too hard on her, so I was hard on her, because I was afraid for her. I was afraid." She paused, strained for breath.

"That damned horse. I told Bill, I told her that horse would just let her keep running away, but he said she needed to learn independence. He was proud of her. But all she and that horse did was run away."

She stared at Brendan. He nodded. He wondered who she was seeing, if she was talking to him or to someone else. Slow tears gathered in her eyes, and ran down her face. He wanted to wipe them away, take her hand, do something, but he sat there paralyzed.

"And then there was Rob, and she escaped again, and I was so damn mad, jealous. All my life I had worked so hard, and there she was, running off like she didn't have a care in the world. But I had Rob, and she had, what, nothing, the city, no family, no home, no one to give a shit about her, and she'd come home looking so beat and exhausted and I just wanted to put my arms around her, tell her to rest, tell her I'd look after her, but I never did. I never did. I never even told her I was proud of her. I never told her. I never told her."

Kathryn was panting now, and the machine above her head was making strange irregular noises. A nurse hurried in, did something to the machine, some adjustment, took Kathryn's wrist, checking her pulse. But Kathryn kept talking as if the nurse wasn't there.

"She wasn't like me. She never was. I couldn't teach her anything. I'd never told her how I really felt, and she thought I didn't care. I know she did. I would have done anything but everything I did was wrong. Everything I said was wrong." She stopped to breath.

"And then she was gone. And I'd been wrong not to tell her that no matter what, she was my girl, she was baby, the sweetest baby you ever saw, with her wild hair and her bright eyes. Oh, God…," she choked and coughed.

"Shhh," the nurse said disapprovingly. "You have to rest now. Don't go getting yourself all upset."

"Oh, shush yourself," Kathryn snapped, still in a harsh whisper. "I'm the one that's dying." She turned back to Brendan. "Do you understand?" she asked. "Do you understand anything I'm saying to you? Do you understand that I was wrong, I was the one who was wrong. It wasn't Mary. It was me. I have to tell her, you see. I have to find her and tell her. Do you understand?"

"Yeah," said Brendan uncertainly. He felt dizzy from embarrassment for her. He'd never heard her talk like this. Then, trying to match her, "Yeah, I think so." Then he said, "Maybe she knew. Maybe she knew you really did care. Maybe she figured it out. There's something like that, in one of the diaries."

He'd seen it, glancing through.

"Don't lie to me," Kathryn said. "Don't make things up. I read them, you know. I read them all. I never knew, until then, what I'd done. I didn't know. I didn't know that she was so hurt. I didn't know."

"I'm not lying, Grandma," he said. "I'm reading her diaries too. She was pretty cool, but, yeah, she was sad a lot of the time. But she didn't blame it on you. It wasn't your fault. You did your best."

Kathryn closed her eyes. "You're a good, good boy Brendan," she whispered. He had to lean over to hear her. "You're a good, kind boy. You look like her, you know. But don't try and make me feel better. I know what I did."

Brendan couldn't stand her looking like that. "Grandma, some of it was her fault too. I mean, she made mistakes. She was the one who left, for God's sake."

"I was her mother," Kathryn said. "A mother should be able to save her own child."

Then she said, "I'm so tired. I don't know if I can ever remember being this tired. I just have to rest a bit. Tell Rob . . . ," and then she was asleep, her breath fluttering uncertainly in and out of her chest.

The nurse was still standing there, watching the machine.

"It's okay," the woman said kindly. "I'll sit with her for a while. You go take a break. Get a coffee or something "

Brendan got up, and wandered down the hall until he found a washroom. He went in, locked the door, sat on the toilet with the lid down, leaned his head against the wall. His throat and chest were on fire. He wanted to cry but he couldn't. He was afraid someone would hear him.

His throat hurt so much he thought he might throw up. He sat there, staring at the white tile floor. Then he got up off the toilet, had a pee and washed his face and went back to grandmother's room.

Dana was sitting calmly by the bed. She stood up, put her arms around him, held on.

"I'm sorry," she said. "I shouldn't have made you do this."

"She woke up for a bit, and talked to me."

"What about?"

"Just about Mary, and stuff, you know. She told me I was a good boy."

Dana smiled, "Yeah, she dotes on you, always has. You and your dad. Your brothers never got the same kind of attention."

They both turned and looked at Kathryn.

"Come on," Dana said. "I'll run you home. Your dad can come back this evening."

"What if she wakes up again?"

"Come on," Dana said impatiently. "I've got to make supper. Your dad will get back as soon as he can. She'll be all right. The nurses will keep a close eye on her."

But Brendan hesitated, then glanced back at the still white form, picked up his jacket and fled.

Chapter Thirty-Four

Brendan had left the diaries across the field at Kathryn's house. After supper he got up, slipped on his jacket, and went quietly out the back door. Dana and Rob were watching television, curled up together on the couch. Dana had her head against Rob' s shoulder. Rob had his arm around her, playing with her hair. It gave him an odd feeling, seeing them like that, it left him out somewhere that didn't matter.

He let himself out very quietly, and went the familiar way, across the fields to the dark and silent house. He went in the back door, and through the kitchen, turning on the lights as he went. The house was cold and strange without Kathryn. It seemed grey and untidy, dust in the corners, the sink cabinet sagged in the corner, the screen door was torn, and the kitchen table already had a thin layer of dust.

He went upstairs, moving very slowly and quietly. He didn't want to be so quiet. It angered him. He would rather have made a noise, crashed and thumped his way upstairs like he was used to doing, but the silence in the house was too intimidating. It felt soft and spongy, the silence, like it was absorbing all noise, except for little tiny noises, like the soft hum from the digital clock by his bed.

He pulled the box of diaries out from under his bed and began to read. He read for a couple of hours, until he got sleepy, then he lay back on the bed, pulled the covers up over his shoulders and slept in his clothes.

He half woke in the middle of the night. He was sure, just before waking, he had heard the back door slam. He lay, hardly breathing. Then he took a deep breath, relaxed, rolled over, pulled the pillow over his head and dozed again. Probably his mother had come looking for him. He wanted to open his eyes but he was so tired, drifting in and out of sleep. He heard footsteps on the stairs and lay still waiting for his mother's voice, his mother's hand on his shoulder. The footsteps, continued, paused outside his room, then the door opened and he felt someone sit down on the bed. He wanted to open his eyes and look but he was too tired and he dozed off again. Whoever it was stood up and left the room and he thought sleepily, it must be Kathryn. She's left the hospital and come home, he thought, and was momentarily happy that he would see her in the morning, and then he went back to sleep.

In the morning, he woke to sunlight, blue sky and the sounds of birds. Damn, it was probably late. As he finished waking, he remembered the footsteps in his room. The door was closed. Probably it had been his mother. He got dressed and ran again across the field, ducked under the fence and went into his mother's kitchen. She turned from stirring something on the stove.

"Oh, honey," she said, "The hospital phoned this morning. They said Kathryn was back in a coma. They don't seem to think she's going to last much longer."

"I slept over at Grandma's house," he said. "I heard you come in and check on me last night. At least I heard someone come in. Maybe it was dad."

"No," she said. "We thought you were upstairs. We didn't hear you go out. We thought we'd let you sleep in because this is so hard on you."

"It's not hard on me," he said. He shifted around on his chair.

She put a plate in front of him with toast, eggs, bacon, and a half grapefruit on it. "Eat up," she said. "I've got to get moving."

He was going to tell her about reading the diaries but she had already left the room. He cleaned the plate, dumped it in the sink, and went outside, wishing he had a smoke, some dope on him, anything.

She came back downstairs, opened the screen door, came out on the deck, into the bright sun. "Are you coming?" she said, looking at him critically. "You should go change. You look pretty rough. Did you sleep in those clothes? And when did you wash your hair last?"

He shrugged. "Maybe I'll come in later."

"Don't hitchhike. It's not safe."

"It's okay," he said. "I do it all the time. I'll be all right."

"Go and change," she said. "I'll wait for you."

"I have to go to Johnnie's," he said, not looking at her. "I left some stuff there. I'll come by the hospital, later, I guess," he added awkwardly. She was silent.

"I'll drive you," she said.

He turned away and then turned back. "Hey, Mom," he said, "Can I ask a favour?"

"What now?" she said.

"Can you loan me a few bucks?"

"Brendan!" she said. She sighed. "Oh, all right. I don't like you wandering around with no money." She opened her purse, took a twenty from her wallet, handed it to him.

"Now, hurry," she said.

He took the stairs two at a time, changed, combed his hair with water, and came back downstairs, whistling, got in the car.

"What did you mean about someone coming in your room last night?" she said.

"Someone came in," he said, "opened the door, sat on the bed, went out again. I thought it was you so I didn't look, I didn't even really wake up."

"After your great-grampa died," she said, "Kathryn complained that he was always wandering around the house. And you know her. She never made things up. She said she could always smell the greasy old overalls he used to wear."

"Maybe it was Mary," he said. "Maybe it was my real grandmother. No one even knows for sure how she died, right?"

"Well, we found the canoe," Dana said. "But no, we never found her body."

"So, did she ever come walking around?"

"Not that I know of," said Dana."But your dad used to dream about her. He said he saw her at the window one night, looking in, looking so sad."

"Maybe it was her," he said. It gave him a queer kind of thrill, thinking about his unknown grandmother coming to see him.

"It was probably the cat," said Dana, briskly.

"No," he said. "I think it was her. I think it was my grandmother Mary."

"Oh, come on." she said. "Why would you think that?"

"I don't know," he said. "I just want to. I miss her, in some kind of weird way."

"She wasn't much of a mother," said Dana coldly.

He didn't say anything, just stared out the window. He felt the red mounting in his face. He kept his face turned away from his mother, so she wouldn't see. He remembered all over again that sometimes he hated his mother. He didn't want to argue with her anymore; he didn't want to talk to her at all, ever. She never understood anything anyway. The only attention she paid him was trying to stuff him with food, like some kind of pet goose. He imagined trying to tell her about his poetry, his thoughts about Johnnie, his long black and solitary walks along the highway at night but gave up. As if she would care. He decided he would read the rest of the diaries later tonight. He hadn't understood everything he'd read, but he'd felt seared raw and sick with the pain that scorched from the pages. Nobody had given a shit, apparently, or even noticed what Mary had gone through. What the hell kind of a family, did he have, he wondered, that could let that kind of pain and not even notice? What the hell was wrong with them all?

Chapter Thirty-Five

Rob was making plans to meet with Sunita. He was on a way to a meeting. He knew she'd be there. The thought was making him drive too fast, drumming his fingers on the steering wheel in time to the music.

He was making excuses. He knew it and he said, out loud, to the dusty truck panel, the radio, the earphones hanging on the mirror, the litter of saw files and his lunch bucket, "I don't care, goddammit. It's just to say hello, maybe have lunch. Not like I'm ever going to do anything."

These forestry meetings had been going on for a while and he knew she was on the committee. He had every reason to go. The other loggers looked up to him. He'd been asked several times to come to the meetings and he'd even gone once or twice, but he'd found himself itchy with boredom and irritation. Jeezus, couldn't they just get on with it, he'd end up thinking to himself, doodling on the useless notebook in front of him.

But there was a new issue on the table, an urgent one. They were planning on logging the mountainside above his and Kathryn's properties and he knew that Kathryn, if she'd been up to it, would have demanded that he go. Dana couldn't disagree with his decision to go. In fact, she was right into it, nothing got Dana riled fast than the idea of a threat to the land, or the water, or in some way, the future of her precious children.

The other night, it felt like he could have talked to Sunita for hours.

"Sunny," she'd said, or rather drawled. "Just call me Sunny."

Then she laughed, like it was a private joke. She'd never said that before, even though he'd known her for years now. She'd always called herself Sunita. They'd gone out on the deck together to look at the moonlight on the lake. Dana was inside pouring coffee. The other two women were in the kitchen with her. Their husbands were deep in conversation about types of cement. He wondered if anyone had noticed they'd gone outside together.

They hadn't stayed long. When she said that, his whole skin prickled, a kind of chill went over him. He could hardly breathe. He'd never noticed before that her eyes were the strangest colour blue and green. They hadn't said anything more, just turned and looked at the moon's shimmering trail on the water. Then they'd gone back in. He'd poured her more wine and they'd talked, about something, God, who knew. Once or twice he felt Dana's eyes on him but he didn't care. He was just having a conversation, for God's sake, nothing wrong with that.

After everyone left, he had lain in bed beside Dana, thinking of Sunny. He wasn't thinking much, just sensing what it was like to be with her, thinking what he might say the next time they met, part of his brain playing a furious staccato beat about him making a fool of himself, being too old for this, knowing that Dana was no fool. She could smell things going on, she had a nose for it, she always said that she could smell out gossip and affairs in the community, she always knew when someone was prowling around. But all he was doing, he told himself, was lying here thinking about what he might say to Sunny, what she might do, how she might look, all innocent, but thrilling and for him, new.

Chapter Thirty-Six

"Kathryn. Are you awake?" Dana sat down on the chair beside the bed. Kathryn opened her eyes.

"I have to ask you something."

Kathryn nodded faintly. Her breathing was irregular but she was alert now.

"Rob and I need to know about the will. Someone needs to take care of things. You've never told us if you even had a will. You can't, I mean, you need to tell us what you want."

She waited. Kathryn went on breathing. Then she smiled but she still didn't say anything. She closed her eyes.

"Kathryn?"

It was her own fault, Dana thought. She'd let this business of the will go for far too long. But she'd been afraid and she'd waited for Rob to do it. It wasn't any kind of easy thing to bring up.

"When you die, you should let Rob have the land." That's what she felt she should say. Rude, but realistic. Somebody had to be realistic. Rob should have taken care of this. She'd asked him about it, often enough. Of course, he'd never confront Kathryn about anything. He went along with her on every damn thing. Dana was his wife, for God's sake, and Kathryn was only his grandmother, not even his mother.

For another thing, Kathryn had never paid that much attention to the other boys. All her attention went on Brendan. Luke and Jason came a dim third to their little brother, and she'd seen the hurt in their eyes. She was damned if she'd see them lose out yet again, see Colin, that useless drunk, walk off with everything. There were lots of alternatives; Kathryn could leave the land to Rob and Colin jointly, she should make sure that Rob kept control and that way, they could give Colin something, put a trailer somewhere for him to live in on the rare occasions he came up from the city.

God, the way land prices were going up and the way lots were going along the lake, the land would be worth a fortune one of these days. Actually, it was already, but neither she nor Rob nor Kathryn were interested in selling. The problem was, they didn't know about Colin. What if he wanted to subdivide, turn all that beautiful land which should be growing food into houses and garages and pavement. What a nightmare. The guy was such an idiot, he'd probably want to make a trailer park or some other abomination. Kathryn would never rest easy in her grave if anything like that happened. She loved that piece of land, no question about that.

Before Kathryn got so ill, Dana had tried to urge her to take time off, pointed out that her own garden was really big enough for all of them, tried to get her to give up keeping chickens and cows and picking fruit. So what if it all fell on the ground? The birds and bears and coyotes would happily clean it all up. But Kathryn had worked like a dog her whole life and couldn't stop, seemed to think it was something close to mortal sin to waste so much as a green bean or to actually spend money to buy food when you could grow it.

And now that Kathryn was in the hospital, it would all go to hell anyway. They'd have to get rid of those stupid old chickens, most of them were too old to lay anyway. She and Rob would have to do them in, put them in the freezer. They'd do for soup anyway. She could freeze the soup in cartons, give some to Luke and Jason, and Mike and Arlene. She had lots of extra onions, beets, she could make the soup like borsch, only with chicken. Where had she left that good borsch recipe she'd gotten from Rita Melanoff the other day?

Chapter Thirty-Seven

When Brendan woke again, the stereo was still on. He was dizzy and desperately thirsty. Things blurred and twisted in his gaze. With some enormous effort, he got off the couch and made it to the kitchen, found a glass, rinsed the cigarette butts and ashes from it, let the tap run for a while before he managed to fill the glass.

Jeezus, I'm really stoned, he thought. His eyesight blurred and twisted like blowing smoke. He went back to the living room but it was littered with prone bodies and the sight disgusted him. He turned and stumbled outside. Three or four dogs came with tails wagging, sniffed his crotch, watched to see what he'd do. Brendan wondered if they knew he was stoned, if they approved, if they cared or if their brains never extended past food, going for a walk and begging for attention. He sat on an ancient dusty chair on the corner of the porch, trying to remember where he was and what had happened.

Yesterday afternoon, he'd been at Johnnie's house. He'd tried talking to Johnnie about how pissed off he was but the guy was an idiot about some things. He didn't get it at all. He didn't get why Brendan was so mad at his mother, or what it was that was so important about this dead woman, about her death, about why she had died and about how she had died.

Johnnie just said, disgusted, "God, Brendan, you're so obsessive. You're stuck on some groove or other. What the hell. It was a long time ago. Who cares?"

Brendan didn't understand it himself. He'd have to think about it some more. Right now, he just felt again like he should go away, should have gone away, should have split when he had a chance, should get away from the whole family mess, could even now be living free and easy on the streets of Vancouver, hanging out, like he had seen in his dreams. To hell with this business of family and school and living right and doing things right and listening to what too many goddammed old people had to say about what he was supposed to do and say and think and believe and eat and drink and fucking breathe, for God's sake.

"C'mon," he had said, standing up, restless, pacing the orange rug stretched over the concrete basement floor. "C'mon. Let's go out for God's sake. Let's go get some smokes, find someone to hang out with."

They left, walked the mile and a half into town. It was raining, a thin stinging spring rain, and they walked through it in their t-shirts, their hair wet and water trickling down their faces. Brendan hoped like hell they wouldn't see his mom and they didn't. They made it to 7-11, ducked into the noisy chattering warmth, the door beeping its warning. The younger kids looked up from the video games, nodded in shy and deferent acknowledgment.

"Hey, Judy," Johnnie said to the counter girl, large, her long blond hair her only pretty feature, huge breasts spilling down her front inside her ugly standardized 7-11 t-shirt. "Hey, what are you doing later? Wanta come with us, party party, eh, gonna blow some smoke, maybe make some music, come on, have a little fun, eh?"

She smiled, resentful even while she was delighted at the attention.

"Oh, shut up," she said, and giggled. "You're such a jerk."

Johnnie and Brendan sauntered past her to the comics, even though they had already read most of them, looked desultorily through the rest of the magazines. Then Brendan bought subs, cokes and cigarettes with the twenty his mom had given him and they went outside, sat on the sidewalk and ate. Other young men showed up, sat down, lit cigarettes, watched the traffic pass.

"I could maybe get my mom's car," Colin, one of the other boys said after a while. Brendan and Johnnie said they'd go buy beer with what was left of the money. A few other dollars fluttered into their hands. They got up, sauntered across the parking lot. The younger kids watched, curious, and jealous, from inside the large windows of the store.

Colin picked them up later, as they sat on the corner sidewalk downtown by the bakery, and they all piled in the car.

Brendan slumped in the back and Johnnie handed him a beer.

"Where we going? Let's go to Billy's. Billy's always got a party going. C'mon, Jeezus, let's have some fun for a time. This is the most boring goddam town ever made, I swear. Maybe we should just blow the fucking place up. Kindest thing you could do, just drop a fucking bomb on it." The others turned and looked at him, surprised. Brendan was usually quieter than this. That the town was boring and dead and stupid was such a truism among them that it wasn't usually discussed. Brendan sucked down the beer and took another one from the case. Johnnie looked at him but didn't say anything.

They arrived at Billy's place, piled out and sat in the kitchen of this trailer, which sat in the middle of a large lot just off the road on the way out of town to the lake. They lit joints and smoked and drank the beer, and Billy, who was a large, red faced man in his early thirties, went and fetched more from the full fridge on his porch. He always had beer and dope. He dealt small time in motorcycle parts, old cars, worked part time as a mechanic and gas jockey. His main ambition was to join a motorcycle gang. He was kind hearted and stupid. Brendan and his friends despised him and liked him at the same time. They knew he was always good for a bed and a meal if they had nowhere else to go. He had a huge and expensive stereo system and an up-to-date collection of the latest CD's. He had once had ambitions that way, had played in a small time rock band that did gigs in various bars around the region. But the band had dispersed, its members gone elsewhere. Billy kept his guitars but never played them. They knew he wanted them to come around; it made him feel popular, groovy, like he still knew something, had something going.

After the beer and the joints, they lay around the living room, hardly speaking, music blasting from the stereo. Eventually, someone roused enough to go out and get more beer. There was a noise in the front yard, and two more cars full of people arrived; they came in, settled themselves. The kitchen filled with empty bottles, smoke and full ashtrays. Brendan drank steadily, smoked joints and cigarettes. Someone handed him a tab of acid and he swallowed it. Eventually, he fell asleep, lying on the couch, the stereo speaker going full blast next to his ear.

Now the acid was hitting with full force. His legs twitched with energy. He stood up, wandered down the driveway towards the road. He had some vague idea of hitchhiking somewhere, he didn't even care, he'd let fate decide, he thought, whoever came by. He staggered out onto the highway, giggling a little at his inability to walk a straight line. He wove his way out onto the white lines and tried walking down them. A couple of cars went by and honked. He waved, but mostly the road was dark and deserted. He wondered what time it was; it must be late. From where he was walking he could see down the valley towards the glow of the lights from the town. He could see the other scattered lights from houses. A dog barked. A coyote yipped and yowled.

Suddenly, he shivered. The night was full of menace and fear. His grandmother was dying in the hospital and his life was just beginning, but hadn't begun, yet, walking down this black and deserted road, too far from his home, from anywhere normal and safe. The night was black around him, like a huge mouth, a huge waiting presence, waiting to swallow him.

He stopped and began to walk back the way he'd come, his whole body rigid and tense, waiting for whatever it was that was waiting out there to come after him. It had no face, only enormous, pulsing colours, constantly changing, and voices which he couldn't hear but which he knew could tear him apart forever.

He walked and walked sweating now, but he was caught in a time trap, and no matter how far or how fast he walked, he seemed to get nowhere, and he tried walking faster, but that made no difference. He began to panic, even more confused, wondering if the night had caught him somehow, if he would get away, or if he was doomed to wander down this strange road forever that would just get stranger and stranger, and then he heard a rushing roaring noise behind him, lights flashing red and blue. He knew it was not a monster at all, but reality forcing its way into the foolish cocoon of dreams where he had been wandering so long. He tried feebly to run but the cops grabbed him and then, out of fear or anger or something he couldn't define, something which came boiling up from some very deep sore and explosive place, he began to fight, swinging wildly and calling them names—pigs, fucking assholes, goddam cops. From far away he could hear himself crying and screaming and cursing and part of him wanted it all to stop, wanted only peace and quiet and to lie down, sleeping, in a dark quiet hidden place, but he went on with it anyway. The cops didn't say much, subdued him with little effort, twisted his arms behind his back with enough force to make him cry out again in pain, forced his head down and into the back seat of their car and took him off to jail.

He lay for hours in the small dim cell, curled and shaking on the narrow bed, holding on to himself as tight as he could while monsters came and laughed at him from the narrow corners of his mind. He kept trying to get control. He got up and walked back and forth but the walls billowed in at him. He sat on the bed, hung on to the bed but even it sank under him. He held on so it wouldn't disappear from under him, leaving him sitting in mid-air.

"Help," he whispered. His stomach was shooting green sharp agonizing pain through his body. It radiated into his whole body like a poisonous star. "I'm sick," he whispered. He curled up again, wrapped the blanket around his head. It smelled of mold and age. Finally, sleep claimed him.

In the morning, when he woke, he was stiff and shaky and his mind kept flickering like a bad movie. He lay on the bed and tried to remember the events of the night before. Someone came to the door, one of the cops from the night before, opened the door and let him out.

"Go on," the guy said, disgust apparent in his voice, his body. "Get the hell out of here, you little prick. You're not worth feeding. But just watch it. Next time we pick you up, we won't be so nice. We're no baby-sitting service for you little morons."

Brendan found himself outside in the concrete steps, in the grey dim morning. It was early enough that the town hadn't awakened yet. He felt in his pockets. He still had some change, not much, enough for a phone call and a cup of coffee. He went to 7-11, got some coffee.

"Jeez, you look like hell," said the attendant, a young fat guy he didn't really know, except that his name was Ray. Brendan looked in the mirror in the washroom. He did look like hell. His eyes were huge and staring out of his face, which was both muddy and bruised. He felt tough and sad and romantic, all at once, came out of the washroom with his shoulders up. At least he had a hell of a good story to tell; he just had to find Johnnie and the rest of his friends, get some food, some sleep.

He left the store and began walking, down the main street, out along the highway, past the strip mall, the auction mart, the linoleum and furniture shops, the A&W, the truck and car places, which finally gave way to hay fields and then a stretch of forest broken by occasionally driveways and houses.

When he got to Billy's, people were still sleeping. The dogs barked and leapt at his face. When he let himself in the house, Billy came down the hall, yawning.

"Hey, man," he said. "What the hell happened to you?"

Brendan shrugged. "Cops picked me up," he said. "Kicked me out first thing this morning."

"Well, your mom keeps phoning," Billy said, peevishly. "Got me out of bed twice already. Wants to know where you are. Dunno how she figured out you were here. Must be some kind of detective. Anyway, she wants you to call."

At the thought of his mother, a deep convulsive shiver went over him. He sat down. God, he was tired. He was so tired. He remembered all at once that Kathryn was dying and his father was a shit, and he hated his goddam mother. He didn't want to phone but he wanted to find out about Kathryn.

Billy handed him a cup of coffee with a shot of whiskey in it, and he took a long drink, feeling it burn all the way down, hit his stomach, threatening to come back up again. He needed to sleep, was falling asleep on the chair; his legs felt thin, weak as wet spaghetti. He finished the coffee, went in the living room, found an empty corner, a blanket, curled up and slept.

Chapter Thirty-Eight

Dana woke him up, shaking him. She looked around the living room, disgusted.

"Jeezus, Brendan. What a mess! What are you doing in this dump? Wake up, for God's sake."

Brendan woke up enough to realize that his mother was crying, or at least, that she had been crying. Her eyes were puffy and bloodshot.

"Wake up," she said again, pulled at the blanket.

"All right, all right," he muttered. His arms hurt when he tried to move them. The light glared. "What time is it?"

"Afternoon," she said. "Around two. I can't find your dad. He didn't come home last night. I've phoned everyone I can think of. I went up to the hospital but Kathryn was asleep and the nurses said he hadn't been there. He was at some meeting last night and he didn't come home. The cops haven't seen him. He hasn't had an accident. He didn't go to work. I'm absolutely frantic."

Her hair stood out in a frizzy halo around her head. Her clothes were rumpled and stale looking.

"Oh for God's sake, come on," she cried impatiently.

He got up and stumbled to the bathroom. His eyes had blue circles under them, his hair stood up in wrinkled odd shaped puff. His upper arms had large bruises on them. He combed his hair and borrowed a toothbrush that looked unused. He took a long time in the bathroom; he could hear his mother pacing outside the door. Finally she went outside, sat in the car with the motor running.

Finally, he went out, got in the car.

"Jeezus, Brendan," she exploded. "You could tell me where you're going and what you're up to, once in a while. You never showed up at the damn hospital. I waited for hours. Kathryn's the same. She just mutters something once in a while. I tried to talk to her but she wouldn't wake up. I need to talk to her. There some things that still need to be settled, stuff about the land and the will. And just when I need your father the most, he disappears."

"What are you talking about?" Brendan said. "What about the will?"

"If I don't do something, that shit, Colin, will inherit everything. You kids won't have a chance. You'll be cheated out of your rightful inheritance. Colin doesn't care. He hasn't come home for years. He doesn't give a damn about that place. We're the ones who've always looked after it. It should be ours. Your father should have done something about it years ago, but did he. Oh no, no way was he going to go against that old biddy. Colin will just sell it and booze the money away."

She was almost shouting.

"Did Grandma make a will?" he said.

"I haven't seen one. I know there's something. Probably scribbled on the back of an envelope. But your dad says everything will probably go to Colin. I can't stand it. The price of land these days . . . you kids need places to live. You're going to have families someday."

"Not me," said Brendan. "I'm getting a vasectomy."

"Don't say that," she cried. "You don't know what you're talking about. You don't know anything."

"Yes, I do," he said. "I'm getting the hell out of here, that's what I'm doing."

"What about school? You're almost finished."

"Who cares?" he muttered, staring out the window.

There was a furious silence in the car. After a while, Brendan roused himself. He was almost asleep.

"Where are we going?" he said. "Aren't we going home?"

"We're going to the hospital. You're going to sit there with Kathryn while I figure out what happened to your father. The only thing I can figure is that he got drunk with someone last night and was too embarrassed to come home. This thing with Kathryn is hard on him and he won't talk about it. I'm going to check out the bars, see if anyone saw him."

"Oh, for God's sake," Brendan said. "Just go home. He'll show up. Don't go in the fucking bars." He groaned with embarrassment. "I'll come home with you. He's probably there. I'm not going to the fucking hospital."

"Fine," said Dana. "That's just fine. You just do as you goddam well please. You always do!" She slammed on the brakes, skidded the car to the side the road. A couple of other cars pulled around them, honking. She yanked the car around, went back the way they had come, driving too fast.

"Just don't tell me you give a shit about this family. Just don't try and tell me that. You're the most selfish brat I ever saw. We give you everything and you just take and take it and give nothing back."

Brendan huddled in the side of the car, shutting out her furious voice, trying to will himself back to sleep, trying to will himself into a place of black quiet, far away from his mother.

"BRENDAN!" she roared.

"What?"

"How can you do this to me? How can you not even listen when I'm trying to talk to you? How can you just turn off like that." There were tears in her eyes again.

"I dunno," he mumbled. He closed his eyes. "I'm tired, okay?" He wondered what she'd say if he told her about the cops, about the bruises on arms. "I didn't get much sleep."

"Yeah, God knows what you kids were up to. Brendan, are you taking acid?" she asked sharply. "Pot is one thing but acid is dangerous. It can really screw you up."

"Naw," he muttered. He turned his head away from her, into his coat collar.

"Brendan? Brendan?" she repeated. He said nothing. Then she too fell silent. When they pulled into the driveway, Rob's truck was there.

"Oh, thank God," she said.

The house was quiet. Brendan escaped immediately to his room.

He could hear their voices through the floor. He couldn't tell whether or not they were fighting. He heard his father finally, because he was standing at the bottom of the stairs. Rob said, "Oh just leave it alone, for God's sake."

Brendan heard the door slam and the long silence after. Then he heard his mother in the kitchen, the familiar clashing of pots, pans, a spoon hitting the side of the mixing bowl. His stomach began to rumble. He came downstairs. Late afternoon sun slanted in the kitchen windows. Dana was putting a roast in the oven, slicing apples for apple crisp, his favourite dessert. There was fresh coffee and chocolate chip cookies on a plate.

"Your brothers are coming to dinner," she said coldly. "Do you think you could manage to stick around long enough to say hello?"

"Dunno," he mumbled. In spite of himself, his hands reached out for cookies, poured coffee, reached in the fridge for the cream and honey. There was the remains of a cold chicken in the fridge, and he brought that out as well, plus bread and butter and mayonnaise and pickles.

"Where's dad gone?" he said finally.

"To see Kathryn," she snapped.

She finished the apple crisp in silence and slipped it in the oven beside the roast.

Brendan was thinking if his brothers came he could get a ride back to town with them. It meant sticking around longer than he wanted but it also meant not having to stay the night.

He stood up, went to slip out the door.

"Where are you going now?" Dana said.

"Over to grandma's."

"Brendan, stay here. Talk to me. No one in this family talks to anyone anymore."

"I'll come back," he said. "I just want to go check on things."

He made it out the door before she could say anything more.

Left in the kitchen alone, Dana poured coffee and sat at her table. Rob's explanation was that he hadn't come home because he needed time to think, that he'd slept in his truck. What bullshit. They'd never fooled around on each other. They never would. She'd asked about the meeting, who was there, what was discussed. He'd been vague. It wasn't like him. She'd asked him again about the will and that's when he'd left.

The coffee was bitter. She stood up, went to the sink, poured it out, went back to the table, sat there as if her legs no longer had the strength to hold her up and carry her from place to place.

Chapter Thirty-Nine

Rob was on his way to see Kathryn, and then he turned and started to go to Sunny's and then he turned again and went to the bar where he drank a lot of beer, fell on the floor on his way to the washroom, cursed jovially and loudly to one of his crew about what bitches all women were, passed out for a while, woke up again, and managed to drive himself home to Dana's where the remains of the family dinner were still sitting on the table surrounding his empty clean plate, knife, fork and spoon.

Chapter Forty

Dana lay in bed seething. She went over and over in her head, any number of things she should have said and was going to say, when she got the chance, to all of them–Brendan, Rob, Kathryn. Even her wonderful boys had been horrid this evening. They'd gulped their dinner, talked nonstop about work and trucks, sat in the living room watching TV while she and Andrea did all the dishes, except for Rob's plate, and the bowls of food which she covered but left sitting the table. Brendan hadn't showed up at all. When they left early, she had a bath, went to bed. It was all her fault for marrying into this godforsaken abnormal miserable family. And no matter how hard she tried, she could never make things right, could never, never make up for the past to Rob. But that was no excuse for being such an asshole. Nothing was.

Chapter Forty-One

Brendan lit a fire in the cold damp lonely smelling house, turned on lights, ran water and put a kettle on to boil, then went up the stairs to the box of diaries. The cat came running, frantic for company, even though there was still food in the bowl on the back steps. The upstairs was too spooky; he brought the box of diaries back downstairs, sat at the table drinking herb tea and reading until he got sleepy, which didn't take long. Then he went and curled up on the couch under the afghan. His arms ached fiercely. The cat curled itself beside him purring. A black curtain of loneliness descended over him and even asleep, he turned and tossed, uncomfortable, trying to ease his arms, until the cat gave up and moved to a chair.

Chapter Forty-Two

Kathryn lay in her high narrow white hospital bed, surrounded by yellow curtains, and escaped restlessly, from one dream into another. A nurse, coming in, hearing her muttering and turning restlessly, checked her IV tube and turned up the level of her pain medication. Kathryn wanted more than anything else to get herself back to the edge of the dark water, where she had last seen Mary, but she had gotten lost somehow, kept going down weary paths that turned into improbable dead ends, kept trying to open her eyes, say something, call out, but found herself wrapped in dense fog that covered her in icy cold.

Section Eight

Mary

Chapter Forty-Three

The apartment was too small, she said, when Gordon demanded to know what the hell was wrong with her this time. Or maybe she needed to go back to full-time work. Maybe she'd call Elaine, see if there was anything at the art college she could do. Her depression followed her in and out the door, to work and back home, sat at dinner and again at the breakfast table. She lay beside Gordon at night, one leg touching his, listening to him breathing. Beside her side of the bed was a pile of books, a notebook, a jar of pens and pencils, a drawing book, an untidy pile of magazines, a tiny book light, and a makeup kit. Beside his side of the bed was a clock radio.

Sometimes, carefully, she turned on the tiny light and read. Sometimes she got out of bed and stood in the living room at the window just behind the drapes and watched the city, or she would sit in the living room, in one of the big chairs, tuck her feet underneath her and sit there staring into the darkness.

"I miss Rob," she told Gordon. "I miss the farm." It was true. It meant nothing and everything. But she had missed Rob and the farm for eighteen years.

She had gone home for his graduation. Her heart broke all over again at what she had missed. He was tall, handsome and at ease with his friends. He danced with her once, before he took off with a gang of kids in a car and she scarcely saw him again all weekend. Kathryn only wanted to talk about the farm, and whether she should sell and whether Colin was ever going to come home. Mary wandered around. Things were going downhill fast without Bill. The fences were sagging, the grass needed cutting. Things looked overgrown. She stayed an extra few days and did what she could. Rob came home periodically. She began to wonder if he was staying away just because she was there. She had bought him an expensive suit for his graduation; she wanted to get him something more but she didn't know what, and she wasn't sure about spending so much of Gordon's money.

Gordon and Rob had met a couple of times, but it had resulted in no more than bare politeness on either side. Gordon had come to the farm and had met Kathryn. Mary had tried nervously to show him what she saw but she knew, before the first day, that it wasn't working, that it was never going to work. She could see, through Gordon's polite eyes, the peeling paint on the house, the rusted cars and tractors behind the barn, the heap of junk parts that Bill was always going to clean up and never did and the straggly garden. She could see his ever so slight raised eyebrows at the ancient bathroom, the scratched and stained sink in the kitchen, the worn carpet in the living room, and Kathryn – her rough voice and rougher hair, her worn red plaid shirts and torn ancient men's pants, her slouching walk and gnarled hands.

She took him to the beach, which of course, he pronounced beautiful, very picturesque, and they wandered along the rocks for a while, hand in hand, but Gordon had the wrong shoes and the wrong legs for such a thing and they went back to the house for tea and carrot cake, and Gordon stretched out on the dusty couch in the living room and tried not to look too bored.

He came back again for that Christmas, their first together, and that was the last time he came to the farm. She should go whenever she wanted, he said. He understood that the place had some kind of hold on her. Rob could of course, come and stay with them whenever he wished, it would be good for him to spend some time in the city, widen his horizons. But Rob never came. Mary was afraid to ask him again. She had asked him once and he had merely looked at her, said, "No, that's okay. I like it better here."

Sometimes, before she woke in the morning, she felt deliciously light, free, fantastic. Sometimes she couldn't remember where she was or what she was doing here. Then she woke fully, felt Gordon's body, heard him breathe and turn over, heard his alarm and then the bed springs as he got quietly out of bed and went to the bathroom. While she lay there, the black cloud would float in again; she would think of painting and her heart would sink. There was almost nothing she could think of about which her heart didn't sink. The news from the farm continued to be bad. Kathryn was poor and getting poorer. Mary sent her money. Rob was working; that helped. No, he didn't want to go to university, what was the point when he could make so much money working in the bush. Mary had once allowed herself to cherish vague dreams of Rob finally coming to the city, of her showing him the university, of him settling in with her and Gordon and gradually becoming someone with whom she could share her dreams, her hopes, her endless aspirations for fame and fortune, which always seemed like they might happen and always and endlessly, eluded her. The dealer who had bought three of her pictures hadn't bought anymore. She had pictures in a few galleries but none of them had found buyers recently.

She had a genteel job in a secretarial shop, typing. Gordon hadn't said anything, but she knew he didn't really want her to waitress anymore. He didn't want her to work but she said she needed to get out. He asked her why she didn't just stay home and paint. She didn't, couldn't tell him about the weight of the stifling afternoons in the apartment, the rain against the windows. His place was too warm, too stuffed with too much furniture. The fridge was full of food she couldn't stand to eat, couldn't stand to look at.

She couldn't tell him some afternoons she went and wandered along the wet streets, a stranger in this city where she had lived so long, that she drank coffee in seedy restaurants until she felt people staring at her, and then she came home again and sat by the window and watched for Gordon's car to pull into the parking lot at the back of the apartment building.

And she couldn't tell him either of the times she didn't use her diaphragm during sex. Twice now she had missed a period for almost six weeks. Then unexpectedly, she had felt warm red liquid trickling down her thighs at the most hideous of moments, once on the bus coming home, once in the supermarket.

Sometimes she fantasized Gordon not coming home, either a car accident or something unknown carrying him off—a tragic accident, the sky falling, something vague. She could bring herself to tears with this.

Or she fantasized going home. As she sat by the apartment window, the winter days would darken into light spangled dusk. She closed her eyes and saw again the mountains across the lake from the farm, the sound and smell and colours of the water, the light shimmering on the rocks, the black cedars with the wind breathing easily through their branches, the way the tiny waves broke, little white crests, against the black curve of the beach.

Gordon usually came home late. He worked hard and he often went for drinks with other people from the university, or for a seemingly endless number of meetings, so she never knew when he would arrive. She made dinner when he came home, something easy, fried pork chops and baked potatoes, an anemic salad. She knew she was a bad cook. She tried to improve but nothing about cooking interested her. Often, instead they would go out to dinner. Gordon was used to eating out. He liked it. He could afford it.

She sat opposite him at the dinner table and silently soaked in his reassuring presence. She liked how he looked; she liked his masculine wrists below his shirt sleeves, the smell of his stale male sweat in his white shirts after a day at work.

She loved his solidity. Beside him, she felt thin, wraith like, unimportant. What he did was important although she didn't know much about it.

She couldn't paint. She couldn't paint. She didn't tell Gordon this because, in fact, she was still painting and she carried paintings off the galleries which dutifully returned them in a few months. Even Elaine couldn't see what she had to complain about.

"You're painting. You're working aren't you. They're pretty good," she said, looking them over. "They're okay. They're pretty. They ought to sell. Be patient. Someone will discover you someday, old thing." Sometimes, one of them actually did sell, but she had learned that the first quick exhilaration of such a sale quickly turned to bitterness.

There was nothing wrong. She sat and stared out the windows as the lights came on over the city and dread seized her heart and wrung it like a dishrag. But there was nothing wrong.

She dreamed of escape. She had money saved now; she could get on the bus, or even hitchhike, and go away, far away where no one had heard of her and didn't care. She dreamed every night of a lonely cabin, by itself, by a lake, and only herself there, and the endless silence.

Each night she dreamed it more perfectly, the size and shape of the lake, the changing, endlessly changing colours of the water, and hills, and trees and grass; she dreamed the pine needled slope at the front of the cabin, the granite rocks and cattailed shallows, the loons and beaver passing. She dreamed the inside of the cabin, the scent and look of bare wood, bare floors. All she would need, she thought, would be a foamie and a stove to cook on. She dreamed, endlessly dreamed, of the silence there, and how she would be in it, thinking, doing nothing, until some kind of understanding or illumination descended and the black fear went away forever, and she could come back, if she ever decided to come back, to Gordon and Rob and the city as a profoundly changed and finally wise person.

Sometimes she thought she wouldn't even need a cabin, just a hollow, a clear space, ground to sleep on, stars to watch, a fire, water nearby. She would lie there, curled, alert and watchful and understanding as any animal, until she came to know something, and then she would return.

One night she was lying there awake, and dreaming awake, trying to lie still and breathe quietly, when Gordon shocked her by turning on the light, sitting up, and saying wearily, "What the hell is wrong? Why won't you tell me?"

"Nothing's wrong. What do you mean?"

She resented him breaking in on her fantasy, interrupting her in the middle of her long and wandering hike into the middle of nowhere.

"Night after night," he said, "I get this sense of you just lying here being quietly desperate. You never say anything. You never ask for anything. When I touch you, you feel about as excited as your average jellyfish."

"I'm sorry," she said.

"Sorry!" he snorted.

"Yes, sorry," she said, in sudden fury. "Sorry I'm not the happy little wifie you thought you were getting. Sorry nothing I do makes you happy. Sorry my sexual performance isn't up to your standards. Sorry, sorry, sorry!"

"I was only asking what was wrong."

"Nothing," she said, and tried to smile. "Nothing is wrong, Everything is just fine."

He stared at her in silence then turned his light off, rolled over. She lay beside him shaking. After a while he relaxed. His breathing slowed and deepened. When she was sure he was asleep, she got up and went and sat by the kitchen window, looking out at the parking lot, where the light sparkled and danced on the wet pavement, and only an occasional cat came and went.

The next day they were both polite and she thought desperately that she must do something about herself and she went and took the unusual step of having her hair done and even buying a new outfit. She tried hard to be a better cook. She went shopping for food and flowers and things to fix up the apartment. For a while again it was all right and they went out to dinner and came home and life was harmony on the surface and only her dreams sang troubled songs.

Gordon had to go away again. He went every year but usually only for a few days. These days he flew to Toronto, and back. It only took a weekend. But this time someone had died. He might be gone a month, he said. He looked at her, troubled, "Maybe you should take some time off," he said. "Go home for a bit. Go see your mom."

It was what she most wanted to do.

"No," she said. "I need to work. Why would I want to go home? Nobody there cares if I come and visit."

"Oh, come on," he said. He came and put his arms around her, rubbed his cheek on her hair. "Come on," he said again. "It'll be okay. Cheer up. The time will go by fast. You've got your painting. You can go see Elaine."

"Yeah," she said. She rubbed her cheek against the roughness of his tweed jacket.

"It'll be okay. You go. Don't worry about me. I have a new painting in mind, a big one."

After he left, she started it. "You've got to paint," she scolded herself. "You've got no excuse. You've finally got all the time and space you wanted. Just work, for God's sake. Stop making excuses."

She tried to keep a schedule, slept in on those mornings she didn't have to go to work, and then got up and made a huge pot of strong coffee and went in the spare bedroom she kept for a studio and stared at the white space in front of her and went back out and stared out the window at the rain and then back to the white square of canvas. After a while, she started to sketch in an outline, a young boy swimming, only the body and the water, blended together in overlapping slabs of colour. For three weeks, she worked on the painting in her spare time, held herself together, got to work and back home again, made food, and ate it sitting at the window, lay in the bathtub and got into bed where she slept in the middle, the blankets bunched against her side with Gordon's pillow, which still smelled faintly like his hair, under her head.

At the end of three weeks, exhausted, she flung down her brush and phoned Elaine.

"Can you come over?" she said. "Come before I scrape it off and throw it away."

Elaine came that afternoon, looking worried. She stared at the painting for a while, shrugged.

She said, "It's one of the best things you've done. What's the problem?"

"I failed," Mary said miserably. "I was trying to do something new and it didn't work. It sort of worked but it's not what I wanted."

Elaine went back and looked again.

"Well, I like it," she said cheerfully. "I think it's lovely. I'd buy it myself if it matched my drapes, but Glen said absolutely no more art until we pay off the car."

"I'll give it to you," Mary said. "You can have it. I can't stand to look at it. All I can see is what it's supposed to be and what it's not." She sighed deeply, went to put the kettle on. Mary had made an effort, bought cinnamon buns and Elaine's favourite tea.

They sat together through the long afternoon. They talked and laughed as they used to and hadn't for a long time and then Elaine hugged her and went home.

After she left, Mary sat in the silent apartment. The painting brooded, a presence even behind the shut door of the room. Finally, Mary got her coat and went out. She walked and walked and walked, past bright windows, lit televisions, parked cars and sodden black squares of lawn.

Elaine's words, the painting, her own doubts, went round and round in her head, like the useless cheerless horses on a merry-go-round. She was pleased and scared by Elaine's comments and by their cheerful afternoon together. She walked until her feet were soaked and she was shivering. There were lights ahead. She had walked over the bridge and into the downtown core along a seedy row of hotels, bars, pool places, clubs. There were occasional groups of men in doorways; she felt a small ache of fear. This was not a good place to be but she was here and she continued with some vague idea of getting through it to one of the wider, more brightly lit streets where there were coffee bars and all-night bookstores.

Someone lurched toward her, into her a path, a wild figure, ragged long trench coat flapping, long hair, long arms spread as if to keep himself from falling. He came towards her and she realized he was singing, or rather chanting to himself, that the widespread arms were some kind of mock dance, and then he turned towards her, his face turned upwards to the ghastly blue glow of the fluorescent lights and she saw it was David. He hadn't changed much. His hair was the same ratty twisted swinging straggle, his face still thin and behind the open laughing red mouth, the wide blue eyes, the same seriousness.

She tried to turn her head and hurry past him and then she heard his shout behind her, "Mother Mary, mother Mary. Hey," and his running footsteps. Reluctantly, she turned.

"Hey, long time," he said, still laughing at something mysterious. "But I knew this was my lucky night, I knew. I knew. The right numbers came up and I knew that the changes were coming." He was taller than she remembered.

He was terribly thin and as annoying as ever. He fell into step alongside her.

"C'mon," he said. "I owe you. What's your pleasure. Pizza, Chinese, Italian, a whole city full of restaurants. I love it. Hey, I know a great place, truly groovy food."

She remembered she hadn't eaten. She was suddenly terribly hungry.

She glanced at him. He looked different. Maybe he had grown up. They found the restaurant, went in, her eyes dazzled at the lights, after the street. It was a dingy hippie place, the kind of place Gordon would never come. It was full of posters, odd looking people in a wild variety of dress, plants, music almost too loud to talk over. The waitress slouched over with menus, nodded to David, looked curiously and with a slight sneer at Mary and wandered away again. The food, when it came, was surprisingly good. She tried to make social conversation with David, but he acted as though their last meeting had been yesterday, began talking about people and events that she had never heard of and wasn't interested in. She was quickly bored.

"I've got to go," she said.

"Hey, wait a minute, okay," he said, leaping up from their table. He made his way to another table. She sat there amused but determined to get the hell out of there. Then he was back, excited.

"There's a great party happening," he said. "Wow, it'll be strange. Lots of cool folks. People down from the country, people I know, maybe I'll go back with them. They've got this groovy thing going, kind of a commune like, wouldn't that be cool, get a piece of land, grow food, grow your own dope, God, I knew my numbers were coming right, oh mother Mary, you're lady luck, that's who you are."

She tried to ask him more about the people from the country but he was vague. Mary felt curiously paralyzed but calm. She was still sure she ought to go home, but she felt light, detached, she could ditch David anytime. In the meantime, she could go along on this crazy journey, this wacko trip into another world, a place she hadn't visited before.

They left the restaurant and threaded their way through a maze of alleys. Mary began to wonder if David actually knew where he was going or if they were just going to tramp around all night, or if in fact, there was no party at all and she was wandering the back streets with some lunatic.

Eventually, they came to an odd tall house, all gables and turrets and bright lights, fitted in between two apartment buildings. There was a flower-painted milk van on the street outside, another Volkswagen bus, an old converted school bus. They went to the house, walked in the door to a barrage of music, noise, voices; no one paid any attention to them. They threaded their way through the crowd, found the kitchen, got a beer, were casually offered tokes from a number of joints being passed around. Mary cautiously took a deep drag, shook her head at the other offers, and went back into the other room, found a position against the wall, where she could watch and listen.

A woman was sitting next to her in an armchair, nursing a baby. A boy of three or four leaned against her knees. The woman had long silver hair, tied back in tousled braids, a low slung purple velvet top, a long skirt of some dark material. Braided moccasins stuck out from under the skirt. Mary watched, fascinated. The baby's mouth was fastened on its mother's small competent breast. The baby stared at its mother who alternately stared back or stroked the curled blond hair of the boy at her knee. Sometimes, she lifted her hand and accepted a toke from a neighbour, or leaned over to listen to the conversation of the people grouped around her, who seemed to all be staring worshipfully at the trio of mother, baby and son. Mary stared as well. The woman began talking about her life.

"Well, it's like a commune, eh. There's like, three or four families. We're each going to build our own house, and then have a communal kitchen and laundry and shit like that. We figure more people can come as the word gets out. It'll be very cool."

"What about rules?" someone asked, someone uncool.

"Rules," she said scornfully, leaning back in her chair. "Man, we're going to be like, you know, free of all this shit." She waved her hand, whether indicating the house, the party, or the city around them was unclear. "This shit'll like, you know, eat you up. All this concrete. We gotta get out of here, start something new. A new way, y'know? We think we might call the place that, new dawn or something like that. Neat, eh?"

Mary wondered how old the woman was. Her hair was silver but her face was smooth, unlined, with round blue eyes, and full red lips.

The baby finished nursing and began to shift around, fretting a bit. She lifted it with a practiced hand, laid it over her shoulder, and pushed at the boy. "Abole, go find Mica," she said. "Tell him I need him." The little boy clung tighter to her knee. "Go on," she said. "It's cool. He's in the back somewhere." Reluctantly, the boy, who was three or four, let go of her knee and began to thread his way carefully through the sea of adult legs.

Mary leaned over. "He's a beautiful little boy," she began awkwardly. "What do you call him?"

"Abole Rainbow," the woman answered. "It's an African forest god." The woman's breast was still outside of her shirt. She looked Mary up and down. Mary was suddenly aware that her jeans were paint streaked, her sweater was baggy, her hair rainsoaked and messy, and that she was in her late thirties, middle aged and dumpy and obviously out of place.

She began again. "I'm sorry," she said. "I couldn't help but overhear. You have some land somewhere?"

"Yeah." said the woman. "Near Stony River. 160 acres. We're going to build a house, y'know. Log and stone, cut the logs ourselves. Or maybe we'll build a dome, or maybe like a whole series of huts, kind of African."

"I used to live on a farm . . .,"Mary began.

"Oh yeah?" the woman said, uninterested.

A man was coming towards her. She lifted the baby towards him, adjusting her shirt to tuck her breast inside.

"Let's split," the woman said. "This party's a drag. Put Karma in the bus and we'll go find some action."

They left and Mary sat alone, paralyzed. No one talked to her or even looked at her. Finally, she decided to leave. She began to thread her way to the door, but just as she was leaving, David came after her, following along again, as naturally and cheerfully as a homeless puppy.

"Wow, that was so cool," he said. "Far out. There's some people there who are raising chickens and goats. It's so fantastic. Man, that's the only way to live. Free as a breeze. Man, oh man."

"It's not that easy," Mary said shortly.

They walked back across the bridge and along the silent streets to the apartment. Mary let David come in with her and then instantly regretted it.

"You'll have to sleep on the floor, or somewhere," she said. "I'm exhausted. I'm going to bed." She threw him some blankets, went in her bedroom, shut the door. She could hear him moving around, singing, then she could hear dishes, the smell of cooking.

She came out of the bedroom. "What the hell do you think you're doing?" she said.

He looked at her, puzzled. "I was hungry," he said. "Hey, it's food, right ? Food should be for the people."

"It's not your food."

"Mother Mary, mother Mary," he said. "Don't be uptight. It's only food. We're learning to share, right. It's the new way."

She turned on her heel and went back to bed. Gordon would never understand, she thought. He'd never understand any of this. She tried to imagine his reaction to David in the apartment, cooking food in the middle of the night.

Oh, God, she thought. She didn't understand it either. It must be because she'd lived in the city for so long. Her lungs, her muscles and her bones were full of concrete, dragging her down. She tried to turn her attention to her cabin, to her journey into silence, the silence of the great trees, the northern woods, the high secret mountains, with their hiding places, their hidden trails. But then David came and lay down on the bed beside her. She said nothing. She only wanted to be far away. When she thought he was asleep, she went from his intrusive breathing snorting warm presence and lay on the sofa, staring at the wall.

After a while, she fell asleep, and woke again, and dozed, restless and uncomfortable, her thoughts weak and useless and confused.

She'd have to get rid of David in the morning; she'd have to decide what to do with the painting. She'd have to decide what to do with her life. She couldn't go on living like this, but she couldn't leave Gordon. She'd die if she left Gordon. She'd die of loneliness. She knew she would.

In the morning, David left without her needing to say anything, promising cheerfully that he'd see her again, but he seemed almost serious about going to the country with the people from the party. He'd made a huge mess in the kitchen. She left it sitting there, untouched.

Instead, she sat at the window in the kitchen, beside the fake maple table with its tidy place mat and its tidy salt and pepper shakers and its barren vase of dried flowers in the middle. It was raining again. She watched the parking lot. It was bound by a chain link fence, sagging at one end where it had been pulled down and trampled on by kids on their way to school or the corner store. The grey cat which lived in a house opposite walked along the fence and back again. The corners of the parking lot were always full of debris, dried bunches of angry looking weeds, plastic bags, food wrappers, sometimes broken toys or appliances which seemed to end up there with no human assistance.

There was a grate in the middle of the parking lot. It was sloped so the rain ran down into it. She could hear it, a distant rusty dribble of water, washing the filth and dust of the city, down and endlessly down into the sewer, and from there, she imagined it running endlessly, under the city, collecting into larger and larger streams, until it ran finally down into an increasingly filthy and polluted sea.

Section Nine

Rob and the Family

Chapter Forty-Four

When Rob woke in the morning, Dana wasn't there. He groaned and rolled over. Two nights in a row he'd gotten drunk. His body felt like a skidder had run over it. His mouth was parched and sticky.

Well, he'd brought it on himself. The night before last, he'd gone to the forestry meeting. Afterwards, he'd suggested casually to Sunita that they grab a late beer after the meeting and she'd said, sure, she'd be glad to, and so they went over to the bar, him slightly hyper and feeling a bit idiotic, like a kid on a date, but what the hell. And then over a beer and then another beer and another, they talked about all kinds of stuff, the meetings, forestry, hikes, places they'd been in the mountains and places they wanted to go.

Then some other people came by and Sunita, to his disappointment, smiled and waved and invited them to sit down, two men and a woman. At first, he figured the woman had to be with one of the men. Sunita introduced them, and they all began talking. They obviously knew each other pretty well, but Rob didn't know them at all. He wondered if they were new in town. The talk turned to environmental issues; these new people seemed to think things were a hell of a lot worse than he did. They were ranting about multinationals and conspiracies and earthquakes and UFOs and other shit that didn't make much sense. He began to wonder if he should get up and leave before he lost his temper and told them they were full of shit.

The other woman made him uneasy. She was tall, with short hair. Looked like a goddamed guy, he thought. But a beautiful guy. Lots of silver jewelry. Dressed like a guy as well. Leather jacket, blue jeans. Big hands. It appeared she had a motorcycle.

"What kinda bike? "Rob asked.

"Harley," she said. "I rebuilt it." He was impressed. He talked with her about motorcycles for a while, and then the talk turned back to the news and the generally rotten state of things.

Then the tall woman, whose name was Karen, stretched.

"We'd better go," she said to Sunny. "I gotta get up and go to work in the morning."

The two other guys made similar sounds of agreement. They said good night politely enough. Rob watched them leave. The two men went one way, towards the back entrance, Sunita and Karen went the other. He could see them out the window getting on Karen's motorcycle. Karen leaned over and kissed Sunita on the lips. A long kiss. Then they got on the motorcycle and roared away.

For a while, he sat there, shrugging and drinking another beer. The joke was on him. He figured he'd just been visited by the queer club of the town. Actually, come to think of it, he had heard rumours about Sunita, but he'd put them down to her lifestyle. But Jeezus Murphy, the woman had sons. He started to feel sick.

By closing time, he realized he still didn't want to go home. Dana would want to know where the hell he'd been and he wasn't about to tell her about Sunita and the humiliation the bitch had just visited on him. He got in his truck and drove very carefully, up the hill to the hospital. The last goddammed thing he needed to cap off his night was a ticket for drunk driving. He rang the buzzer at the hospital, but no one came. He leaned against the wall, waiting, and finally, someone, a nurse or a doctor, left and he slipped inside the door before it fully closed. No one was around. He wove his way down the hall to Kathryn's room.

Kathryn was asleep, or looked asleep, under the white cover, her gnarled knotted blue veined hands lying on top of the covers. An IV tube needle was stuck into one arm and another tube was taped under her nostrils. Rob sat down by the bed and waited for the room to stop whirling. He put his head on his chest and dozed for a while. What he wanted more than anything was for Kathryn to open her eyes, wake up, growl at him for sitting there like dumb drunk fool. If he told her about Sunita, she'd laugh at him but he wouldn't care so much. She'd never scared him even when he was little and first went to live with her. Somehow, she'd always been on his side, despite her sharp tongue and sarcastic views. He reached over and took her hand. It was thin and cool. He could feel the bones in it, sharp and angular. He put it down again, laying it carefully on top of the covers.

Once after Mary had taken off and he'd been only living with Kathryn and Bill for a little while, she'd heard him crying at night. He used to cry himself to sleep a lot, until he got used to Mary being away. Then he just got mad instead. But Kathryn had heard him and come in and all she did, night after night, was sit with him and tell him stories, simple silly stories about the farm she'd grown up on, and a pet horse she had, and rabbits and kittens. She'd sit there until he fell asleep and she never mentioned these times to him or Bill.

Then he went through a stage where he hated his mother for leaving him and when he'd say anything, Kathryn would only shrug and say, "People have to live their own lives. Your mom just wasn't made to be tied down. Some people are just born like that." So after a while he accepted it, or he thought he had, until Mary came home and began interfering, or trying to interfere, in everyone's life again. She came home with all these bright ideas and high hopes, books full of ideas about organic gardening and back to the land kinds of stuff. After a while, she shut up about it all. She went on painting, though.

The problem was, she had no money and she couldn't get a job, despite her years of experience as a waitress. No one in town would hire her. People barely spoke to her. The town was full of weird looking people with long hair and funny clothes and somehow Mary got lumped in with them. Rumours flew about why she'd left Vancouver and what she was doing back in the valley, that she was a junkie, a drug dealer, that she'd gone crazy, that the man she was living with had kicked her out and she'd run out of places to go. After a while, Mary started staying out of town and the rumours died down. After all, with the numbers of other weirdos and freaks around, she wasn't that interesting.

Kathryn always had suggestions for stuff Mary could do, things she ought to try, jobs she could apply for, businesses she could start, stuff she could grow on the farm to make money. Mary did try selling fruit and vegetables off the farm, but she never put much energy into it and no one was interested anyhow. She had her paintings for sale at one of the new craft stores in town but she wanted too much money and they were too much for most people.

She just seemed to get lonelier and lonelier and more withdrawn, didn't make any attempt to make friends, alienated people who tried to help out, like Kathryn and Jim. And then she was gone. And it was his damn fault.

Rob knew it was his fault. He'd never told a goddam soul that it was his fault, but it was. Mary had tried. She'd called and invited him over. Once she'd bought him an expensive shirt he didn't need and she couldn't afford, and what the hell had he done? He'd ignored her, that's what he'd done. Like a perfect shithead, he'd avoided her, never gone to her house, never even thanked her for the damn shirt, never acknowledged the pain and frantic desperation on her face, in her eyes. She had no idea how much he had wanted to do just that, go over, sit by her side, put his head on her lap, be held by her, drink tea, admire her paintings, which he still thought were the most beautiful things he'd ever seen, just like he thought she was beautiful, dressed up, her hair flying, a gypsy shawl over her shoulders, beads and earrings flashing, colours like maroons and deep greens and turquoise and hot pink all somehow working together.

She was extraordinary. And he wasn't. He was a just a plain goddam guy, trying to work and keep his nose clean and keep a job, a few bucks coming in and his old truck on the road. His mother was an embarrassment and mostly he had wished to God she'd go back to Vancouver so he could go on dreaming about going to visit her someday and never actually doing it. Until she was gone and then he would have sat by her side forever if it would just keep her alive and in one piece.

All his life, when he was a kid growing up on the farm, after she left and he felt so damn alone, someday, he was going to go visit her. But he had to have something to show her, something with which to measure up to the standard she'd set, something where he wasn't just a dumb asshole kid and later a dumb asshole logger with sawdust for brains and no money. He dreamed of driving to Vancouver in his new truck, showing up at her apartment, ignoring her dumbass boyfriend and meeting her, finally, as some kind of equal.

He wanted to meet her on some kind of equal ground, where he could look her in the eye, and say, look, I survived without you, I succeeded without you, I made it without you, I didn't need you then and I don't need you now and what the hell do you think of that? And then maybe they could have talked and understood each other enough to become friends.

He groaned and shook his head. He should be at home. Dana was going to have a fit when he finally showed up. He didn't want to think about Dana. God, he didn't want to think about anything. He was supposed to be getting up to go to work in an hour or so. But he couldn't even bring himself to think about that. The guys in the bar would pass the word that he was sleeping off a hangover. They'd think him a wimp for not making it to work just because of a lousy hangover, but what the hell. He'd go find somewhere to curl up and sleep for a while. He'd go over to Joey's trailer. Joey worked for him so he'd better damn well have gone to work. He wouldn't care if Rob hid out there and slept for a few hours. Then he'd have to go home and deal with the shit there and then try to figure out what to do with his life, and the empty sick loneliness in his gut that just made him want to curl up and hide and not give a shit about anything, anymore, ever.

Which he'd done. He'd slept at Joe's for a bit, got up and gone home, prepared to face the music, only to find Dana on a rant about the will, the land and how it should be their's and not Colin's, how he was supposed to have talked Kathryn out of the land years ago and hadn't bothered. She had hardly seemed to notice that he'd been gone all night. His useless twit of a kid Brendan was there took, sulking upstairs, trying to be invisible and not even bothering to say hello or how the hell are you. The kid looked like hell, from what he'd seen of him. But Dana had sure picked her moment. The last thing he wanted to hear was Dana going on about Kathryn's impending death and what they ought to be getting out of her, after he'd spent half the night sitting watching her breathe, and praying that she would just go on doing that simple thing, breathing, one long deep breath after another.

Then he was told that he'd better goddam well show up for supper because the boys were coming over, and that's when he'd lost it, slammed out of the house, got back in the truck, drove to town and proceeded to drink himself into a stupor all over again. This time when the pub closed, he drove home, drunk, against all common sense and everything he'd ever told his kids, that if he ever caught them in a vehicle driving drunk he'd kick their butts all around the block.

He knew he had to get home, sober up, make peace with Dana, to whom, when all was said and done, he knew he owed her his whole goddamned life. He was goddamned sick of the looks he was getting around the bar, where he'd never been known as much of a drinker, and goddamned sick of the glee among the assholes he was drinking with—their stupid jokes and stupider sick drunk bragging, stories he'd heard before, too many times, He'd left and come home to his plate and supper sitting reproachfully on the table. Goddam Dana, anyway, she always had to have the last word.

And now here he was, waking up alone, missing a second day of work, worried about Kathryn, for all he knew, she might have died anytime and no one would have told him.

He got dressed. He figured he'd better go to work, even if he only made it for a bit. Word would be everywhere that he'd been drinking but drinking and not working was bullshit, was weakness. He got himself, with some effort, in and out of the shower. He was stiff and sore and lazy. Shit, he thought. I used to be able to party all night and work all day. What the hell.

He got in the truck, sat listening to the radio while the diesel warmed up. It was another sunny early June day. The weather report was for more hot sunny weather. Well, that meant it was only a matter of time before work shut down anyway, before they kicked the loggers out of the woods because of the fire hazard.

God, it is dry, he thought, as he drove towards the mountain road leading up into the logging site. Too dry, for so early in the year.

Been a dry spring, the snow pack had been low. Bill had had a thing about fire, used to mutter about it, go around filling barrels with water and muttering. The other side of the lake had burnt when Bill was a kid and he'd never gotten over it. Told the story over and over whenever the weather got dry which of course it did every summer, but the old man had been right. It was always a dangerous time.

Chapter Forty-Five

Someone sat down on the bed, picked up Kathryn's hand. Kathryn could feel the warmth of this other person's hand coming into hers, like tiny jolts of electricity, little flickerings of blue fire which entered in and joined and added to the flame already dozing fitfully inside her.

Kathryn kept struggling up and up, towards some kind of light and air, demanding of her lungs that they keep breathing, struggling to open her eyes, and then the darkness, the weakness, would take over and she'd sink back down into invisibility again. She was exhausted by this very struggle, and thought that perhaps if she gave up, simply rested, something would happen and she would regain some kind of control, some kind of understanding of what was happening.

Various kinds of noise swam towards her and went away again. Sometimes she could see the people attached to the voices, even with her eyes closed. It was very confusing. She wanted to talk to them, spin out a thread of connection that would pull her up and out of this dim place and into the bright noise and colours of that other world. And behind all of it was the sense of something else that she was supposed to do and hadn't done, had failed to do and had to keep trying to do—but she was too tired to remember. She was so tired but under the tiredness was a bright and bitter anger at her own helplessness, like a flame struggling with pitchy wet wood, gusting and flickering and sparking but not going out.

Voices swam towards her again. These were familiar voices, which added to her sense of struggle. She tried again to open her eyes, reach out her hands, get out of this narrow hard scratchy bed, get up and out of this place, wherever she was, get up and go home. I want to go home, she thought. She tried to say it out loud but the effort twisted her body into painful knots.

"Kathryn," a voice said. "Are you waking up? Can you hear me? Can she hear me?" the voice went on. "It looks like she's trying to say something."

"It's hard to say," said another voice. "She seems to be drifting in and out of a coma, a kind of twilight sleep. It's hard to say how long she can hang on. She's a pretty tough old girl. She may even come out of it again. We're just monitoring the situation from hour to hour. She hasn't actually had a stroke and that's good news."

"Grandma," said a voice. The voice was Arlene's. "Grandma, I just want you to know that we're all praying for you, and we're all here, your family is here, and we all love and care about you very much. We want you to feel free to do what's best for you. If you want to go now, if you want to go away from us, then you should go. We can let you. If you wake up and stay with us for a little while longer, that will make us all so happy."

Kathryn would have laughed out loud if she could. What a drip Arlene was. She had always been. She was too much like her mother, a large foolish blond woman who had giggled too much and made silly cooing noises over the animals on the couple of occasions she had showed up at the farm, and only stayed with Colin long enough to present him with a child she couldn't seem to manage to care for and had eventually disappeared into some ghastly unknown fate.

Experimentally, Kathryn tried again to move her head, to say something at least to tell Arlene that she'd leave in her own good time and didn't need someone's damned permission. All that came out was a kind of moan, a low hideous sound, rather like a cow. She was embarrassed but tried again, and this time her head flung itself to one side, rather suddenly, like a tic or a kind of twitch.

"Are you all right, dear? Can you hear us?" said the other voice, a bright overly cheery kind of voice. Kathryn pictured a big fat blowsy kind of woman, a red faced woman in a long housedress, and then the picture in her head faded and the darkness came in again.

Much, much later, she opened her eyes or rather, her eyes sprang open without her volition, with no act of will on her part. There they were, wide open and staring around. The room was dimly lit. The curtains around her bed hung white and still. The air she breathed seemed dry, harsh, as though it was full of a fine dust, too fine even to see, which coated her lungs and throat and made it ache, made her want to cough, but when she tried, nothing happened, only a small rasping noise, like something sliding, sand paper, rough skin on skin.

Her eyes were dry and sore. She lay very still, rediscovering her body, the ache in her arm where the needle went in, the weakness in her legs, her far away legs, which barely seemed to belong to her, her hands, bent, curled, numb at the tips of her fingers; her stomach, lungs, heart, beating, beating, trudging steadily, if tiredly, onward.

No, she thought.

No I don't want to be here. People die here. Bill died here. Or had Bill died? She wasn't sure. Perhaps he was waiting at the farm for her, impatient for supper, wondering where she'd gone. Perhaps he was there, with the children, and it was late and dark and she wasn't home. She tried again to move but her body didn't respond. She started to get frantic, afraid of the dark, of her children being alone in it without protection, of Bill wandering through the dark fields looking for her, and then, quite suddenly, she knew what she had been trying to remember. She knew now where Mary was. She could see her very clearly. She was at the beach, squatting on the sand, and the slowly falling sun made a pink and gold nimbus of her hair. She was squatting at the edge of the creek that ran over the sand and mud. She was shaping the mud with cold reddened hands into roads, dams and houses, peopled with stick people. She was humming to herself. Kathryn could hear the tune, a silly mindless tune that she couldn't quite recognize. But she could see that Mary was happy and waiting for her to come.

Section Ten

Mary

Chapter Forty-Six

"Oh, for God's sake," Kathryn said. "Nobody could live here."

"Well, I'm going to," Mary said. "It's here, it's cheap. I don't need much."

"You'll freeze next winter. Who do you think is going to get up wood for you and thaw the pipes when they freeze? "

"I can run a chainsaw. I'm not just a helpless city slicker. Remember. I grew up helping dad do every damn thing. I helped him get wood and feed the cows and do whatever we had to do to survive. And now I have to survive. So this house is it."

Kathryn didn't say anything, just turned away, resumed peering around at the house. It was discouraging enough. The floor still had linoleum on it, but it was worn and covered in a litter of dust, broken glass, rat shit, paper, old clothes. The walls were stained, the wallpaper, what was left of it, torn and fluttering in strips, the painted walls grey and dusty, with occasional broken holes in the gyproc. The windows were single pane, cracked and dusty, several broken.

"It's basically intact," Mary said. "It just needs a lot of work."

"Where are you going to get the money?" Kathryn said briefly.

"Oh, for God's sake," Mary said. "For years you wanted to me to come home. You said I was a lousy mother and you and dad were going to sell the goddam farm because no one was here to help out. Well, here I am, okay? I'm trying to remake my life and it's not easy and all you can seem to do is bitch and criticize."

"You made your choices. We did what we could to help out."

"Yes, I know you raised my son and thank you very much.

You don't have to keep reminding me over and over how much I owe you. Just shut up about it."

"Well, that's just fine and dandy. I guess I've got lots of work of my own to do at home and you'll just do what you want to do anyway. You always have. Come over later if you get hungry."

Kathryn vanished out the door. She would have slammed it if it hadn't been blocked by debris. Mary stared after her. "Just leave me alone," she muttered. "Just go away and leave me alone."

After Kathryn was out of sight, Mary tried to turn her attention back to the task in front of her. She spent the afternoon shoveling and sweeping the debris off the floor and arguing in her head with her bitch of a mother. It was late August. The sun shone in the dirty windows, grasshoppers buzzed and whirred over the dry yellow meadow grass in the front yard. The lake was still, burnished blue steel under the sun. She'd go swimming later, when she finished cleaning the floors. She hummed and sang defiantly as she swept. To hell with her mother.

She could have the house indefinitely, just for fixing it up. The owners lived in California; they were elderly now. Once they'd thought they'd make a fortune speculating in Canadian real estate. Well, they'd made half a fortune. They used to come around when she was a kid, but they hadn't been to visit in years. They'd sounded surprised when she phoned, but pleased as well to have someone in the house caring for the property. It had sat empty for years. Rumour had it that they had no real heirs, only a distant set of relatives somewhere. At least they had no plans to sell.

Various people had lived in the house over the years. They'd come and gone. Each set of tenants had left the house slightly mangier. There was a row of dead vehicles out back, mouldering under grass and new trees. Grass had grown over the cast off tires, machine parts and tin cans in the yard. A few flowers and trees had survived it all.

She wondered if Gordon would ever come to visit. She'd tried so hard to explain to him why it was important, why she had to leave, move, get out of the city and change her life. She wanted him to come with her, but they both knew there wasn't a chance in hell of that happening. He'd helped her move, even given her enough money to live on for a little while. They'd spent one night, the last night before she left, lying together, wrapped in each other's arms, weeping. He hadn't actually been as broken up as she thought he would be. She'd given him that last painting after he said he liked it.

Then she'd packed everything in her little brown car and driven home, driven into Kathryn's yard, arrived just as Kathryn and Rob were sitting down to supper, sat there and told them she'd come back, she'd come home for good. She saw the shock and unease on their faces. They didn't say much. She sat with them, ate supper, wandered, after the dishes were done, down to the lake, sat there fighting with the mosquitoes while rising fish dimpled the still water and the last of the sun lit the granite folds of the rocks behind her. She came back up to house after it was dark. Rob and Kathryn had already gone to bed. She sat out on the porch but the mosquitoes attacked in savage clouds and finally she went in, went up to the little hot stuffy room at the top of the house, and went to sleep.

During that summer, she was possessed by feverish, boundless energy. Nothing fazed her. She took over the garden from Kathryn. She went to the beach in the afternoons, lay in the warm golden-green water and luxuriated in its silken ripples over her breasts and between her legs. She took the old green canoe out in the evenings, fishing, and brought back shining brown speckled trout, with rainbows fading along their sides. She picked fruit and helped Kathryn can and make jam. She was full of ideas for the farm, passionate and evangelical. She ran into their stubborn solid silent resistance, their eyes which looked at each other and left her out, their unspoken thoughts and uneasy shrugs at her ideas. But for that summer, at least, she didn't care.

There was so much she had forgotten. She welcomed it all back inside; she fitted it all into the empty places. She missed Gordon, but she thought of the city as loneliness itself, when she thought of it at all. It seemed to have disappeared somewhere far beyond the ranges of blue misty mountains ranged between it and her. She knew it was out there somewhere and she was content to leave that knowledge undisturbed. When she thought about it at all, she was amazed at how fast it had all slid away—her city manners, her city talk, her city pace, slid off like shed skin.

In the meantime, there was the drowsy heat on her back between the raspberry rows, endlessly picking the tiny sweet berries, a job she had once hated, bending under the drooping canes for the last overripe berries hiding underneath, the raspberries dwindling now in the heat, despite the rainbow flashing of sprinklers. There was carrying the raspberries into Kathryn's, then putting them away in plastic bags in the freezer against the long cold winter. There was so much else, the long orderly rows of the garden with more weeds than her father ever would have tolerated, but still productive, full of their own secret power; the gathering and swelling and budding and breaking open; the round fat grapes, and the apples, plum, peaches, pears, pulling the tired trees down with their weight.

"There's so much," she said to Kathryn. "God, what people in the city pay for a few poor wizened apples, or a bunch of grapes." Kathryn shrugged.

"That's their outlook," she said. "They chose to live there."

She and Mary had arguments about pesticides.

"Mom, they're poison," Mary protested. "Besides you don't need them. There are natural methods. I bought a book on it."

"Well, if you can teach them damn worms to read the book, more power to you. In the meantime, I don't want to open a jar of cherries and find a layer of worms on top, eh?"

"But pesticides are destroying the environment. Especially that stuff you're always spraying around for mosquitoes. It's bad for eagles and things."

"You'll be the first one complaining when the mosquitoes get bad around here. How are we supposed to work out in the garden if we don't use something to knock them back a little? What the hell, are we just supposed to let the damn bugs take over and eat us out of house and home?"

"No, but . . ."

"Well, if you'd do a little more practical work and a little less reading, maybe you'd figure a few things out. Those damn books must have been all written by idiots with a little back yard garden in the suburbs somewhere. Not for people who have to get real work done because if they don't, they damn well won't have anything to eat come winter."

"Oh, for God's sake, I only meant we could try something different for a change. What the hell would it hurt? "

"Well, go ahead, go ahead. Who's stopping you? Do whatever the hell you want. You always have."

Mary turned away, unable to continue, a sudden loathing and rage against her mother rising up furious and fast. "I've got to go," she said. "I've got stuff of my own I have to do." She hurried across the path to her own house, went in and shut the door, leaned against it panting as though she had escaped from something. But once she was through the door, she couldn't find anything she wanted to do and ended up sitting by the window, staring out at the flattened trampled grass, the weed ridden remains of ancient flower beds, until she finally got up, fetched a piece of paper, began to list chores she ought to be doing and then gave up, got another piece of paper and her drawing pencils, began a series of tiny sketches, all around the edges, lost interest in that as well, and got up, went back outside and down to the lake and along the rocks and back again until it was almost dark.

Chapter Forty-Seven

He overheard something about a fire. It came in over his radio, a couple of truckers talking to each other, while he was still working. It came almost at the end of the day, which had been long, hot, and weary. Rob kept going, kept up with everyone else working, even with his headache and his still aching stomach, but he hid it. He snapped at the other guys, once or twice, mostly because they were being even stupider and more moronic than usual. They seemed pleased that he was so hungover. It made them feel more on a par with him.

He didn't pay much attention to the talk about fire. It could be anything, anywhere, a lightning strike, a garbage fire or some idiot burning trash in a barrel, too stupid to realize in weather like this, sparks could ignite almost anything hundreds of yards away. Goddam tourists, city people, idiots.

Then he heard the lake road mentioned. He put down the saw, went over and called in to the forestry office. Sure enough, they'd gotten a call from some terrified cottager, who had lit a fire for his kids to roast wienies on the beach, only it had then lit the driftwood and brush twenty feet away and was now climbing up the hillside behind this dork's cabin. Forestry had called for a bomber and a spotter plane. They didn't have a crew available. They weren't sure just where the fire was on the lake road, couldn't tell him much more.

It was probably nothing. It could be anywhere on the fifty miles of lake road, nothing to do with him. But his head was aching, his back and hands hurt and it was damned near five. He chucked his saw in the back of truck, went over and told one of the guys that he was on his way, he'd see them in the morning.

He saw the smoke long before he reached the fire. It was three miles from his house, in a brushy wooded draw below the highway; it didn't look too bad, despite all the smoke. The smoke was good. It meant the fire was smoldering, burning slowly, working its way through the brush and leaf mould. As long as no wind came up and they could keep it below the road, it would be okay. The shore on either side of the draw was rocky, steep, with only a few trees. It was a situation that could easily be controlled with some quick action and common sense. He drove down the driveway to the cabin. There were a few cars and trucks parked in the yard, a line of people stopped on the highway, stupidly watching the fire like it was some kind of show.

People were carrying water up from the beach in buckets to throw on the fire, and a few people were ineffectually beating at the burning brush with shovels.

"Where's the owner?" Rob asked some skinny potbellied creature in Bermuda shorts.

"Over there, on the phone," the guy stuttered. The owner of the cabin was indeed, talking on a cellular phone. He slammed it shut in frustration as Rob came up to him.

"There's no fire department," he said out loud in general disbelief. "What are we supposed to do now?"

"Forestry's sending a bomber," Rob said. "We need to get these people out of here and off the highway, and then get some pumps going. Have you got hoses here?"

The man stared at him in stupefaction.

"Rob Mangerton," Rob said, holding out his hand to the phone. "I'm one of your neighbours to the north. If you'll let me have that thing for a bit, I'll round up some pumps and some help and this shouldn't be much of a problem. Pretty dry these days. How'd it get started anyway? "

"Damn kids," the man muttered, meekly handing over the phone. "Must have been playing with matches or something."

"Well, guess forestry will figure it out when they get here," Rob said cheerfully. "You know they charge the cost of fighting the fire back to the property owner if they find out it was his fault."

"Jesus Christ," the man muttered.

"Organize someone to get that traffic up above moving," Rob said. "Keep it moving in case the smoke gets too thick." The man went off, and Rob called Jake McFadden, an older guy who served as the local fire warden. His wife answered the phone and assured him that Jake had already left with a truck full of equipment, and would pick up four or five other neighbours along the way. Rob called Dana, who answered with ice in her voice, but agreed to phone Luke and Mike, round up Brendan, and get them down here.

Rob left the phone on the picnic table on the deck of the cabin and went up the draw to the fire. It was burning hot and fierce, had made it to the top of the skinny birch and alder in the creek, was crackling and roaring through the green leaves which exploded like popcorn as the fire reached them. The few people trying to fight the fire were dressed in bathing suits, shorts, halter tops and sandals.

Jeezus Murphy, Rob thought to himself. Do they think it's a goddam beach party?

"Okay," he roared above the noise of the fire. "We've got help on the way. If you're not dressed or trained for this kind of work, the best thing you can do is get your cars out of here and make room for the crews coming in." Reluctantly, but with obvious relief, most of them turned and began to head back down the draw, picking their way with difficulty over the broken rocky ground. He saw the cars begin to pull out, saw, gratefully, Jake's truck pull in and the grizzled old man begin to pull equipment from the back. He went over, nodded to Jake, helped him carry the clumsy heavy pump and a roll of hose over the creek.

"Helluva mess, eh?" he shouted cheerfully. Jake was getting deafer year by year.

"Ah, she'll be okay if we don't get no wind. We get a south wind, you better get on home and starting wettin' down the roof."

They both stopped, looked south towards the distant end of the lake, then Jake nodded over to the other side of the lake, where black clouds laced with purple had settled in the valleys.

They both shrugged. If a wind came, they were in trouble. If not, they could probably have the fire out in a couple of hours. They got the pump up and running and squirting water just as the spotter plane came over, circling and banking steeply to avoid smacking into the mountain.

"Don't think they'll do a drop here," yelled Rob. "Too steep. No room for a run."

"Ah. he'll come along the shore there."

"Might not be able to. He might be too close to the trees."

"Ah, them guys, they'll fly anywhere."

"Better get the rest of these damn tourists out of here."

He left Jake holding the hose and walked up to the highway. There were still cars stopped, people gaping over the edge of the road, some with cameras.

"Better get going," he told them. "Bomber's on its way. Make a hell of a mess of your cars, not to mention yourselves."

Reluctantly, they moved away, got in their cars and drove away, one by one. When they were all gone, he went back down the hill. Another truck had arrived and a second pump was being set up. The edges of the fire were already blackening, steaming where the water had hit. Three or four other men, neighbours from farther along the lake had come with shovels; they were working their way up the hill, covering the edges of the fire with dirt, moving it in on itself.

Rob nodded. It wouldn't be long. They'd have the fire contained by night, when the cool air coming down the mountain would slow it even further. They'd have to watch it closely for three or four days. No matter how much water they poured on it, the fire would smoulder in the leaf mould and rotted fallen stumps for days and spring up again if they weren't there to catch it.

The spotter plane circled again then flew off to the south.

"Guess they're not coming in," said Jake. "Too tight probably. Well, we'd better make sure she's done before dark."

Another truck arrived and Rob's heart leapt when he saw his three sons walking together towards him.

My boys, he thought. My sons. His heart swelled and he took a deep breath. He wanted to swoop them up, tousle their heads as he had when they were young, but instead he only nodded to them.

"Hey there, old man," said Luke cheerfully. "Thought we'd come see if you needed some help." He looked around. "How'd it get started anyway?"

"Guy wanted to let his kids roast wienies," said Rob briefly. "How about a couple of you relieve Jake on the pump. He's probably ready for a break."

Luke and Jason moved off. Brendan was left facing his father.

"Haven't seen you around much," Rob said.

Brendan shrugged, but said nothing.

"You know," Rob said. "You could let your mother and I know what you're up to, now and then. She gets kind of worried about you."

"I'm here, aren't I?" Brendan said.

Rob was tempted to hit him, right there and then, so tempted his fists curled at his sides and then he unclenched them and said levelly. "And where the hell were you earlier when you couldn't even bother saying hello? "

"I've been reading my grandmother's diaries," Brendan said. "I read them all. I finished them this afternoon. You fucking bastard." His eyes were suddenly bright with tears. He blinked, turned away, and went up the hill after his brothers.

Rob took several steps after him then stopped and went back to the house and the cellular phone. Dread clogged each step. What the hell was that in Brendan's eyes? Contempt, more than anything. He never thought he'd see that in the eyes of one of his children.

Oh, God. Brendan, he thought. He knew he had to phone Dana. They'd need food and coffee to get through the evening. She'd probably already have it organized. But at least he could let her know what was going on. He went on up to the cabin. A woman came to the door.

"Yes?" she said stiffly, as though he were some tradesman come to bother about a bill.

"I need to use your phone again," he said. "Call the wife and let her know what's happening. She'll be bringing some food down, later. Appreciate it if we could maybe use your deck here to eat on."

"I suppose that would be all right," the woman said. "I'll get the phone."

Shit, Rob thought. Anyone with an ounce of hospitality or common sense would be already making coffee and food, inviting them in. This woman handed him the phone and then carefully shut the screen door, as if he carried some kind of contagion.

Dana's voice was still cool. She and Jake's wife would be down with coffee and food in an hour or so. And knowing Dana, it would be a lot more than a few sandwiches. Keeping his voice down, he explained the hospitality level at the cabin.

"Okay, paper plates," she said. "No problem. We have some and I can get more if I need to."

He knocked on the door and handed the phone back, nodded politely to the woman and went back to the fire. He thought of asking her if her husband wanted to come out and learn to really play with fire, and then he thought of Brendan and his heart sank again.

Section Eleven

Brendan

Chapter Forty-Eight

Brendan had volunteered to stay and watch the fire through the night. Everyone had agreed that the danger was over, as long as a wind didn't come up. The people in the cabin had packed and gone as well, with barely a word of thanks to the people who had showed up to save them from their own stupidity. Dana and the other women had come with coffee, plates of chicken, pots of stew, pies, fruit salad, and they had all eaten together on the deck of the cabin, the men spelling each other off on the hoses from the pumps. Dana had brought some foamies and sleeping bags and hauled them out of the car for Brendan. During supper, he managed to avoid both his father and his mother, avoid looking at them or catching their eye, managed, almost, to pretend they weren't there at all. He sat apart from everyone with his plate of food. The people around him were people he had known his whole life, but they didn't know him, he thought.

They all stood around, shoveling food into their mouths as fast as it would go, saying the same damn things they'd all been saying to each other for years and would go on saying to one another until they died, and seemingly endlessly contented to go on uttering stupidities to one another until then.

Finally they all left. Of course, Dana had to make a fuss, come over and put her arms around Brandon, say something stupid and irritating like "be careful." Rob said nothing to him at all.

After they left, Brendan wandered back up to where the fire still smouldered. He stood in the dark, watching it eat its slow and relentless way through the leaf mould and rotted ancient stumps. It was amazing how much of the fire was left after the gallons of water that had been poured on it. Every once in a while, a small bright clear flame would flare up and catch a leaf or a twig and shiver and shake into momentary life and then wink out again. His dad had said Forestry would send a crew in tomorrow to finish it off, clean everything up.

The words he had said to his father still echoed in his head. "You bastard," he had said. "You fucking bastard." At the moment he had said those words, he had felt something tear open inside, and he had had to stop himself from going on and on, from saying more and more unspeakable things. Rob had stared at him as if he were someone strange, someone brand new, just discovered.

He walked away from the glowing worms of the fire and down to the black edge of the water. The small waves slapping the sand always sounded louder at night. There was still a black bulk of clouds massed in the cleft between Castle and McGregor Mountains, and heat lightning shimmering behind it. The moon had risen and the moon trail danced in a long track that led away south to the distant end of the lake.

He was used to the lake being beautiful. He was used to it all. It was just scenery. He'd told himself that before. He'd seen it all his life. But now his heart squeezed tight inside him and faltered and stammered like a shy child. It was all so goddamned amazing, he thought. It didn't matter how much he had seen it all his life. It was just so amazing.

He kicked his shoes off, waded into the water, which was icy cold. After all, it was onlyl late June. The lake never really warmed up until August. His feet began to ache and he went back and stood on the sand, which still held warmth from the day.

The thought came that if he spread his arms, he could widen out, grow thinner and thinner, enormous enough to embrace the whole amazing breathtaking scene, take it inside himself, and then his sense of himself began to shrink and vanish and realized it was the other way around. It was him who was spreading and dissolving and being absorbed into this earth, this ground, until all that he was or thought he ought to be would disappear forever, into this golden hazed and darkening world.

He waited, holding his breath, almost disappointed when he didn't disappear, but instead went on standing on the beach with the small waves licking and sucking at the sand and the rocks and driftwood. He didn't know what he felt or understood anymore. He only knew that somehow the boundaries between himself and the valley had thinned and disappeared. God, I really do love this place, he thought. I'm part of it too. That was one of the things that Mary had written about, how the valley had caught and held her, how it had made her what she was. He didn't know what that meant, only that in some way he might spend a long time trying to understand, it was true for him as well.

Finally, the night stopped entrancing him and he got tired enough to go back up to the cabin. He spread the foamie and got in his sleeping bag, and lay there for what seemed a long time, staring at the stars, before he fell asleep.

The thunder woke him. While he slept, the storm had circled around to the north and now, as he watched, a lightning bolt crackled across the whole sky and crashed into a cloud on the opposite side of the valley. The thunder broke above him and rumbled and echoed through the mountains before grumbling into a silence in which Brendan could hear the rush and roar of the wind behind the storm coming down the valley. The lake was already running with whitecaps. He sat up, uneasy. He had always been afraid of lightning storms. The moon was still out, hanging just of the top of the mountains, but about to be swallowed by a black and solid wall of cloud. Another flash of lightning and thunder, more distant. He waited, worried, counting the seconds, hugging his knees, trying to figure out what to do. The wind would stir up the fire, but the storm would probably also bring a drenching rain to put it out again. Plus there wasn't much he could do on his own. He had a cellular phone. He could always call his dad.

Another lightning crash. This time, a fork of lightning lanced down and hit the mountain top opposite him across the valley. A whole section of trees on the tip of the peak suddenly blazed up like a giant torch. The light from the burning trees reflected on the wavetops of the lake.

"Jeezus Christ," Brendan muttered. Lightning hit the mountainside somewhere behind him. The wind smacked into the trees around the cabin and went roaring on by. He didn't want to get up. He didn't want to walk, upright and vulnerable, under this violent sky, up into the trees and brush where even from here, he could already see flickers of light from the fire.

Thunder rolled and boomed, the wind roared in the tree branches, the waves were now banging onto the beach and the rocks. The lightning was almost continuous, crackling all around the valley. He told himself it was just a thunderstorm. They happened every summer, every year. He had lived through all of them. The lightning wasn't after him. It only hit the tops of the mountains, or big trees. Not him. He was a small and very insignificant part of it all.

He forced himself to reach for his shoes, put them on, stand up, forced himself to walk towards the fire, which had jumped up into some dry brush. As he watched, it began to lick across the ground and then jumped again into a tangled clump of alder and small cedar which exploded into flame. Shit, shit, he thought again. The south side of the small peninsula where the cabin was situated was all pine and fir. Once the fire got out of the alder gully and into the pine trees, it could make a hell of a mess.

He ran back down to the cabin, jumping rocks and stumps in the dark, found the phone after scrabbling around on the deck for it, dialed his home with shaking fingers.

Rob answered, sounding sleepy.

"Dad," Brendan said, trying to control his voice.

"Hey there, son. What's happening down there?" his Dad said. "Pretty windy here. Your mother is worried. Thinks I should come down. How does it look to you?"

"The fire's come up in the wind. It's taking off a bit," he said. He had to talk loud over the wind and the thunder. "It could get into those pines south of the cabin. It's headed that way. Doubt if it could get across the highway, but it's starting to take off." He could hear Rob yawning. There was a long silence.

"Dad?" he said doubtfully.

"Yeah, yeah, keep your shirt on. Guess I'd better come on down and take a look. Be there quick as I can." The phone line clicked. He tried to figure what had been in his dad's voice. Was it fear, or just calm reassurance? He didn't know whether he had a right to be scared, or whether, when his father showed up, he should just pretend nonchalance. After all, it was still only a small fire. The rain would show up soon. He was probably getting worked up and scared about something over which his father would just shrug.

A pine tree up the hill from the cabin suddenly exploded into flame. Brendan jumped. He began to shake all over, uncontrollably. The lightning seemed to be stabbing, stabbing, at the hillside above him, probing down blindly, looking for him. Another tree went up. Burning needles and bits of ashes and sparks blew ahead of the fire, on the wind. Where was the rain?

More and more trees were going up. The fire began to twist into a series of small tornadoes whipped by a fury of their own. A spark landed on his hair, stung as it sizzled and went out. He began to worry about the cabin, but mostly now, he was worried about his home, the whole lakeshore, what could happen if the fire really took off, got above the road, various hideous scenarios flashed through his mind, panic stricken animals, fleeing people, burning homes, people hiding from the fury of the fire by retreating to the lake, at what point should he give the alarm, start phoning everyone, call in the Forestry, the army, someone, and meanwhile, he stood here paralyzed, waiting for his father to come and save him.

Uncertainly, he started up the hill to where he knew the pumps were and stopped. The pumps were behind the fire's direction, not much use. What was needed, he thought, was a crew above the road, in fact, maybe he could take a shovel up there and put out any spot fires that might jump the road, and he started to go find a shovel, and stopped again. Not in the dark, and on that steep slope above the highway, and above the fire, he'd be trapped, helpless, if the fire did jump the pavement and come roaring up there, he'd be a fool to try to get in its way. Maybe he'd better stay here and try to save the cabin, although, what the hell, the guy was probably heavily insured and from what Brendan had heard, it was probably all his fault and he deserved to lose the place. There were sparks on the roof even now, he could see them glowing. Damn.

He began to pace back and forth and back and forth on the flat graveled turnaround just below the cabin, and because he couldn't do anything else, because he was trapped and frustrated and terrified, he began to think again of what he had read that afternoon, lying upstairs in Kathryn's sad empty house, reading Mary's journals of that long bleak winter after she had come home, of the aftermath of family dinners and parties when she had come back to her cold house and written in her journal about being lonely, suicidal, invisible, extinguished, feeling ignored by everyone, Rob, Kathryn, Arlene, the neighbours, and then how she had run out of money, and couldn't get a job, no one offered her any work at all, although she applied everywhere, and the thought, the humiliation of crawling into welfare haunted her like a nightmare, but she got through the winter somehow. Gordon sent some more money and she sold two paintings, and she lived on what she had put by from the garden, on meals at Kathryn's, and showing up at her other few friends at meal times and kept on painting.

The car needed repairs and she left it sitting in her driveway and hitchhiked everywhere. There were plenty of other people doing the same thing, so that didn't matter much, and there were plenty of places where an extra mouth for a meal was hardly noticed. Some parts of life in the valley were free and easy, in those days, but she was too old, too stubborn and too bitter to fit into the easy foolishness of hippie life, either. More and more, she stayed home, huddled in her house, gingerly feeding the stove, needing to husband the small amount of wood she had gathered.

And Kathryn and Rob and Jim and Arlene (who was only a teenager) never noticed at all, went on living their lives and assuming she was living hers, and so she did until the day she put the canoe in the water and disappeared. She had been canoeing before that day, had canoed a lot, all winter and had written about the clear and glossy surface of the water, with little ice bangles all gently cohering into a surface film through which the canoe wove a black and solitary trail. Brendon remembered that image because he thought it was so beautiful and he wished that he had thought of it himself.

Her journals got increasingly bitter and yet she wrote about how happy she was to be home, she wrote about moments of joy—about waking up to new snow, about the taste of canned peaches. She wrote about optimism, about things improving in the spring, about planting a new and bigger garden, new fruit trees, about getting some chickens. But she was bitter, and she blamed herself for all of it; over and over she reviewed her life, and all the mistakes she had made, and choices she hadn't made, and lamented all of it. She berated herself for it and for the fact that Rob never came by, and when she broke down and invited him, he came with his friends, stayed very briefly, and was polite. She stood at the window and watched his truck drive out of the yard and her heart broke and she knew it was all her fault and there was no going back.

But she hadn't given up. That had struck Brendan over and over, her fierce sense that somehow it would all come around – that she and Rob would find their way through to some kind of understanding, that she would rebuild this old neglected barren weed-sown piece of ground into some kind of thriving farm, that other people might eventually want to join her, that she would finally fit in and belong somewhere, and that even she and Kathryn might learn to speak some kind of similar language.

He lifted his head and as he did, the first raindrops hit his face. At the same time the headlights from his father's truck came down the winding driveway.

By the time his father stopped and got out of the truck, the rain was getting stronger but had not yet erupted into the solid downpour which usually came with such a storm. Instead, the wind was picking up. He waited for Rob and together they walked up through the thick smoky dark to where the fire was hissing under the impact of the rain.

Rob had to shout over the background roar of the fire. "It doesn't look too good. I'd better call Forestry, make sure they get a crew out here right away, keep them here for a few days until it's safe.

Damn close thing. If the rain doesn't come, if this wind keeps up and it jumps the highway and gets up on the mountain, we'll be in one hell of a fix. A little rain won't stop that. We'll just have to wait for a bit, see what happens."

They were both silent watching the fire."You know,"he said, "I been thinking a lot about your grandmother lately too. I mean your real grandmother, Mary."

"I'm sorry," Brendan started to say. "I shouldn't. . ."

"Oh hell, it's nothing worse than I've called myself over the years. She was so goddam beautiful. And strange. She scared hell out of me. She scared everybody. We didn't know what to say to her. So we left her alone. Too much, I guess. The hell of it is, I would have done anything for her, anything to get her to notice me, anything so as I could understand her. Anything but what she needed. Just plain and simple human comfort. So all these years, you see, I figured," his voice choked and stopped. "So all these years, I figured it was pretty much my fault that she died." He paused, went on. "I tried to read those diaries, but I couldn't do it. I just couldn't. I wanted to burn them but I couldn't do that either. So I put them away and tried to forget about them, about her. And then you look at me and you look so much like her. . ."

His voice choked off into sobs. Brendan stood frozen with horror, listening to his father, his immovable giant mountain of a father, weeping. After a while, he put his hand on his father's shoulder.

"It's okay, Dad," he said. "It's okay," which sounded stupid and insane but he couldn't think of anything else to say.

His father stopped, wiped his nose on his sleeve.

Finally Rob stirred, shifted uneasily. "Let's walk up the hill," he said, "see how close it is to the road."As they got closer to the highway, they could see the fire boiling up in a clump of small firs. As they watched, the fire raced to the top of the trees, jumped to another larger tree, which exploded, roaring and whipping in the wind.

"What'll we do?" Rob yelled. "Should we phone people, wake them up?" Brendan stared at him, startled; his father, asking his advice? Another fir exploded, and sparks from it blew across the road, landing in the brush. A flare started in the tall dry grass, then another and another.

"Go," yelled Rob, shoved Brendan. "Call everyone north of here. Get down to the lake. You'll be okay there. I'm going for the farm, get your mom up. I'll get on the phone as well, call Forestry and the cops." Together they ran back down the long dark driveway. Brendan's heart pounded in his ears. He sprinted for where he had left the phone. A phone book. He needed a phone book. His heart was still pounding and he found himself moving slowly, despite his panic. There should be a phone book in the cabin. He'd have to break in. He grabbed a board from the beach, went to the cabin, smashed a window, stepped in through the splintering, crunching glass and found a light switch. The cabin seemed calm and quiet after the chaos outside.

He found the phone book in a drawer, called the first neighbour past their farm, finally got a sleepy sounding voice. "Mr. Wilson," he said, "This is Brendan Mangerton. There's a bad fire down here at Boulder Creek. Looks like it might jump the road. My dad and I are calling to warn people."

"Oh, thanks!" said the voice, startled. "Want me to call anyone else?"

"Oh, sure," Brendan said. "Maybe call the neighbours on either side." The man said he would and then he'd have them call their neighbours. Brendan hung up, went on phoning. People reacted, were shocked, scared, but fairly calm. When Brendan phoned someone who had already been called, he hung up and went back outside.

The fire was across the road racing up the mountain, heading north. Sparks and ash drifted down towards him; he could feel the heat from the fire, crisping his skin. He retreated back down the beach to the lake. He was on his own now, the road would be closed. No one would be able to get through to pick him up except by boat. He stared at the fire, then at the sky. Perhaps it might still rain. But an effervescent gold star shone between the blue black clouds which still covered the sky like old bruises. The wind kept up. White foam curled off the tops of the waves and slithered hissing onto the sand. The wind was warm on his skin. He thought of his mother, their house and his room, and then his mind switched to the animals fleeing the mindless alien greed of the fire—of horses and cows trapped in fields surrounded by wire, of small helpless animals underground, in trees and huddled under brush. He went on staring while the fire climbed steadily up the mountain, roaring, exploding, spitting, noise like a jet plane continually taking off. He wrapped his arms around himself. He was shaking all over like a whipped dog.

Another noise broke through the roaring which enveloped him. He peered out at the water, could see a light, bobbing, disappearing again, coming towards him. It was no night to be on the lake in a boat. Some idiot was taking a huge chance; the light struggled on towards him, it was obviously coming towards him. When it got close enough, he could see his father grinning at him over the windshield. Brendan waded out into the water, jumped, caught the side, and Rob gunned the motor, backed away from the heaving wash off the beach, and they headed back towards the farm.

"Everything okay?" Brendan shouted over the engine noise.

Rob yelled back, "Forestry has a crew on the way, the bomber will be here at first light, looks like this rain is going to continue for a bit which will keep the fire down. Damn close thing. We'll all have to watch it, stay on alert, get ready to run. The RCMP is on their way; I guess they're telling people to get out. Your mom was worried sick that I left you down here."

Brendan nodded. He was still shaking. Now he was shivering as well. Rob was maneuvering the boat through the waves, quartering them. The bow of the boat slammed down hard into each wave trough, covering them with spray. More than anything else, Brendan wanted a cigarette, a joint, or both, but he still couldn't bring himself to smoke in front of his dad.

From out on the water, he could see the fire, still steadily climbing the mountain, trees exploding, the fire spreading as he watched, but going up the mountain, not north along the shore. Thank God.

By the time they made it home, Brendan was almost nodding off despite the cold and wet, looking forward to the warmth of his bed, the familiarity of his room. They crawled into the relative calm of their own bay, tied up the boat, made it up the path. But Dana met them at the door, her face white. "Don't relax yet," she said. "The hospital just called. Kathryn's got out somehow. She's escaped. Or at least they can't find her."

Section Twelve

Mary

Chapter Forty-Nine

Fall 1974, Mary is coming home at last, turning down the long drive past the faded For Sale, Lake Property sign, down past the rows of huge cedars. Getting out of the car at last, stretching. Everything familiar, even the air touching her face, familiar air. Inside, the house smells of food and her mother's magic coffee. Comfort, comfort in every black drop, gingersnaps fresh out of the oven of which she eats until she feels stretched and round and too full.

Then she goes out to the garden, the long sweet green rows, plants growing and unfolding, more food. She lingers here, grazing, greedy, gobbling; asparagus, new leaves of lettuce, strawberries. Then continues to the orchard, the peach trees, with tiny green folded globes of future sweetness, ancient apple trees, branches like twisted pythons, the secret shadowed places to hide underneath in the thick springing grass, where deer lie down at night, turning around and around to make matted round beds. She and her brother used to play there, make tunnels in the grass, become deer, or foxes, rabbits, mice, snakes.

And as always, her favourite pilgrimage, on down the path to the beach, coming out of the line of black firs into the open, the light pouring over her, over the wrinkled grey loaves of granite, folded along the edge of the water, over the sand with the creek flowing through, the long thin lines of driftwood, piled against the rocks. She sits on the rocks, staring into the green depths of water, and over the wind sheened surface, across to the mountains, blue humped familiar shapes.

Then the slow meandering back to the house, solid under the cedars and the giant walnut tree that stood there since before she can remember. And the city, vanished from memory, even Gordon, his face as she was leaving is gone, vanished behind the mountains.

Back in the house, her mother, brisk and harsh as always, her hands, long, bluish veins, wrinkled, the knuckles enlarged and purple, is washing, cooking, cleaning, feeding. Mary slumps back down at the table, pours another coffee she doesn't need, has another cookie.

"Things look good," she says. "Garden, orchard, everything's in good shape."

"We're barely keeping up," Kathryn snaps. "It's too much work. I don't know how we can keep going. Rob works so hard, and he has his school to keep up. I don't know how he does it. But it won't be for much longer. Once he graduates, he'll want to get on with his life, get a job and a place of his own. Someone phoned the other day, wanted to come look at the place. But they sounded too snooty on the phone. I told them I'd think about it."

Mary says nothing. Her head is full of hopeful resentful words. But I'm here now. I can help. She says none of them. Instead, she carefully casually changes the subject.

"Seen Jim around?" she asks.

"Oh, he still comes by now and again. Brought us wood this winter. He seems so lonely though. He needs somebody. He never got over you."

Mary sighs, "Mom, leave it, will you. Jim and I are friends."

"Well, if you're going to be seeing him, tell him to come over for Sunday dinner. Rob will be glad to see him."

"No he won't. They don't even like each other."

"Of course they do. Jim got Rob that job slashing last summer. You don't know. You haven't been here."

"I know, Ma, I know I've missed a lot. But I'm here now. I told you, I've moved back."

"Right," says her mother, "until you take it in your head to fly off somewhere else."

"I told you, it was a sudden decision. I just came. I couldn't stay in Vancouver anymore."

"Well, you've stood it for a long time. You stood it after your dad died. Didn't bother you then."

Mary takes a deep breath, held it, holds in the bright rage that rises in her throat, which flowers and rises in her belly.

"I'm here," she says very carefully. "I never really left. It's my home. I'm going to live here and paint and have some peace in my life."

"Peace!" says her mother. "This is a farm, not a damn peace camp. If you want peace, go join those silly hippies living up on Mercy Road. Not that they get much peace with all the babies they keep producing up there."

Taking a deep and heavy breath, Mary gets up and for the first time in years puts her arms around her mother, noticing her tininess, her thin bones and the tension that rises from her humming like electric wire. They stand there in the silence of the room, the good smell of food surrounding them, and hold on to each other; two women holding together inside the waves and currents of sorrow and confusion which they have made and can't evade. They break apart, embarrassed. Mary goes outside to the garden where she hangs on to the old metal gate made from an ancient thresher wheel. She hangs on, not crying, just staring at the ground until she sees Rob coming down the hill from the bus, from school. Then she hurries to pick some lettuce, kneels on the ground for just a moment before coming into the house smiling and laughing for the sake of her son.

Chapter Fifty

When Mary woke, the particular blue from the dream stayed with her and flavoured the whole length of her waking. The blue was the bright colour of the plastic tarp which, in the dream, had stretched over her head, while she had curled warm, in a kind of nest somewhere beside the old rock wall in the orchard. The rock wall was gone now, hadn't been there for years; her father had taken it down to make a larger hay field. So, for that matter, was the orchard, but in her dream, she had found a kind of hollow beside the rounded blocks of the wall protected by thistles and wild roses, a hollow as comfortable and warm as a cradle. Then a strange dog, large and black, came and sniffed her out, crawled in, wet and dog-heavy, on top of her, licking her face. But the dog gave away her hiding place. Arlene came and peered under the tarp.

"Go away," Mary yelled at her, full of rage and fear at being discovered, "go away, go away," and Arlene had gone. So then Mary could pull the blue tarp back over her space, over the hollow there at the edge of the field by the hill, and lie there in the utter relief of being finally alone in the blue peaceful light. When she looked around, she was surrounded by her tools – her paints, canvas, art books, sketches, all stacked and tumbling from shelves while she lay in the middle of it all, cocooned and warm, hidden, curled away at last from everyone's prying eyes, and interruptions and people wanting things, expecting her to do something miraculous.

Outside, in the bleak yellow field, her mother wandered, lost, calling for her, but her mother couldn't find her, not any more, not as long as she stayed, cunning, in the blue room, hidden and safe.

When she woke from the dream, she lay still, curled in a knot under the blankets, reliving its peculiar bright vividness. She wanted it back, mourned for the safety, the pervasiveness of that particularly luminous blue. Then the red ragged irritation that had been there under the surface of the dream also flooded in, her rage at silly Arlene, her rage at her mother. The voice with which she had tried to blast Arlene and all the rest of them away boiled inside her.

Why did they always have to show up and drive her crazy? God, she wanted to be back there, if it were only possible, alone under the blue light with everything important in her life surrounding her, and her mother's voice fading away over the yellow hay stubble.

But even as the dream receded, as she curled herself in the warm hollow in the middle of the ancient sagging mattress in the cold room, the state she was in, a state she would just as soon have forgotten about, flooded in, inexorable, a needling, nagging presence, reminding her of all the things she had kept at bay by sleeping.

The house was freezing. She could tell that from the numbness on the tip of her nose, now poked above the covers. It was late fall, time, to start dealing with fires and kindling, wood and ashes.

She had better get a fire going or she would be chilled all day. Her knees hurt when she pushed herself up, and swung her legs over the side of the bed into the cold air, descending bit by bit into the air as into cold lake water. Finally then she stood upright, straightened herself with an effort, threw the ancient yellow chenille bedspread over her shoulders and around her sagging breasts, and sagging sad aching forty-four year old body and stomped, creaking, she swore she could hear her damn knees creaking, down the stairs. She put the kettle on, split kindling, lit the stove, made coffee , and stood over the stove while it warmed up. She gulped her own terrible coffee, cutting its bitterness with a heavy dose of cream, listened to the radio and watched the grey light over her mother's pasture, as the morning dragged itself into motion.

My mother, she thought to herself. My mother, but nothing went any further than that. She didn't want to think about her mother; her mother was just there, a presence, like weather, unpredictable and all pervasive.

Quite suddenly, then, she remembered another part of the dream, which she had forgotten, where she had accused her mother of killing her cat, a cat she'd had as a pet when she was little. Her father was there as well, and they had both nodded. Of course they'd killed the cat, as they had all the right to do and Mary no room to disagree.

And that was the point in the dream, she remembered even further, where, vengefully, even gleefully, she'd told her mother she thought about killing herself, thought about it every night as she went to sleep and every morning just as she was waking up, told her that it was her comfort and her litany, that the possibility of dying kept her alive every morning for one more day. She told her how she thought of death as a stiletto of shining glass, shaped like an awl, but bright, shining and thin. It glided into her heart, effortlessly and with no pain, and stopped all the grief and noise there forever.

When the feel of the dream finally faded, the day became an ordinary day. After coffee, after the house had warmed up and the frost had gone off the grass, she went out in search of the last of the elderberries, thinking she could at least make juice or jelly, something useful. She shambled past the stupid dead car in the driveway which she couldn't afford to fix, plodded, increasingly wet footed in her worn running shoes, from corner to corner along the outside edge of the pasture fence. She clipped off the dusty blue clumps of elderberries, which were beginning to wither and shedding berries with each touch, then came back to the house with them. It was already noon, she noted with surprise. Somewhere the morning had drifted away without her noticing.

She ate some crackers and cheese, then left the elderberries sitting and went back outside. The grey heavy lidded clouds had lifted, temporarily, and thin bright sun poked down through holes and lit up patterns on the mountains, gold and pale grey blue patched with white where the first snow had already come and stayed to settle in, gilded light on the alder and maple and the blazing yellow tamaracks.

She picked some late flowers in what was left of the tangled ancient garden. There were still chrysanthemums, and even some buds on the roses. Then she went inside and sat down, staring out the window and the heaviness that had been waiting for her all day came and sat on her shoulders, crushing her down into the old burgundy chair with stuffing growing out of the arms like lichen. She sat there for a long time, listening to the clock tick in the kitchen and the metal in the stove clicking and creaking as the stove cooled off.

Finally, moving like a blind person, she got up, got her sketchbook and began doodling shapes of leaf and shadow clusters, trying to see the shapes and the relationship between them, page after page. She drew steadily for a couple of hours, while the light changed and shifted, grew dull, opaque, until finally she noticed that the house was cold and she was hungry. She got up, stretched and went to split wood while the evening came down around her.

For a moment, she thought she might call her mother, maybe even run across the pasture for dinner. There was always food there. Her mother always made sure there was extra food in the house because someone was always dropping in to eat it. She had hardly any food left. A bit more of the crackers and cheese. Some noodle soup. Some frozen ancient vegetables in the fridge freezer. Butter, popcorn, coffee and tea. Her staples.

But irritation rose again in her throat and nose and on up into her forehead between her eyes, until she could barely see. No, she thought, I won't go, I won't go over there, and watched her rage dance and shimmer over the bare dry pasture.

She thought how peaceful it must look to someone from the outside, the twilight sifting down over the gold burgundy shaded colours of fall, while in reality, over these fields, invisible battles and torments and agonies raged and rang. She could almost see her the confusion of her feelings about her mother, floating like black smoke towards her house. Kathryn was thinking about her again. She knew she was. Thinking of more good advice to give her. Probably found her a totally unsuitable job somewhere with someone she'd never work for in a million years. No, she couldn't go over there. It was easier to go hungry.

Instead, she lit her fire and sat down again by the window. When it was finally dark, the deer came into her yard; she could barely see them, dark shapes, drifting like shadows under the apples trees, looking for the last windfalls.

The house was silent, shadows gathered around the fire, which spat and crackled softly in its iron box. There was no other sound. There was no one else anywhere. Bitterness seeped from the walls like water, burned her skin like acid. For the thousandth time, she wondered what she was going to do with winter coming on so fast, no money except the little that trickled in here and there. She might sell a painting. There was always that ridiculous mocking possibility of selling something, or she could ask for help. If Gordon or Elaine knew what a lousy time she was having, they might help. Or Kathryn or Jim or even Rob. They might. But they'd know then, too, the mistake she'd made.

She began to play with her favourite dream, the dream of swimming and swimming, the dream of being alone, in the dark, in the water, not drowning exactly, but no longer part of the world, no long weighted down by it, swimming like flying, wondering if she would ever have the courage to do it, to swim and swim, to somehow swim free of the demons and problems surrounding her. She sat on the floor, her head in her hands, rocking and rocking.

Chapter Fifty-One

By the middle of December, it was obvious that she would need more wood, a lot more wood. That was one problem.

There were lots of problems, none of which she could seem to do much about. There was the car, which needed brakes and tires and a new battery, which she couldn't afford. Hitchhiking was all right in the summer; in the winter, it was crazy. Kathryn let her borrow the truck, sometimes, but if she borrowed it too often she had to hear the whole lecture about what a waste of time and gas and money it was to be running off to town all the time for nothing important.

She had applied to every business in town for job. After a while, she got the message. No one was going to hire her. No one phoned her back. No one even mentioned her applications.

Then there was the whole business of food. She had stored some. But it was hard to make a dinner out of a plastic bag of frozen beans. You needed butter and almonds and really high quality rice and perhaps some chicken and a bottle of wine. That was dinner. At first, she had tried for a while, well, a pretty short while, to live without eating meat, without drinking tea and coffee, without white sugar. She had drunk, instead, endless cups of herb tea after which she immediately wanted a cigarette and an entire pot of very strong coffee. Kathryn laughed at her, made sure she had coffee on and perking whenever she saw Mary heading across the field to her house, made sure, when Mary came by just before mealtimes, to have steaks laid out or a pork roast in the oven, or raspberry pies cooling, or an angel food cake in the pantry.

For a while, Mary ate there almost every night. Her mother was lonely; there was always too much food and Rob seemed to hardly ever be home. Then she did the dishes and watched TV and came home over the dark fields. After a while, she stopped going over for meals. She sat in her kitchen and ate plain rice and steamed broccoli and watched the lights from her mother's window and the glint of water from the lake. Somehow, her own loneliness seemed more bearable than her mother's loneliness. Mary had no TV. In the evenings, she lay on the floor and read, or drew things, or simply lay there in the silence until she was tired enough to go to bed. Sometimes she wrote letters to Gordon. After a while, he wrote her a polite note asking her to please not write anymore as he was seeing someone else and he didn't think it was such a good idea. She tore the letter in two and threw it in the stove. She sat on the floor by the stove for a long time, her head on her knees, holding on to her legs with her arms and hands.

Christmas came. Mary had no money to buy presents or a turkey. She made things. She thought she might give Rob a painting, and she worried for weeks over whether that was a good idea and finally she picked her most recent painting, a vivid pastiche of colour, and wrapped it in newspaper. She traded another painting at the craft store in town for a carved wooden candle holder for Kathryn and a jewelry box for Arlene, and she went to Christmas day at Kathryn's carrying her presents and a couple of jars of canned beans and they had a nice enough day . Then Mary came home and stared into her fire and thought again of Rob's polite face when he saw the painting, how he had laid it aside, how Arlene had looked at the box and said, puzzled, "But what's it for?" and how Kathryn had put the candleholder on a shelf, with no comment at all.

After that the snow fell and fell, in tangled snarling coils that drove Mary inward and inward. It left her sitting dazed and chilled beside the small dwindling fire in her stove. Day after day, she stayed home, stayed inside, only went out for trips to the woodpile, and back in. She hung blankets over all the doors and windows, moved a sleeping bag and foamie into the living room beside the stove and lived in two rooms. She had no energy to paint, no energy to do much of anything. She had congealed and frozen into ruts, like the muddy ground of her garden, like the icy slope of her driveway. It was impossible to believe there would ever be heat in the world again, that she would be warm enough to lie on the grass, to walk around outside in the air in only shirtsleeves and jeans. Kathryn phoned every day but everyone else she knew seemed to have disappeared. She heard Rob's truck pull out every morning as he left for work, saw him come back at night, saw him go in and out doing chores. Her bathroom was too cold for baths; she couldn't even stand the thought of washing her hair. She sat in her greasy sawdust littered living room, and tried to keep warm, waiting for spring.

Jim came by. She made him coffee and they sat at her table and tried to talk. She was ashamed of her littered house and her greasy hair. She wanted to tell him about her nights when she lay under all the blankets she could gather, listening to the walls tick and creak in the cold. She wanted to tell him about the fear that crept in under the blankets and kept her huddled there, but she said nothing. She smiled and made conversation. He didn't stay long.

She got through January and then February, and March teased and tortured with sudden days of warmth and light and then long weeks of rain and mud and green sprouts appearing from under the mats of leaves in the garden. She began to draw and she wrote long hopeful letters to Elaine and waited for spring.

Which came. Which came with a rush and an uplifting uprushing sudden warmth and birdcalling and water running down the gravel litter pavement. People came out of their houses, dazed and lifting their faces and walking around, bent over, amazed and thrilled over small discoveries, snowdrops, and tulip leaves and the tiny swelling buds on forsythia and lilac. They stood talking outside their houses, or at the mailbox, or wherever they found themselves.

Mary walked around and around outside her house, carrying her teacup, peering under bushes. She found violets, daffodils in unexpected places; tiny yellow flowers she had never seen before that had sprouted through the last crusts of leftover snow. One day, she agreed to come to Kathryn's for dinner, and she ate and ate, drank wine after supper, leafed through the new spring catalogues, discussed gardening and went home through the soft dusk, feeling more hopeful than she had felt for as long as she could remember.

But she was frantic about money. Still frantic about money. She hadn't believed that she had lived this long with no money. Bits of money trickled in; she got another cheque from a gallery in Vancouver. Elaine had sent her money for Christmas. Kathryn tried to give her money for work on the farm but she decided she hadn't gotten that desperate yet. The fear of no money was a black hole with no bottom; it was the biggest part of what kept her awake at night. It made her fearful of the mail, of bills coming in, of phone calls from people wanting to be paid, of going anywhere, doing anything.

Things had snowballed over the winter into larger difficulties. She ran out of paint and canvas; she couldn't afford to send paintings to galleries, she couldn't afford to make phone calls, she stopped going to town, she stopped calling people she knew, she stayed on the farm and felt the world going away from her, going on without her, leaving her. But when she thought of going to Vancouver again, her heart sank.

But as spring came, as she walked and sketched, she began to feel more hopeful. One morning in April, she got a call from the gallery to which she had sent paintings, asking if she would consider getting together enough work for a whole show. That same afternoon, she got a call from someone she barely knew asking if she would come to a meeting in the town to help form an arts organization.

She let Kathryn loan her enough money to buy paints and canvas and food in return for helping to put in the garden. She worked through her days with feverish energy. She painted in the morning, gardened in the afternoon, and late in the day, she went canoeing on the still frigid waters of the lake.

She went through her days, frantic but singing. More money came from the gallery owner in Vancouver, enough to pay her phone bill, enough to let her buy some groceries, enough to let her think that there was a chance, a chance that things were finally, finally, getting better.

She watched the water creep higher in the lake; she sat in the sun and combed her red hair and sang as she dug in the garden, planted the new rows of peas and spinach and broccoli. In early May, the seeds sprouted, the grass was thick and green, tiny belled strawberries began to show on the plants, the gallery sent yet more money and Mary began to let hope creep into her heart.

In late May, the weather turned hot. Mary worked in the garden at Kathryn's and came home and ate supper, watching the lake and the mountains. This summer, she had decided to sell fruit and vegetables from the farm at the market in town. She would make another effort to get a waitress job in the fall. Or maybe she could give painting classes to the children of the women in the artist's guild.

The lake was high, full of brown water, littered with slowly drifting rafts of broken trees and twigs and reeds which had come down the river. In the late afternoon, she went to the beach. When she went to put the canoe in the water, she hesitated, as she always did. The water almost covering the whole beach, was burning cold. When she was a kid, she and Colin loved this time of the year, spending hours along the beach, looking through the driftwood, sometimes making rafts or simply finding logs that were long and flat enough to serve as quasi-canoes, which they paddled with sticks or fragments of boards. Because the water was so cold, they had to keep their feet balanced on the top of the logs but they never tipped over. They simply grew expert at balancing.

She pushed the canoe out and stepped into it, careful not to let the water come over the tops of her heavy rubber boots. After pushing off, she always had this momentary exhilaration, this sense of freedom flying free from the land, of serenity and floating peacefully on the flat silver surface of the lake. She noticed that water was seeping more freely than usual into the bottom of the canoe. Well, it was old and getting rotten, decaying, and needing to be replaced. Only it couldn't be replaced, of course, because all such things cost money, and the way things were going, she was never going to have very much.

Well, but who knew, maybe she would, someday, when some collector, some brilliant rich person saw her paintings and fell in love with them, some brilliant rich person. They would drive up to her door someday, chequebook in hand, come into her ratty old house, look at her work, and transform her life with money, money, money.

And then the town, the community of small minded narrow ignorant assholes who ran everything and wouldn't give her the time of day, the people who wouldn't give her a job and the morons who looked at her paintings in the craft store and said snidely to each other, "But what is it?" would realize what idiots they'd been all along. Reluctantly, they'd have to face the fact that they had ignored a kind of greatness living in their midst. They'd have to acknowledge her somehow. She'd be nice about it, the surest way of making them eat dirt would be her own graciousness, and the fact that she didn't have to care one iota about what they thought because the outside world, the big world, the real world, the one that counted, would be at last singing her praises.

The air was clear and hot and she could smell the water. Normally, she stayed fairly close to shore in the canoe, always fearful that a wind could come up, catch the high sides of the canoe and she'd have to fight her way home through it. But today the lake lay smooth as glass; the lake was her friend, her sister, and the mountains were old smiling grandmothers. Her heart lifted and swelled within her and she began to sing as she paddled, trying to open her eyes as wide as she could, to take in the colours and textures and swirling masses of light and shadow all around her until they came into her like music, like the softest and most delicious of food.

Winter was long gone, and the summer was soon coming upon her and even though nothing real had changed in her life, even though she still had no money and Rob still ignored her, in fact he had a new girlfriend she hadn't even met yet, and she still couldn't get a job, and she'd have to do a ton of work if she was going to survive the next winter and she still had no idea how she was going to survive here for the long term and Jim was ignoring her as well, because he had a new girlfriend, what the hell. She looked outward, the patterns that had made up her life swirled around her, but she had survived. She had won.

She turned the canoe towards the center of the lake following an arrow of light that moved ahead of her; dancing, sparking glints of light. She had survived. What was it her mother had said? Her mother said over and over, the only thing that mattered was to get by, to survive. She never said anything that really mattered, nothing about beauty or love or friendship or trying to care for one another. No wonder Rob passed her by like a stranger. He'd been brought up to be normal, to work, to kill things, to hide his feelings, to be a block of concrete.

The world would be an easier place without her mother in it. Without her mother, she would be free. Without her mother, the ghosts that haunted her would leave. Without her mother, she'd be free to breathe in this world, without looking over her shoulder, with no one to please and no one to fear.

She drove the paddle deep into the water pushing the canoe faster and faster. There was the farm; she could live there by herself. She could farm and paint. She would be alone except for Rob. Maybe someday she would finally find someone to talk to about that day in the cabin in the woods, someone to tell about the suffocating terror that covered her every time's Gordon's weight came down over her chest and belly. Maybe someday she would be able to let it go, maybe someday she would let it all go. Maybe someday she would even open that deepest and darkest of places, the place she'd long ago stopped thinking about; how had she done it, let that man steal her life, her chances. She'd never stop looking for him. She would recognize him again in an instant. Sometimes she wondered what she would do if she saw him again. Kill him, probably, somehow.

She heard the bump before she saw anything, and then she saw that the crack in the bottom of the canoe had broken wide open, and the dark water was swelling up in it like blood. She looked down, unbelieving and saw the stub of the branch sticking through the hole. She had driven the canoe over a stub of branch on a log floating just under the surface of the water. She hadn't been looking, she'd been dreaming.

She looked back, shore was far away, farther than she realized. The sun beat down on her head. The water seeped inexorably into the canoe and she realized that she would have no choice at all but to swim for the bitter futility of the shore, try dragging the canoe with her, try making it to shore before the cold got her, before the water ate her up like a cold grey shark. The best thing to do would be to turn the canoe over, get on top of it, and try to drift with it into shore.

But it was too cold and her hands kept slipping. The bottom of the canoe was slippery with algae. Her hands and legs hurt too much. She couldn't stand it. She had to get to shore. She had to get warm. She had to get back to Rob, back to Kathryn, back to the beckoning promise of land.

She hurt too much to think. She let go and began to swim, heavy handed and awkward, and as she sank into the black water, she remembered desperately, she had forgotten to take off her heavy rubber boots.

Section Thirteen

Kathryn

Chapter Fifty-Two

It was dark outside the hospital and cold. Kathryn wrapped her arms around herself, trying to stop the shaking. She stood under a tree, a Douglas fir, leaning against it for support, watching the lights from the hospital. But the sense of urgency that had gotten her out of her bed, given her strength to pull her old sweat shirt and pants on over her hospital gown, gotten her outside past the temporarily empty nurse's station deserted her. She leaned against the tree, afraid to sit down, afraid her legs would fail and she would never get up again, or that she would descend into that darkness which had overwhelmed her again and again in the hospital.

She remembered her vivid dreams of another place, another time, of her grandmother, the fire by the hearth and the music skirling over heather covered hills. She lost herself for a while in reverie, beginning to follow the path again that led to the dark pool of water, but then she remembered, she had something else to do, something urgent, something to do with Mary, who was lost and crying for her, as she had cried and cried at every little thing when she was a toddler, clung to Kathryn's legs and cried and refused to be comforted, until Kathryn, in exasperation, gave her a swat and made her sit in a corner where she sobbed herself into exhaustion.

But she never would, Kathryn remembered. She never would be quiet. When she got older, she began to run away instead. Kathryn would have to go look for her, march her back in the house, both of them in a sullen fury at the other. She'd usually find her just before it got dark, leaning against the back porch, sitting in the dust under the walnut tree or out in the barn with the red mare.

She had to get somewhere, somewhere far away, back to the farm, that much she remembered, had to get away from this horrible building which shone and reeked of fear and death. If she could get to the farm, if she could get to her house, to the sanctuary of her kitchen, her chair at the table, her stove, her blue teapot, her garden, the old cat rubbing her legs, the pictures of Mary and Colin and Bill hanging on the walls, the ticking of the grandfather clock in the hallway, the rocking chair that had been her mother's, the braided rag rug she had made from Mary and Colin's outgrown childhood clothes—all the artifacts of her life without which she had no life.

She pushed herself away from the tree, and began to walk down the hill, turned and went down the alley, past the sleeping houses, the dreaming flower-filled gardens and back yards, the hedges and parked cars and garages and the occasional suspicious dog. She walked slowly, furious at her shuffling feet, still stuck in ridiculous pink slippers, at her wobbling legs and her shaky hands. When, when had she gotten this old, this feeble, this helpless?

She made it for several blocks, and then exhaustion rolled over her again like a dark wave and she stumbled across someone's lawn to a wooden garden swing under a huge black fir. A little black and white dog with fuzzy ears and a matted tail came growling and cringing and sniffing at her drooping hand, and then retreated back to a doghouse under the people's porch. The sky was now grey, rather than black. She thought she would just rest a few minutes and then push on.

"And how are you going to get to the farm, you silly old bat?" she asked herself out loud, trying to sit up a little straighter and not creak the swing, and not wake anybody up who might be a little concerned at finding some lost and senile old woman swinging in their backyard. She remembered a dream she used to have when she was a child, a dream of not being able to get home, of walking and walking down a strange road, trying to find the road to her house, or finding it and then finding it blocked by a landslide, or a rushing river, or some other kind of obstacle. It had been the most terrifying nightmare of her childhood, and now she was living it. She began to wonder if she was really awake or if this was just some other variation of that ancient dream, in which case, she wanted more than anything else to wake up and find herself in the small attic room she had shared with her sister when she was a child. She remembered that room so clearly—the rough board floor, the tiny dusty window, the green and red patchwork quilts their grandmother had made for them, the pink flannel pajamas they wore at night, the cold in the winter, the sound and sour smell of her pee puddling into the bucket they kept in the corner.

And her mother, calling through the floor to come for breakfast. Her mother wrapped in her ancient worn-thin blue robe, would be making the oatmeal for breakfast, always oatmeal and sometimes boiled eggs or biscuits. They never had fruit in the winters; they couldn't afford it. They had apples, which shriveled and finally froze in the small root cellar outside across the yard. Then there was nothing green or fresh, the monotony of boiled cabbage or carrots or turnips, canned tomatoes, canned beans—canned everything.

She was so tired. Oh God, she thought. I want to go home, she said, still talking out loud. She got herself up and on her feet again, wandered out of the yard and back into the alley. "I want to go home," she mumbled indignantly to herself. "You can't keep me in that damn place. I'm going home. I am, I am, I am going home."

Chapter Fifty-Three

"What the hell?" Rob said. "Disappeared? Jeezus H. Bloody Christ. The old bat. You mean they just let her walk out of there. Well, have they at least looked for her, done anything at all? Useless idiots."

He rubbed a hand over his face, shook his head. Brendan just stood there, beside him, stupefied, with his mouth open, like someone half awake.

Dana's hair was standing up on end, her face was bare of make-up; she had wrapped herself in her pink housecoat, but her feet were bare. "All they said was she had disappeared and they wanted to know what we wanted them to do, if they should call the police, or if one of us had taken her."

"Taken her?" Rob turned away in fury. He was yelling now. "Taken her! Good God, what kind of idiots run that place. Us take her. Why would we take her? Do they think we're into kidnapping our own bloody relatives. Of course they should call the police. She could have fallen down, broken something, be lying in pain somewhere. She might have died out there, all alone, with no one around." He spun around, grabbed the door handle, just as Dana grabbed his arm.

"The road's been closed, you idiot," she said. "I had the radio on. They said they'd let local people through. You just have to wait. You've got to calm down a bit. You're not much use to anyone in this state. You're totally exhausted. I'll pour you a coffee, and I'll run and throw some clothes on. We'll drive down and see if we can get through. Brendan can stay here and keep an eye on things and listen for the phone."

"Calm down, eh?" he said, with fury. "Sure, easy for you to be calm. She's not your mother."

"She's not yours either." Silence fell in the room, heavy and thick.

Finally, moving heavily, like someone in pain, Rob sat down at the table. Dana poured coffee and put it in front of him.

"It's the time of year, isn't it. It's the same time of year. Twenty-one years ago." He put his head in his hands.

"I'll be dressed in a moment," Dana said, and headed for the stairs. Brendan wanted to leave too. He kept having the feeling they were all trapped in some terrible television drama, with people entering and exiting according to some prearranged script, and that sooner or later, it would all start to make sense.

Dana came back downstairs; she went to Rob, put her arms around him and they held on to each other. Moving together, they went out the door, got in the truck and drove away. Brendan poured himself coffee. He hated the taste of coffee but he felt he had better stay awake. He had better be responsible. He sank into the chair by the phone. The coffee sat untasted on the table. His chin sank onto his chest and his eyes closed.

It was dawn, thin light seeping down from the clear sky. The storm had gone. Rob drove the truck and Dana sat beside him and held his hand as she had when they were young and going together, when she first saw the life they could build together, when she knew that with Rob she could have all the things she'd always wanted, and the idea filled her with passionate energy. She'd known, even then, exactly what she wanted, had a scrapbook full of house pictures, knew, even then, she could have strong children, that she would feed them properly, they'd look up to her.

They came to the fire site. Cars were parked along the road and people were staring up at the burning mountain. Smoke was roiling up from it in huge brown furious lumps. A RCMP officer was stopping cars on the road. They pulled up, the cop came over. Rob explained. At first the guy shook his head, then shrugged, waved them through. They went on, passed a forestry crummy, full of men in hard hats, driving towards the fire, and Rob waved, sighed in relief.

Dana sighed too, shuddering, "Is it going to be all right?"

"The fire's gone up the hill," he said. "It's going to take a while to get it slowed down. They'll bomb hell out of it all day. But if the wind stays down, we're probably all right. Sure as hell hope so."

"Rob," Dana said after a while. "She hates that damned hospital. She's afraid of it. She hates the feel of it. She hates feeling helpless. After all, she's been so tough and strong her whole life. Better she should be with us. We can bring her things over from the house so it feels more familiar."

"All right," he said. After a while, he added, "Thanks." Then he said, "You know, Brendan's been reading her diaries, Mary's, I mean. He called me a bastard last night. He thinks it was my fault she died."

"Of course it wasn't," Dana said, her voice sharp and tight.

"Yeah, it was."

They drove in silence. There was a lot of traffic, people going to look at the fire.

"I never knew the whole story, just that my dad was someone she met, some useless bum, according to Kathryn, and he disappeared and there she was, seventeen and pregnant and terrified. She never had a chance, after that. She never belonged here . . . she never belonged anywhere else."

"And now there's Brendan," he added heavily. "Kathryn always says how much he looks like Mary. I don't want him wasting his life, wondering who the hell he's supposed to be and never getting it straight. And those friends of his. . . useless idiots. He keeps saying he's going to Vancouver. Wonder how much longer he'll actually stick around? Maybe it's the best thing, he should go, learn a little about reality. Here he's always got us to run to if things get really tough."

"Can't you do something, Rob? Get him some work here for the summer?"

"He's no damn logger. Cut his fool head off the first day. No, he's going to go his own way and God knows where that'll be. But at least he has a home to come back to, if he needs it or if he wants it."

"Your oldest son's girlfriend is pregnant, you know," she said.

"That's what we were going to announce the other night, when I made dinner."

"Christ, I'm sorry, Dana. I was just pissed off, is all, fed up with things, worried about Kathryn, you know. Pregnant. Jeezus, are we ready for this? Are we that damned old?"

"I know," she said. "I do know . . . you're still going to have to talk to Kathryn about the will."

"Yeah, yeah," he said. "If we find her. Where the hell could she have got to?"

"Not far," she said. "Not in the kind if shape she was in. Unless someone picked her up. But surely they'd figure out who she is and come tell us, or phone the cops or something."

They drove in silence, swaying to the familiar curves and twists of the road. It was light now, barely light, but light enough, as they neared the town, to see the slight determined figure shuffling its way along beside the pavement.

"Oh Jeez," Rob sighed, drove past, swung the truck around, pulled up beside Kathryn who refused to look at them but shuffled along with her head up. Finally, he pulled ahead and parked and both he and Dana got out of the truck and came up to Kathryn.

"I'm going home," she said. "Don't put me in that place again."

"No, we won't, Mom," Dana said. "You're coming home with us. You can stay with us until you're feeling better."

"Have you seen my Mary?" Kathryn asked. "Do you know my Mary? I was going to meet her. She was at the beach."

Dana and Rob looked at each other.

"No, we haven't seen her," they said together. They all got back in the truck and Kathryn fell asleep almost immediately. Rob put his arm around her thin light body, and held her, drove with one hand, while the tears ran and dripped down his cheeks unchecked.

Chapter Fifty-Four

"I'm going," Brendan announced the next morning. "I'm getting out of this dump. I'm going to Vancouver."

He'd gotten up late and then he had gone in to see his great grandmother. She was sleeping when he came in but she woke up when he sat on the bed and touched her hand. He leaned over and kissed her cheek. She smiled.

"Grandma," he whispered. "Grandma. Are you okay?

"You're an idiot," she whispered. He winced. Her voice was hoarse. Dana or Rob might hear and come to see. "Of course I'm not okay. I'm dying. Never done it before. I thought I would hate it, but I'm tired. I'm so tired . . ." Her voice trailed off.

"Grandma, I'm going to go away for a little while," he said. "I'm not sure how long."

She studied his face."You're leaving? Why?"

"I just have to for a while. I can't stay here and I can't stay at your house. I'll be around if you need me."

"No, you won't," she said. "You're leaving me too. Brendan, don't go. Stay with me."

"I can't."

"You think life is some kind of adventure," she snorted. Her voice was a hoarse whisper. "You think you're going to discover something. You're not. Life isn't about discovering anything. It's about surviving. It's about surviving and family and helping each other and getting by on what you have. Why are you going?"

"Because," he said. "Because there has to be more than that. There has to."

"Go then," she said peevishly. "Don't listen to anyone. I'm ninety-one. What the hell do I know ? Go. I'll bless you for it but I won't forgive you."

Brendan's eyes filled. "I love you, Grandma," he said. "You're the best."

"Yeah, yeah," she said. "I'm the best but I'm old and worn out and useless now. Go," she said. "Get out of here. I'm tired. I have to sleep." She closed her eyes and when her breathing was regular, he stood up and crept backwards out of the room.

Rob had gotten up after an hour's sleep, done the chores, driven down to check on the progress of the firefighters, and had now come in the kitchen, whistling and cheerful. He checked to see that Kathryn was still asleep upstairs. Then, after a while, Dana had taken her a tray and she had drunk a bit of tea and gone back to sleep. Dana had phoned the hospital and talked to Kathryn's doctor, who sounded so pissed off that they weren't bringing her back right away that he barely said anything. Dana fumed as she slammed the phone down, and went out to the kitchen to make pancakes for lunch.

Now they were all sitting at the table together while the sun shone in the windows and lit up their faces. They were silent after Brendan's announcement. He kept his head down, wouldn't look at them. He was thinking about Johnnie. He needed to get to Johnnie's house, he needed to talk to him. He wanted Johnnie to come with him, but if he wouldn't, he'd go alone. He'd hitchhike. He'd decided that now. He had a couple of hundred dollars which wasn't anything, but it would have to do.

The silence stretched on. Finally Rob stretched.

"There's your grandma," he said. "What about her?"

"Fuck you," said Brendan. "Don't lay that shit on me." He got up, left the room and they heard his footsteps on the stairs.

Rob put his head in his hands, felt the tears start and shook them off. Not again, he thought. I'm not crying again.

Dana stood up, poured them both more coffee, sat again.

"Kathryn seemed better this morning."

"Yeah, it's good she's here. I'll tackle her about the will, Dana, as soon as she's a bit more awake. You were right about that."

"He'll come back, Rob. He's eighteen. He doesn't know a damn thing. He's just mad about everything. Although I don't know why he's so damn mad at us. All we've done is give him everything he wanted, his whole life."

"Maybe that's the problem, we were just too good to him. So now he thinks the world owes him something."

The steam from the coffee rose up and bathed their faces and mingled with the dust motes dancing in the sunlight which poured in the windows like melted butter. They sat on and on, waiting for something. Then the front door slammed and the logs of the house shook and rang from the impact.

"Bastard," said Rob. "If he thinks he can just waltz in and out of here whenever he feels like it, he'd better think again. He's in for a good dose of reality, that one. Wait until he's on the road somewhere, cold and hungry and shit out of luck."

"At least it's summer."

"Yeah," said Rob, "it's summer, it's bloody hot and dry and someone's got to keep things watered and weeded or we can kiss the garden good-bye." He stood up, stretched.

"Did you forget what I told you last night? About Luke? Grampa."

"Makes me feel old," he said, putting on his hat by the back door.

"You'll get used to it," she said. "I'll call, see if they can come for dinner."

Outside the lake was deep blue under the wind, light bouncing and skittering in a giddy glitter across the wave tops. Despite the distant threat from the fire, the valley was green and blue, round and safe and enclosed, like a giant bowl sitting full of ripe round fruit on someone's kitchen table, holding everything that anyone could ever need; the alfalfa was coming up, an emerald and purple fuzz in Kathryn's field. The garden blazed with flowers. The raspberry canes were also in bloom, buzzing and vibrating with bees like a row of green rockets about to take off. The lawn needed cutting and he had better get some irrigation going on the hayfield or there wouldn't be any hay. He'd better get moving. Instead, he sat on a rock under the walnut tree, an offspring of the one in Kathryn's yard, closed his eyes and let the sun warm him, warm his bones and blood. He closed his eyes and sat on and on.

From far away, he could hear the phone ringing. It rang and rang but he couldn't move himself to answer it. He heard Dana's footsteps on the stairs inside the house, a distant rapid thumping, like a drumbeat. Then the screen door creaked and Dana came across the lawn to where he was sitting. He went on sitting, staring at the lawn, at the grass, at her feet coming towards him in their brisk sandals, her slim brown ankles. Finally, with great effort, he raised his eyes.

"It's your Uncle Colin," she said. Her voice was flat and weary with resignation. "He's at the bus station. He wants to be picked up."

He tried to lever himself to his feet and realized at that moment how tired he was. He'd been up all night, he hadn't slept much the previous two nights. His legs and back ached.

"You have to talk to Kathryn before he gets here," she said. Her voice was shrill. "It's ours. It should be ours."

"Oh, c'mon," Rob said. "You don't know what`s going to happen. You don't know what Colin's got planned. You don't even know what's in Kathryn's will, or if she's got a will. At least give the guy a chance. We haven't seen him for years. We don't know what he thinks about anything."

He rubbed his forehead. "Maybe I can grab a nap this afternoon. He's at the bus station?"

"So he said."

"What'll I do if I see Brendan hitching? Put him on the bus as Colin is getting off, I guess." He got heavily to his feet. "I'll grab a coffee to take with me." He went off to the house, putting his feet down heavily and slowly, like an unconscious parody of an old man walking.

Chapter Fifty-Five

Colin lumbered heavily across the kitchen and sank into a chair. He had thickened and sagged and grown grey since they had last seen him, after Mary's death. He had never come home again after that long two weeks, although he sent Christmas cards and occasional postcards from the southern US in the winter. Dana poured him coffee.

"God, what a night," he groaned. "No sleep, some damn kid crying."

He held the cup in both hands. "So, you two are looking good."

"Can't complain," Rob said. Dana put a plate of cookies on the table and Colin grabbed two of them. He stuffed them in his mouth, one after the other, then slurped at his coffee. It spilled on the table but he didn't notice.

"Work going good, eh?" he said. "Got a nice new truck, I see."

"I've had it a while, Uncle Colin," Rob said. "I'll probably have to replace it soon."

Dana wondered when he would actually ask about Kathryn. He finished his coffee and held up his cup like she was a waitress. She poured him a second cup.

"Excuse me," Dana said. "I've got to catch up on my chores."

She went upstairs into her bedroom, began making her bed. She had already made up the other room with fresh sheets. After a while, she heard his footsteps on the stairs. He blundered into Kathryn's room. Dana went and stood behind him.

"Hey Ma, how're ya doing?" He sank onto the bed. Kathryn's eyes flickered open then closed again. Colin patted her hand and stood up.

"Guess she needs to sleep," he said. "I won't bother her now."

He went back downstairs. Dana finished making her bed and went downstairs. He was back at the kitchen table still drinking coffee. The plate of cookies was empty.

"God, you wouldn't believe what the bus costs these days," he said. "It used to be cheap. The seats are like iron. My back feels like hell. Well, maybe I'll go take a nap."

"I'll call you for lunch," Dana said.

After lunch, Colin went back upstairs to sleep some more. Rob fell asleep in his chair in the living room. Dana cleaned up and then slipped quietly out the back door. She went across the sun warmed hayfield to Kathryn's house.

"Why did he even come?" she had said bitterly to Rob after Colin went upstairs.

"He's her son," Rob said.

"He wants her money, what there is of it. He wants the land. He has some nerve, showing up now, after he ignored her all these years."

"He's not so bad," Rob said. "He just, well, he made a different kind of life for himself. Maybe it hurt to come back, after Mary died."

"Sure," Dana snapped, "and maybe his own mother could have used a little help now and again, instead of always having to lean on you."

Rob got up. "Got stuff to do," he mumbled. "Gotta get some water on that garden."

Now Dana was on her way to Kathryn's house to look for the will. It was obvious Rob was never going to say or do anything. It was obvious, even dying, that Kathryn still had too much power for him to wander into her room and ask her even something as simple as if she had a will.

"The old bitch," Dana said out loud. She was so fed up, pissed off, and worn out.

She'd given Kathryn's old house a good cleaning, spent a whole day over at it. She'd looked for the will then, but hadn't found it, and it was only that night, lying in bed, that she remembered Kathryn saying something about keeping her important papers in the freezer. Now she went straight there, moved aside the frozen tumbling blocks and bags of meat and fruit and there it was, wrapped in brown paper and tied with twine.

She sat at the table and unwrapped the package. The will was there, but it was an ancient one, unchanged since Bill had died. It named Kathryn's sister Eileen, who had died ten years ago, as executor and instructed that in the event of both Kathryn and Bill's deaths, the land was to be sold and the money distributed to Colin and Mary. Did that mean Rob would get Mary's share? She'd have to call a lawyer. There were other papers, the land title, their wedding certificate, birth certificates, and, in a yellow envelope, a folded package of one hundred dollar bills. She counted. There were a hundred of them.

The bills were old. How long had Kathryn been squirreling them away? She had never had any money. She and Bill had always been dirt poor, lived poor, acted poor, and now here was this pitiful wad of money, not enough for anything. Mary had died poor. Rob had said once Mary had died desperate because she had no money, no hope. What a stupid thing to do, save this pitiful bit of money. She folded the money, put it back in the envelope, put everything back in the freezer.

Chapter Fifty-Six

It was late. Dana had to start supper. By the time she got it made and supper on the table, she found herself waiting for the sound of Rob's truck. He was late again. It was the second time this week. He was hardly ever late without phoning her. He knew she worried about accidents. Early in their marriage she'd made him promise to phone when he was late.

I'm under too much stress, she thought. This is too much. The sky was raw and yellow from smoke from the still dying fire. It got in everyone's throat and eyes and made people irritable. Colin had been back for a week. He continued to complain, to wander restlessly around the house, occasionally stopping to look at a magazine, or out the window. She had tried, graciously enough, she thought, considering what a rude self-absorbed pig he was, to find things that might interest him, but television, books, the garden, the state of the land, were all wasted on him. He allowed, in one brief and isolated burst of conversation, that he had stopped both drinking and smoking, went to AA regularly, and had acquired some kind of faith in a "higher power." She felt, momentarily, sorry for him. She put on a family dinner, cooked a huge roast of beef, invited the boys, and their girlfriends, Mike and Arlene, made pies and salads and cookies and cake. The boys were briefly interested in their long lost great uncle, but finding he knew little or didn't care any more about logging, or sports, or hunting, or fishing, had left him alone, which meant he was on her hands most of the time, just hanging around.

Plus she had the care of Kathryn, who woke up enough to get to the bathroom, thank God, but had to have trays and meals and was furious and complaining and confused in those few moments when she was awake. Colin dutifully sat by her side a few times for a short while every day, then wandered downstairs, and into the kitchen again, like some lost and hungry child. He hadn't even spent any time over at the old place, for God's sake.

One morning he came in the kitchen for coffee. He went to the fridge, opened it and peered hopefully inside, then pulled out a piece of leftover strawberry pie.

"Colin," Dana asked. "Has Kathryn said anything to you about the will?"

"She hasn't said anything to me at all," he said. "I dunno if she understands anything. She seems out of her head most of the time. She keeps wanting to talk about Mary. Of course, she never said anything to me my entire life that wasn't nagging me about work or coming home or my duty to the family."

"But you must have talked about the land, what was going to happen to it, especially after Mary died."

"Why should we?" he said. "It's mine now, I guess. Not that I care. There's nothing there, just an old house, run down fields. I hate that damn place. I can't even go over there. God, the work we used to do there just to stay alive. The old man bitching. . . nothing ever pleased him. I got the hell out of it all soon as I could. They always wanted me to come back. Who's going to do the work, they'd say. On and on. Every time they phoned, every time they wrote a goddam postcard. All she ever cared about, all she still cares about."

"Well, it could be fixed up, made productive," Dana said. "It's good land, good for fruit, hay, trees."

"I don't care," said Colin. "I don't give a shit. I don't want anything to do with it. If I can get a pile of money out of it, that'll do me. God, the old man used to get us up at six, go out to pick rocks, pick fruit, do the goddam hay. And for what? He could have made more money working in town anyday. Jeezus. What a life. I don't even want to think about it." He picked up his coffee and lumbered heavily out of the room. Dana heard him slump onto the couch. When she went in later, he was asleep, feet up on her shiny new pillows, his paunch protruding under his polyester shirt.

And every day, she spent worrying about Brendan, who hadn't phoned and who wasn't in town staying with any of his friends, all of whom professed not to know his whereabouts.

"What's the matter with Colin ?" she had hissed at Rob one night, as they were getting ready for bed. "He resents having to do anything. He's still complaining about the work Kathryn and Bill made him do. He's so useless, for God's sake. You think he could help out with something. Gardening, the dishes, anything. I never thought I'd see one of Kathryn's kids so useless. What happened to him? "

Rob shrugged. "Maybe the booze took it out of him."

He was preoccupied thinking about Sunita, who had literally bumped into him on the street at noon that day, when he had come into town to go to the hardware store, had given him a radiant smile, and invited him for lunch. Feeling angry but somehow helpless, he'd gone. Over lunch, she'd acted like his long lost best friend, asking for advice, talking about the forestry meeting and politics and generally being all happy as hell and looking relaxed, while he sat there, smiling politely and trying to make serious conversation, and far too conscious the whole time that they were in a public place, that people had noticed them. He was conscious that she was as attractive as ever, and he had to get back to work with the missing machine parts he'd come to buy and that his crew was waiting for. He didn't understand at all what was going on with her or what she wanted.

When they left the restaurant he said abruptly, "You still into hiking, fishing, all that?"

"Sure," she said, and laughed at him, ran her tongue out of her mouth. "What did you have in mind?"

"Maybe going up Howser Lake some weekend soon, if the weather's good and nothing else is happening. Haven't been in there for a while. Fishing should be good."

"Let me know," she said. "Call anytime. I'm game for anything." He almost laughed out loud. He looked around the street to see if anyone had noticed. But he was already making plans for the trip.

Colin came in the kitchen, sniffing among the pots and pans like a sad hound. Dana took pity on him, dished him up a plate of food, put another plate on a tray and took it up to Kathryn. When she came in the bedroom door, Kathryn was sitting upright on the edge of the bed. She suddenly stood upright, held out her arms to Dana, and then fell forward onto the rug. Her left arm jerked spasmodically. Dana couldn't tell if she was still breathing.

"Colin," she yelled frantically, ran to the top of the stairs, called again. "Colin, get the ambulance. It's Kathryn. She's having a seizure or something." Silence. She scrambled down the stairs.

He was sitting in the kitchen, doggedly eating. She ran to the phone and only after she hung up did he come into the hall, asking, "What, what's the matter?"

They waited for the ambulance together, sitting beside Kathryn's bed, watching her struggle for breathe. The doctor in the hospital took a swift look, shrugged, "Pneumonia. Won't be too long now." He went away again. They waited again. Dana had left a note for Rob. She waited for his footsteps, his voice. Colin left the room for coffee and Kathryn opened her eyes, still gasping for breath.

"You," she said, looking at Dana. "Well, it doesn't matter. Tell Rob . . ." she said, stopped to breathe. "Tell Rob, he's to buy the land from Colin. Give Colin the money. I saved it. I saved it for Rob. The land for Rob…in the freezer. I told him…" she said, "I told Colin…."

She closed her eyes again.

Dana stood up, went to the door of the room, leaning against its cool brown plastic frame. One corner of her mouth curved in triumph. She could hear Rob's voice in the hall, loud, frantic, could hear his footsteps coming like small thunder. She smiled to herself, hid her smile against the wall.

"Mine," she murmured fiercely, crooning it to herself. "Mine"

Chapter Fifty-Seven

Brendan is sitting on the back seat of the Greyhound bus, on the way to Vancouver. The seat is next to the washroom, which gurgles and stinks. Some guy in the next seat is snoring loudly, mouth open, wrapped in the rank smell of booze.

He waited at Johnnie's for three days. For one whole day, he and his friends sat on a hill across the valley from the fire, watching a giant plane roar slowly over the surface of the lake, scoop up a belly full of water, and dump it on the fire. People from all over the valley came to watch the sight, watch the planes and the helicopter with its bucket hanging underneath. The fire had left an enormous hole, a black scar on the side of the mountain, a gaping line in the trees, and then the bombers had left a red rust stain around its edges.

Brendan and Johnnie had laughed at what geeks people were, getting in their cars on a Sunday afternoon and driving out as far as the roped off line in the highway, and the standing around on the road below the mountain, staring at the fire like they'd never seen anything burn before, like it was the most exciting thing to hit the valley since the glaciers.

But then they'd done it themselves. They and their friends took beer and food, and lay in the sun. Heat shimmered off the distant glitter of the lake and distorted the far shore. By the end of the day, they were tired and drunk and bored. Most of them went back to Appleby to find more beer.

Brendan and Johnnie stayed. They lay side by side on the flat rock where they'd been sitting on all day. The sky over the mountains was a dull yellow. The bombing plane had gone home for the day.

"What are you going to do man, if you don't go home?"

"I'm leaving," Brendan said. He kept his eyes closed. He didn't want to look at Johnnie. "I'm going on the bus, maybe tomorrow."

"Go then. You'll be back," Johnnie said. "You'll never survive it, man. You'll hate it. Remember when I went there, couple of years ago. You'll sink under the loneliness. Remember when I spent the winter there? Fuck, I hated it so much, people ripping you off and no one to hang out with. City sucks, man. This place sucks too but it's home. You know who your friends are."

Brendan opened his eyes and looked at the light shining through Johnnie's red hair. He kept his hands at his sides. He and Johnnie had slept side by side through so many nights in so many basements on foamies and air mattresses and couches. Johnnie's breathing had comforted him through such nights. Johnnie had a girlfriend named Heather who came and went in his life. Brendan had friends who were girls who never stayed around because he lost interest in them after almost no time.

I'm okay. It's okay. We're friends, he thought. But he didn't know what that meant either, he knew he didn't want to be a faggot and get jeered at, and he wished he could just say to Johnnie, "Yeah, I love you man, but I've got to go."

His throat hurt. He felt tough and lonely. But Johnnie would always be there. They were friends were for life, forever, and they were both young and strong and they could go anywhere, do anything they wanted.

"Vancouver doesn't scare me," he said. "It's just a place full of people, just like everywhere else."

"No, it isn't, man," Johnnie said. "It's a crock, that place, the whole shitting place. You'd never get me back there again. You won't have a chance. It'll eat you alive."

He wouldn't look at Brendan. He sat up, pulled a cigarette out, lit it. He sat looking across the valley at the still smoking fire scar. It looked like something had taken a bite from the side of the mountain and it was still bleeding.

"So what are you going to do then? Stay here your whole life? You've always said how you hated it."

"It's all right," Johnnie said. "It's not that bad. Guy at the feed shop said I can come work there anytime."

Brendan was silent.

"I'll come back," he said, after a while. "You know I'll always come back. But I'm not living here the rest of life. No way. I've got stuff to do."

"So go then, man," said Johnnie. "I don't give a shit. It's no big deal. Just shut up about it. Don't talk about it. Just go."

"So, I will," said Brendan. "Jeesus, what's your problem? What's the big deal?" Johnnie said nothing. He turned his head away, threw a rock down the mountain.

"C'mon, let's go," he said. "This place sucks. Let's go get bombed. There's nothing else to do." He stood up and walked away down the mountain. Brendan watched him go, then he followed him down the rocky path.

Brendan hadn't heard anything about Kathryn before he left. He had stood for a long time by the pay phone at 7-11, then he walked away again. If he talked to his parents, it would just be another stupid argument. He'd phone from Vancouver, he thought. By then there'd be nothing they could do. He'd be gone. That was it.

Now, he wants, he needs, to not think about her or his family, or Johnnie. He has to get on with things. Now he only wishes he could sleep. He has tried, turning and twisting various ways on the hard plastic seat, his head lolling against the metal wall, thunder from the wheels rumbling beneath him. Nothing works.

He is beginning to get a sense of what Johnnie was talking about. It's all gone, all the stuff he has swum in his whole life, the valley like a warm round bowl, family, friends, school, stick out your thumb for a ride, raid the fridge for food, sleep at someone's house, someone always has dope, music, comics, time to bullshit. He feels naked, stripped, all alone in this dark bus full of sleeping people, watching out the window at the houses, fields, dark shapes of animals, trees and rivers and snowy mountain passes, slipping by in a steady progression.

He wishes he could stop everything, hold it back, just for a while, get off the bus and go into one of those dark sleeping houses with a bed and blankets and there, unknown and alone, stay for just a while longer, stay, hold back the night, hold it in until the next day bursting forth, illumining the rich and shining possibilities that lie in wait.

He bounces on the seat, wishes desperately for a cigarette, a joint, a book, Johnnie's company. He has brought one of Mary's diaries with him, one full of sketches and observations. He brings it out, holds it under the feeble yellow light.

Next to a sketch of a leaf, a pattern of fir needles, a blown dandelion, she had written:

Whenever I think I might be in danger of becoming too smart for my own good, I go home. When I am lost, homesick, depressed, tired, burned out, elated, I go home. I have been doing it for years now. I was created by my home. I was shaped each day, by living in it, by standing still in it, by learning it. It has made me a connoisseur of colour, light, texture, taste, all of it coming in, as real as making love, only this—this has never bored me, never lessened. It was born in me early to want to be a painter, more than anything else, because I wanted some way to capture that utter feat of colour and texture. I don't remember ever not knowing it was beautiful.

It occurred to me the other night, as I looked out the windows of my rented house in a borrowed city, that it is harder to see a place when you don't have a relationship with it. It's like looking at a crowd of strangers among whom some may eventually be friends. I have stood on the mountain at home, looking out and said, I love you as I would say to any utter beloved person, and not felt foolish. I know it intimately, as I could know a lover's body, each curve and bump, each joining and parting, each scar and nick and mole. I grew there, sliding down gravel slopes on my half mad half wild horse; swimming out into the lake. I lived there, explored there—all of it, as far as I could ride and back in a day on my bike, as far as the horse would take me on the logging roads, as far as the lake's edge, and then as far, as deep as I could swim. I tasted and smelled as much of it as I could, beginning with the wild strawberries in June. . .

Brendan closes the book again, leans back against the seat, closes his eyes. "I will," he says. "I'll try. I'll do what I can."

PRINTED AND BOUND
IN BOUCHERVILLE, QUÉBEC, CANADA
BY MARC VEILLEUX IMPRIMEUR INC.
IN AUGUST, 1998